**LEGIONN
BOOK**

THE SEA OF GRASS

By Gilbert M. Stack

Amazon Edition

Copyright 2017 by Gilbert M. Stack
Cover Copyright 2017 by Shirley Burnett

Dedication

I want to thank Patrick Wyman for his vivid podcast on The Fall of Rome and Louis L'Amour for showing us the story possibilities in the Great Plains. But mostly this novel is for everyone who's wondered what the legions would have done if faced with fell and overpowering magics far from home. With your shield or on it, Marcus!

Table of Contents

Dedication
Prologue: Very Little Rainfall and Teeming with Nomadic Savages
Day One: He's Awfully Young
Day Three: We Are Familiar with Your Brother
Day Four: The Men Are Sharp and Well-Trained
Day Five: An Issue of Purity
Day Six: Armor Up
Day Seven: How Bad Do You Think It Is?
Day Eight: Might As Well Let the Savages Kill Us
Day Nine: It's Risky
Day Ten: Why Is It Buzzing?
Day Eleven: We're Surrounded by Sinkholes
Day Twelve: Beautiful and Awe Inspiring
Day Thirteen: What's Wrong with the Fort?
Day Fourteen: Time Is Not Our Friend
Day Fifteen: It Might Get Bloody
Day Sixteen: The Time Things Would Be Hardest
Day Seventeen: We're Not the Ones Who Are Going to Be Dying
Day Eighteen: Severed Skulls Were Not the Ideal Choice of Weapons
Day Nineteen: They Aren't Going Away
Day Twenty: Outnumbered Ten to One
Day Twenty-One: We Are Legionnaires!
Day Twenty-Eight: I Regret to Inform You

Excerpt from *Legionnaire Book 3: The Jeweled Hills*

About Gilbert M. Stack
Other Works by Gilbert M. Stack
Contact Gilbert M. Stack

On the Sea of Grass, Tribune Marcus Venandus once again proved his worth. Thinking only to start his exile in the far off Jeweled Hills, he quickly became entangled in dangers and responsibilities that dwarfed those he encountered in the Fire Islands, once again saving the Republic from a substantial and unexpected threat...
                              Severus Liberus

Prologue
Very Little Rainfall and Teeming with Nomadic Savages

"This interview is a courtesy, Lesser Tribune. I should have simply had you arrested. You were, after all, exiled some six months ago."

"Tribune," Marcus Venandus corrected the rather pudgy Aquilan official who had not even bothered to rise from his parchment-strewn table to greet him despite his talks of courtesy.

"Excuse me?"

"My rank," Marcus explained to him, "is *tribune*. I was promoted by Praetor Titus Virtuus for my actions in saving the thirty-second legion, killing the rebel witchdoctor, Kekipi, and preserving Aquila's hold on the Fire Islands against three subsequent rebel attacks with only a handful of men."

The cool recitation momentarily off footed the self-important official in the governor's office of the port city of Dona, the Republic of Aquila's foothold on the southern coast of the upper continent of Septemtrio. "I, um," he paused to straighten a pile of parchment, then returned to the attack. "I have no information regarding—"

Marcus handed him a rolled parchment in which his former commander had eloquently summed up his accomplishments in saving the island of Mokupani after the previous commanding officer had led the legion to utter ruin.

Irritated, the man snatched the scroll out of his hands and quickly read the document. As he did so, Marcus had the satisfaction of watching his eyes widen in surprise. "I, um, none of this news has reached us here in Dona yet," the man complained when he finished reading.

"How could it, Sir?" Marcus asked him in as friendly a manner as he could muster. "The Fire Islands are nearly two thousand miles away by ship. I've been sailing around the coast of Austellus for nearly two months—I left on the first ship, three days after I received the Senate's decision to exile me. How could anyone have beaten me with the news of my promotion?"

"Well, um, yes," the official agreed somewhat mollified, "but, um, you do realize that the latest information the governor has still places you on the list of proscribed individuals. You're still not permitted to be here."

"Of course, Sir," Marcus agreed. "The Senate probably has Praetor Virtuus' report now, but who knows how long it will take that august body to deal with this rather minor matter when it has so many grave concerns to occupy its time."

"Right, right," the official stated. He repositioned himself in his seat, trying to get more comfortable. "But that means we still have to deal with this exile—"

"It's largely irrelevant, Sir," Marcus told him.

"What?" the outrage on the man's face threatened to bolster his initial antagonism.

"What I mean to say, Sir," Marcus mollified him, "is that I have personal business in the Jeweled Hills. There will be plenty of time for the Senate to rescind my exile before I'm able to return to the Republic."

Marcus' clarification did not fully satisfy the official. "Well then, why are you lingering in Dona then? According to my reports, you've been here nearly ten days."

"I'm having trouble finding a ship that will take me to the Jeweled Coast," Marcus explained. "Apparently there's been a lot of pirate activity of late and we're moving into the stormy season."

"Quite right," the official agreed until he apparently realized that his comment might serve as a justification for Marcus continuing in Dona indefinitely. "But that's not an excuse for you to ignore your exile." He considered the problem for a moment. "I guess you'll have to take the overland route across the Sea of Grass."

"The overland route, Sir?" Marcus repeated. "Forgive me, but I've never been this far north before and I'm trying to remember my lessons from the lycee. I thought that everyone took the sea route to the Jeweled Coast and then traveled inland to the Jeweled Hills."

"No, no, there is an alternative route," the official said. "Let me see here, I think I have a map buried somewhere on this table." He pried at his stacks of parchment for a couple of minutes until he found what he was looking for and stretched it out above his other documents.

"Look, here we are in Dona in the foothills of the Sturm Mountains." As he examined his maps, all the hostility drained out of the man as if he thoroughly enjoyed lecturing on the local geography. "These mountains rise in height as they travel northeast for about four hundred miles. Then they break down into foothills again here and form the Jeweled Hills. Understand?"

Marcus merely nodded, pleased to have the opportunity to study the map and not wanting to do anything that would turn this man antagonistic again.

"For the first two hundred or so miles," the official continued, "the mountains come practically to the edge of the ocean, but after that a very fertile coastline develops. It's some hundred to one hundred and fifty miles deep in most areas. Except for a couple of city states in the southern portion of that coastline which belong to the Trevilian Federation—the so called, Pirate Islands—this area forms the southern third or so of the Jeweled Coast. Normally you would take a ship here, probably to Diamonte, and travel inland to the Jeweled Hills. But there is an alternate route that has become much more popular with the rise of all of this pirate activity."

He pointed to an area north of Dona and west of the Sturm Mountains. "These plains are called the Sea of Grass. They're pretty useless—very little rainfall and teeming with nomadic savages. It's only about four hundred miles north to south, but you can't go the direct route. Mostly you need to follow the water sources and skirt a great salt pan that stretches across the northern half of the plain like a great wound. We've established a handful of forts along the way to protect travelers now that the sea route is becoming problematic. Large caravans of wagons have taken advantage of this to ply the land between the forts. One leaves Dona about every ten days. You can attach yourself to the next one and with a little luck be in the Jeweled Hills in just four or five weeks."

Marcus hadn't heard about the caravans. He and his companions had barely moved from the dockside inn they'd taken lodgings in while looking for a ship to help them finish their journey. He'd never even considered trying to get to his half-brother's home in Amatista by land.

"Thank you, Sir," he told the official. "This has been very helpful. This route is definitely worth investigating."

The man frowned slightly when Marcus did not immediately commit himself to joining the caravan. "I think you'll find this gets you to your destination months earlier than waiting on a ship willing to brave the northern coastline." He hesitated a moment before continuing. "And I'd like to be able to report to the governor that you'll be joining the next caravan. While I hope the Senate will act quickly to reverse your exile, it is technically still in force."

"Yes, of course, it is," Marcus agreed. "If you could direct me to a place I can learn more about these wagons, I'll see about getting out of your hair and completing my journey."

For the first time in the entire conversation, the official smiled. "The man you'll want to speak to is named Burkhard. He's the caravan master. He'll be able to set you up with space in one of the wagons. It may cost a bit more than sailing, but..." He spread his hands as if to ask, *what can you do?*

"You've been very helpful, Sir," Marcus told him. "I hope you will not take offense when I say that I wasn't looking forward to an extended stay in your fine city."

The official finally stood and offered Marcus his hand. "Of course not, you've a journey to complete and until all the technicalities are resolved back in the Senate, we have a proscription list to enforce. I wish you a quick and, well, I can't imagine that traveling across those dry plains in a big wagon will be pleasant, but I hope you have a journey as pleasant as it can reasonably be."

They shook hands, each man grasping the other's wrist in the Aquilan manner. Then Marcus retrieved his scroll documenting his promotion and left.

Day One
He's Awfully Young

Marcus strode to the left of his wagon as it approached the staging point for the caravan as the rim of the sun first appeared over the horizon. There was a frenzy of confusion in the air as dozens of others did as he was doing. Most appeared to be merchants striving to get their goods through to the Jeweled Cities north of the Sea of Grass when the traditional sea lanes were closed to traffic, but there were more than a smattering of other travelers as well ranging in rank from foreign nobles to common folk. There was also a detachment of well over fifty green band legionnaires—without any reds or blacks as far as Marcus could see, but the staging area was large and it was possible he simply hadn't spotted them yet.

He had decided to buy a wagon primarily because he had a significant amount of treasure to transport—the spoils of defeating Kekipi in the Fire Islands. The rebel witchdoctor had accumulated quite a horde of gold ingots, pearls and minted silver coins of the Qing Empire far to the northeast. That last had perplexed him mightily as he could think of no reason for such a horde to exist in the Fire Islands, so he had reported most of those chests to his superiors in Aquila. But as to the ingots, he had passed many out to his surviving men as their share of the plunder and kept the majority of the chests for himself. The pearls he simply hadn't reported.

When he had gotten back to the Aquila castrum in the town of Maleko, he had confiscated the horde of the men who had tried to murder him and his hand—his superior officers, the praetor and great tribune. Again he had kept a significant portion for himself, but used the rest to help him recruit native troops to fill out the ranks of his depleted legion. Generous gifts to influential natives like Makuahine Akela had helped to start the recruits volunteering and regular payment of their salaries had helped keep them from deserting again. He'd turned the remnants—together with a thorough accounting of his expenditures—over to Praetor Titus Virtuus when the man had assumed command of the legion and set his trusty adjutant, Calidus Vulpes, to smuggling out his own treasure less Praetor Titus take it on himself to confiscate it for the good of the legion. The fact that Marcus was owed a substantial portion of the plunder as the de facto head of the legion in Mokupani was unlikely to dissuade the Praetor from depriving him of this significant wealth.

It was Calidus who had suggested Marcus buy one of the large wagons used by most of those traveling with the caravan. He had also insisted they buy a *cargo* of very high quality Teriseti wine to use to camouflage the treasure. Marcus was not really comfortable buying a cargo. Buying wine to transport and sell to others somehow wasn't as reputable as buying land to grow grapes and make wine. However, his adjutant's math was unassailable. With only Marcus, Calidus, and Black Vigil Severus Lupus traveling together there was a significant chance of them being robbed if anyone found out just how much wealth they carried with them. The wine would make them appear to be just like the majority of the other wagons in the caravan and discourage people from examining them too closely.

So Marcus had bought a massive wagon capable of carrying *twelve thousand* pounds in its bed which they used up fast at nearly four hundred pounds to the amphora of wine. He'd also bought a team of four horses to haul that weight, and hired a probably-not-trustworthy local teamster named Kuno to drive the wagon. Now all that was left was to find Burkhard, the caravan master, so he could pay his fee and he'd be off like a merchant to the Jeweled Hills.

He frowned at the thought. How could his fortunes have literally soared so high and sunk so low at the same time? Maybe he could pretend the wine was merely for his personal use or a gift for his brother when he reached Amatista. It wasn't like he needed the money after the plunder in the Fire Islands.

Ahead of him, the caravan master's son, Gernot, appeared with a parchment scroll, pausing to speak with the owners of the wagon ahead of him. Money changed hands and Gernot made a notation on his scroll before rolling it back up, pointing at a place further along on the road, and approaching Marcus.

"Tribune," the young man greeted him with the same perpetual scowl he'd worn through their first meeting two days ago. The boy's father had smiled happily at the thought of collecting a fee for an additional wagon, but his son of no more than sixteen years had definitely appeared less pleased. "You're very nearly late. It's a bad start. I ought to ban you from the caravan."

Marcus took a glance over his shoulder where at least a dozen additional wagons were still rolling slowly toward the staging area. He'd be very surprised if a dozen more weren't still making their way out of town. If it had been up to him, he would have insisted that everyone in the caravan report the night before—but who was he to tell these local *experts* how to run their business?

He turned back to Gernot. "If you turn people away for being on time, what are you going to do with all those who are genuinely late? It will cost you a pretty penny if you lose half your caravan."

The scowl deepened, which intrigued Marcus. He hadn't thought the man's frown could grow more severe. "Don't get smart with me, Tribune. Smart men tend to die out on the trail. They think they know what they're doing but too often end up getting themselves—and others—killed."

Gernot simply didn't like Aquilans, Marcus decided. It was a common attitude out in the conquered territories. The boy's father might not like them either, but he loved gold and silver and knew that there was no profit in antagonizing his overlords. The son did not yet have his parent's wisdom.

"I'll keep that in mind," Marcus told him. "In the meantime, you have a lot of work to do if this caravan is to depart an hour after dawn as your father said he planned to do." In Marcus' opinion, there was no hope that they would leave even by noon. It was a problem Aquila often encountered in the provinces. The discipline so necessary to making any enterprise run efficiently simply didn't exist in most of the world—which went a long way to explaining the success of Aquila's legions in conquering so much of the planet.

"We'll get started when my father is ready," Gernot told him. "Now give me your fee so I can see to these other wagons."

Marcus definitely did not like the young man's tone, but he counted out the silver denari without expressing his disapproval. It did not pay to offend the caravan master on the first day of the journey.

The young man counted the coins into his box and started to leave.

"Gernot!" Marcus snapped having just discovered the limits of his patience.

The young man turned angrily on him. "What is it now, Tribune? I have work to be doing!"

"Record my payment on your parchment," Marcus told him. He spoke slowly and forcefully to make certain the young man understood how much trouble he was courting.

"I'll do it at the next wagon. I'm in a—"

"Now!" Marcus interrupted him.

"Best do as he says, boy," Severus Lupus suggested. It was the *friendly* advice of a Black Vigil—the man in charge of the most experienced legionnaires in a Lesser Tribunes' hand. It was a unique and highly respected position in any legion. The *only* way a man could become a black vigil was to survive in the ranks through his two years in the green band, his twenty years in the red and at least five years as a rank and file legionnaire in the black. Then a *tribune*—not a lesser tribune—could promote him to black vigil, although even then he usually did so only with the approval of his *great tribune*. They were in many ways the backbone of the legion officer corps with the experience to mentor green and red vigils and even lesser tribunes. Marcus had benefited from Severus' guidance from his first day in the legion and he'd been very pleased when the man had agreed to take a leave of absence and accompany him on his journey to the Jeweled Hills.

Gernot whirled even more angrily on the older man. "Who asked you?"

Severus was not impressed. "The Tribune is trying to do you a favor. It's a lesson he often has to teach young officers. Putting off the record keeping in an important task often leads to trouble—and in your case that would be serious trouble. Imagine for a moment what would happen if you *forgot* to record the Tribune's payment. Your father would check that scroll, see the blank next to this wagon, and come to collect it. The Tribune would then inform the Caravan Master that he had already paid. This would put your father in quite a bind. After all, he had trusted you, his *son*, to collect the money, so it would be reasonable for him to believe that the Tribune was trying to cheat him out of his just fee. But does he call the Tribune on this disgraceful behavior? Does he stand up for the honor of his son and refuse to let the Tribune's wagon travel in his caravan? And if he does, what will the Tribune do in response? He'll file formal charges of theft against you and your father and since he was robbed—however unintentionally—and Tribune Marcus is a patrician, you and your father would be *crucified*."

At that final word, Gernot's anger gave way to incredulity as his eyes grew round and wide.

"Now isn't that a lot of trouble to court just because you're in too much of a hurry to note that the Tribune has paid his fee on your scroll?" Severus finished in not unkindly tones.

"But, I, he's," the young man stammered.

"Always listen to a Black Vigil," Marcus suggested in the same almost-fatherly tone that Severus had adopted. "I have never known one to give bad advice."

Gernot removed a quill and ink bottle from his box and quickly made the suggested notation. He then put his implements away and hurried on to the next wagon.

"He's awfully young," Severus commented as they watched him leave.

"I hope he listens to you," Marcus said. "It just might let him grow a little older."

****

Kuno parked Marcus' wagon at the end of the long line and turned to address his employer. "It could be a long wait still, Tribune, but the roads are good for the next twenty miles or so. Even with a late start, we should be able to reach the Sea of Grass by nightfall."

"When do you think the caravan will get moving?" Marcus asked.

Kuno stood in his seat at the front of the wagon, and picked his nose as he looked back at the jumbled confusion behind them. "I'd say before high noon. Not a lot before, but it shouldn't be too much later."

"We were supposed to leave shortly after dawn," Marcus complained.

Kuno shrugged.

"Auxiliaries," Severus complained. "It's the same as with the auxiliaries. Why is it that no one outside of Aquila knows how to organize anything?"

Marcus patted the older man on the shoulder. "Remember that idiot Castor in the Fire Islands? The foreigners don't have a monopoly on incompetence." He checked the sun and figured he had at least two more hours. "Come on, let's see who else we're traveling with." He raised his voice. "Calidus! You stay with the wagon for now!"

Calidus was actually already talking to the owners of the wagon directly ahead of him. He quickly pressed his fist to his heart in the legionnaire's salute to signal that he understood his instructions then went right on talking.

That was fine with Marcus. He trusted Calidus. The man was smart and capable with oodles of initiative—which was why he had made him his adjutant despite not even coming from the equestrian class. He'd promoted him to Red Vigil in the aftermath of the massacre of the legion in the Fire Islands and like Severus he'd acted as a Full Tribune while they rebuilt the legion out of native forces. Calidus would be fine.

Marcus and Severus walked up the long line of wagons taking note of the sorts of people who had joined the caravan. Most were actually Gente of the Jeweled Hills—merchants and their guards he gathered—and sometimes their families. He had a better than rudimentary grasp of the native language and decided to use the trip to further improve his skills. He was naturally gifted in picking up foreign tongues and he didn't think it would take him much time to add this language to the other half dozen he already spoke fluently.

The Jeweled Hills were a strange collection of northern city states. The majority of the population were Gente, but they had been conquered two centuries earlier by a semi-nomadic people called the Gota—not the savages of the Sea of Grass but an entirely different race from the northwest. The Gota had taken advantage of a poorly considered invitation to aid the city of Cuarzo in one of its perpetual wars with its neighbors to get its foot in the door and then rather quickly conquered the rest of the Jeweled Hills. The Jeweled Coast had held out a couple of decades longer but like their inland cousins had not been able to overcome their age-old rivalries to unite against the external threat.

Marcus and Juan Pablo's father had been stationed in Amatista nearly fifty years ago as a minor member of a diplomatic mission from the Republic. His only contribution to the undertaking appears to have been getting a local Gente señorita pregnant so that he was ordered to marry the girl by his head of mission to soothe the social outrage of the mercantile elites. Such marriages were literally meaningless in the Republic since the wife (Juan Pablo's mother) was not a citizen and when the mission ended in failure, Marcus' father had happily abandoned his Amatista family, returning home without them. He'd then repeated the pattern in Aquila so many times that he'd developed a reputation as the most divorced man in the Republic. Marcus frankly couldn't figure out why any woman would have anything to do with him. Supposedly he was quite charming, but his track record should have decisively frightened off any potential mate.

"That one looks awfully young to be a magus," Severus said, pulling Marcus' attention back to the here and now.

Ahead of them, a young man—really a boy perhaps a year older than the caravan master's son—looked about him at all the wagons with a mixture of excitement and apprehension. He wore an expensive green robe with two lines of stars adorning it as if he were purposely calling attention to his magical abilities.

The young man caught sight of them and some of the tension apparent in his face eased away as he almost charged down the line of wagons in their direction. "A man of Aquila," he trumpeted. "Now this is a pleasant discovery. I was beginning to think that I would have to start my sojourn to foreign lands completely surrounded by…well…foreigners."

Much to Marcus and Severus' surprise, he stepped completely past the tribune to try and shake the hand of the Black Vigil.

Severus did not accept the offered hand, but the magus did not appear put off by his lack of courtesy. "I mean, one expects to be surrounded by foreigners when traveling to places outside the Republic, but I just expected there to be more of my fellow countrymen around on the journey."

The Black Vigil took a step back from the overly enthusiastic young magus and looked to Marcus for help.

"And you would be?"

The young magus jumped in surprise, whirling about to face Marcus. "Oh, excuse me, I didn't notice—I mean, of course, I noticed you, but I guess when I saw the strong and experienced face of this gentleman I just naturally assumed…"

His voice trailed off and he wiped his sweaty hands on the front of his robe, then tried to start again. "I am Seneca Liberus," he introduced himself pausing as if he expected to be recognized. When neither Marcus nor Severus reacted, he repeated himself, "Seneca *Liberus*."

Marcus racked his brain for something that might satisfy the young man's ego. It was not the name of one of the great senatorial families which meant the man was probably of the equestrian class. Since magical talent often ran strong in families, Marcus fabricated what he hoped was a polite and accurate guess. "Not the great family of magi?"

"The very same!" the young man pounced excitedly on the answer. "The very same!" Abruptly he seemed to remember his manners. "And you are?"

"Tribune Marcus Venandus and this is Black Vigil Severus Lupus."

"Military officers!" Seneca exclaimed as if there could not possibly be a better answer to his question. "You must be going to take up your commands in one of the forts we'll be passing through on our journey north. Are those your men I saw marching toward the front not so long ago?"

"Alas, no," Marcus told him. "Severus and I are on leave while I handle some personal business in the north. What, if I may ask, inspired you to make this journey?"

This question appeared to deflate some of Seneca's enthusiasm. "My magisters at the Collegium Magicae decided that I would benefit from a period of study abroad—an exotic apprenticeship, if you will—so I am traveling north to the far off city of Amatista to study with the renown magus, Efraín Estudioso. You know, learn a bit about how the foreigners do things to make certain our own magi are up to snuff when it comes time to defeating their magics."

The more Seneca tried to justify his *exotic apprenticeship*, the more Marcus became convinced that the young man was not at all pleased with his assignment. He decided it was time to move along. With a long journey ahead of them, there would be plenty of time to learn more about the apprentice magus.

Clapping the young man on the shoulder, he said, "Well it's good to meet you, Magus. It's always a benefit to have a student of the arts around in case there's trouble on the trail."

Seneca started at the suggestion as if the idea that his magical talents might be needed had never occurred to him, but Marcus affected not to notice.

"We'll have to talk more after the wagons hit the road, but in the meantime, if you'll excuse us…"

The young man nodded vigorously. "Of course, of course, don't let me keep you from your important business. I'll just wait here near my things in Señor Joaquin's wagon. It was very good to meet you both."

As soon as they were out of earshot of the young man, Severus whispered, "I'll bet he did something embarrassing and got himself expelled from that fancy school."

"It's possible," Marcus agreed, "but I'd guess his family really is influential enough to get that expulsion turned into some sort of academic exile. I know if I'd been expelled from the lycee I would have gone out of my way *not* to associate myself with it in the future. It would have been too embarrassing."

****

The wagons began to pull forward a little after the sun reached its zenith. The day was hot and more than a hundred teams of horses kicked up a substantial cloud of dust which both added to the heat and cut down hard on their vision. It also made them readily visible to anyone looking from as far as twenty miles away—more if the viewer had the advantage of a bit of elevation. The heat was an inconvenience which any legionnaire of Marcus and Severus' ranks had long before become inured to, but the dust worried the military men. They'd been warned that the savages were acting up and they hated the ease with which any hostile could mark their passage.

All three legionnaires walked beside their wagon with the easy stride of men who'd spent their lives on their feet. It hadn't even occurred to Marcus to buy them riding horses. Not only would the animals consume their store of water—and Marcus had upset Calidus by insisting that they carry twice the recommended amount of consumables in their wagon—but riding on a cross country journey went against the grain. It was not that Aquila did not employ cavalry. In fact many still viewed it as the elite branch of the service because only the wealthy could afford the horses and kit that the cavalry man required. However, the people of the Republic had long ago figured out that the true legionnaires were the infantrymen who were the decisive factor in *all* of the big battles. The cavalry had important roles to play, but in the end it was the strong shields and sharp swords of the infantry which decided the course of nations. Marcus, raised by his maternal grandparents, had had the option of joining the cavalry as his father had, but had happily passed it by to follow in his grandfather's footsteps.

It was a decision he would never regret.

Day Three
We Are Familiar with Your Brother

The caravan was starting to get a little better organized. On the third day out from Dona they finally got started within a long hour of dawn. Marcus would have never accepted such blatant lack of discipline from his own men, but he had to admit that the problems facing Caravan Master Burkhard were more severe than those facing the typical tribune. Civilians really didn't like being told what to do. They didn't seem to grasp the importance of following orders and immediately obeying those in command. And to make matters even more difficult for the caravan leader, one of his charges was a Gota nobleman who seemed to take it as a point of honor to demonstrate repeatedly that he was not under the commoner's command.

So each morning, men and women got up late, took too long eating their breakfasts and getting their wagons prepped for the trail, and generally moaned and complained whenever Burkhard or his son, Gernot, prodded them to get moving.

Much to Marcus' surprise and disappointment, the legionnaires were part of the problem, not the solution. They were all green—seventy-seven of them—replacements for losses in the northern forts, and they had foolishly all been sent under the command of one green vigil straight out of the lycee. The man was in way over his head and foolishly viewed Marcus and his two experienced officers as a threat, not a potential resource. He'd obviously heard of the disaster in the Fire Islands and feared that any contact between him and the exiled Marcus could taint his entire career. So the three legionnaires watched with a combination of amusement and concern as the Green Vigil continually failed to capture the respect of his men and get them to perform with the efficient discipline of true legionnaires.

The big exceptions to this pattern (aside from Marcus and his men who were always ready to start their wagon rolling an hour before dawn) were a handful of the most experienced merchants. They wanted to get on the road and cover as many miles as possible before they stopped again at sunset. Every day lost to traveling was a day they couldn't be selling their wares and buying the goods they wanted for the return trip. They also knew that provisions could run out on the trail and were always looking for the chance to replenish their water containers—huge ceramic amphorae like the ones that contained Marcus' wine. Too many of the other travelers didn't seem to understand that as they entered the Sea of Grass proper, the opportunity to replenish their supplies would be few and far between.

And so they walked beside the slow moving wagons, making between twenty and twenty-five miles per day, and Marcus wondered what would happen if they actually did run into any savages.

****

"Calidus, please tell me we brought replacement axles for the wagon."

The wagon they were rapidly catching up to had broken its axle and the man standing beside it looked hopeless and lost. He was Gente, by the look of him, with very black hair, a neatly trimmed beard, well tanned features, and an amethyst stud adorning his ear. His clothing was silk—far too fine for the trail—and there was a softness about the man's hands that suggested he had little experience with manual labor.

"We have a dozen," Calidus answered him.

The number was much higher than Marcus had expected. There were four spare wheels tied to each side of their wagon but he hadn't noticed any axles.

Calidus read his surprise and shrugged. "They don't take up a lot of space and it seemed like it was better to have and not need them then to want them and be forced to do without."

Marcus nodded with approval. "Correct as usual, go get one out of our wagon while Severus and I go borrow a dozen legionnaires."

Without stopping to talk to the family in trouble, he and Severus double-timed it up to the straggling tail end of the long line of green legionnaires—all pretense at walking in a column had fallen out of them. They had abandoned their armor—presumably to the wagons—and none even wore a sword. It was pathetic and seeing the lowly state of preparedness brought back bad memories of the lax conditions Marcus had had to contend with in the Fire Islands.

"Green Vigil!" Marcus bellowed in his best parade voice.

Legionnaires whipped around to look for the officer, saw Marcus and Severus striding toward them in their civilian clothes, and reacted in a half dozen different ways—all but one of which further annoyed Marcus. Most ignored them. A few continued to watch warily. Only a few reacted to the voice of command by attempting to fall back into the column formation in which they'd been trained.

From further up the formation, Green Vigil Phanes Kimon turned and made his tired way back down the line of his legionnaires. "Yes," he said with a sigh of impatience, notably failing to salute his superior officer—a bad practice despite the fact that Marcus was on leave. "What can I do for you?"

Marcus had not yet decided how much control he would assert over these troops. This wasn't his duty and the young man's commanding officer would be justified in complaining if Marcus interfered too blatantly with his troops, but Marcus had never been particularly good at accommodating fools.

"I need to borrow a dozen of your men. A wagon has broken down back in the line and the owners are going to need help to get it moving again."

"My men are legionnaires," Phanes announced as if he somehow thought that Marcus had failed to understand that. "They are not common laborers to go fix a broken wagon."

The young officer deserved to have the haughty expression knocked off his face, but before humiliating him, Marcus tried one more time to reason with him. "And yet, when the legions march they are often accompanied by extensive supply trains. Who do you think fixes those wagons when they break?"

Reason did not penetrate the young man's thick skull. "Those are not *legion* wagons. My men do not—"

Marcus reached out, caught the man's earlobe and twisted it hard enough to make it feel like he intended to rip it off.

Green Vigil Phanes screamed in shock and pain, his body twisting awkwardly at his tried to relieve the pressure on his ear. His caught at Marcus' wrist with his hand but failed utterly to force it away from his head.

Marcus dragged the young officer about fifty feet to the side of his disgraceful column and threw him onto the grass while his men and most of the wagon occupants in sight pointed and laughed.

"Green Vigil Phanes, you are a disgrace to the legion," Marcus told him in a remarkably calm and almost uninterested voice. "Your men do not know how to march in column. What is worse, despite the fact that everyone in this caravan has been warned that the savages are acting up, none of them are wearing their armor, carrying their shields, or bearing their swords."

"We're just passengers—" Phanes started to say, but Marcus kicked him soundly beneath the chin to shut him up again.

"Even worse, you antagonized a superior officer by insulting him for making a suggestion regarding the disposition of your men."

Phanes spit out a mouthful of blood. "You're not in my chain of command!"

"No, I'm not," Marcus agreed. "But I am a *tribune* who is going to have dinner with every commanding officer we meet in the forts between here and the Jeweled Hills. Don't you think it would be advisable to accommodate a couple of reasonable requests to make certain I put in a good word to counter the absolutely abysmal impression you will make when your ragtag column of men straggles in?"

"No one really expects us to be ready to fight yet," Phanes protested. "I mean, we haven't even been assigned to our hands and there are no red and black bands to back us up."

Despite the man's arrogance and utter stupidity, Marcus felt his first nudge of sympathy for the young officer. He crouched down in front of him. "Of course you're expected to be ready to fight. You're legionnaires— part of the greatest army in the world. Yes, you have a lot to learn still, but if the savages ride over that low hill right now, you're expected to form your men in ranks and march into battle."

Marcus stood. "Now get up, wipe the blood off your chin, and walk back with me as if nothing has happened. Then call out twelve strong men to accompany me back to the broken wagon. I'll leave Black Vigil Severus Lupus with you for the time being. Listen to what he tells you and you'll have these men doing you proud by the time we reach Fort Prime tomorrow afternoon."

From the sullen expression on the young man's face, Marcus did not expect a genuine change of heart. But he got up and stalked back to his men with Marcus and two minutes later, twelve legionnaires were walking behind the tribune to help fix the broken wagon.

****

Caravan Master Burkhard had ridden back to the broken wagon accompanied by a couple of his guards and was firmly berating the soft-looking man as the last of the long line of wagons rolled past. "No, I cannot wait the whole caravan on you. I told you when you joined that you were responsible for your own wagon. You stupid Gente! If you didn't know how to drive a wagon, you should have hired someone to do it for you."

"I did hire a driver, Caravan Master, but he proved to be a base miscreant and abandoned me yesterday morning. I fear that my father-in-law's competitors must have intervened and paid or scared him off."

Burkhard remained unmoved by the man's problems. "Then you should have paid him more. I can't hold up the entire caravan for one wagon."

"Of course you cannot," the man agreed with great generosity. "But what you can do is not seek such extreme profit from our misfortune. All would agree that you deserve some gain from your foresight in having brought an extra axle, but one hundred denari—that, my good man, is more than outrageous—it is bordering on the criminal."

The flowery speech bounced off of Burkhard's cool uncaring façade. "It's what a good axle is worth out here. You should have had a bit more of that foresight you're praising me for."

"But candidly, my good man, I haven't got one hundred silver pieces. It is—"

Marcus entered the conversation. "And you don't need it." He held up one of the axles that Calidus had brought with them. Burkhard frowned but didn't object in any way.

"Oh, thank you," the man gushed. "Our driver abandoned us yesterday and I'm trying to drive the wagon but I have no experience with the overland route. We had intended to sail up the coast but between the pirates turning the blue ocean red and now the storm season coming to ravage the coastal waters we simply could not find a ship willing to risk the journey. Yet my father-in-law cannot wait for the pirates and the weather to sort themselves out. He will be ruined if we don't get this cargo through to him."

Marcus' head started to throb from the effort of keeping up with the man's rapid speech. Bad enough that he spoke in the language of the Gente, but he formed the words so quickly that each flowed into the other without any clear break between them. He was still trying to formulate a reply when a soft feminine voice added her thoughts of gratitude.

"Yes, thank you, noble stranger. My husband is quite right. It is vital we get this cargo through to my father in Amatista, but our long stay in Dona has depleted our savings and we really have very little to pay you with."

Marcus turned and noticed the Gente's much younger wife—say, nineteen to his thirty—sitting in the tiny bit of shade cast by the broken wagon. She was very noticeably pregnant—so much so that the baby was almost certain to come on their trip north. She wore beautiful amethyst earrings and her fingers were adorned with many rings, but the bracelets that Marcus understood most northern women wore were missing—as if she'd had to sell them off. This was a family in distress, although, perhaps, not quite as grave a situation as they were suggesting.

"Ah, and where are my manners," the woman's husband said. "My name is Señor Alberto Lope and this lovely young flower is my most beautiful wife, Carmelita. And you, our savior, are?"

"Tribune Marcus Venandus." He pulled his eyes away from the wife wondering how people could be so utterly stupid. Was there really no option but to take a pregnant woman on a wagon ride across the Sea of Grass?

"From Aquila?" the man asked as if nothing that Marcus had said could have pleased him more. Then, without waiting for a response, he extended his hand. "My new friend, I am truly pleased to meet you. Your arrival is as welcome as a cool breeze on a hot summer day. Long shall we remember your kindness to strangers that nothing but your virtuous heart compelled you to aid."

"Speaking of aid," Marcus said, "why don't we see about getting your wagon back on four wheels."

"But of course, of course," Alberto agreed.

As he opened his mouth to continue describing just how deeply he was in accord with Marcus' suggestion, the Tribune turned his back on the man and addressed the legionnaires. "What every young man thinks when he leaves home to join the legion is that he's going to spend the rest of his days locked in pitched battles fighting for the glory of the Republic. And it's absolutely true that fighting is the most important thing we do, but—and I want you to listen closely to me here—it's never *all* that we do.

"We train for battle, fortify locations, conduct some more training, build roads and bridges, engage in some training maneuvers, wash our uniforms and polish our armor, and train a bit more for battle."

By this time all twelve men were smiling as if Tribune Marcus Venandus were the greatest wit who'd ever addressed them.

"So can you guess what we're going to do right now?"

"Help these people get their wagon fixed?" one of the men shouted.

"No," Marcus told them. "We're going to train you how to fix a wagon the legion way—get it back up and rolling as quickly as possible. Do you understand?"

"Yes, Tribune!" all twelve men called out, proving they'd had a good foundation of training before they'd joined the caravan.

"Excellent!" Marcus complemented them…and he meant it. Attitude was important when working with green legionnaires. Normally he'd leave a task like this to one of his vigils, but Severus and Calidus were both busy elsewhere and it wasn't like Marcus hadn't served as both a green and red vigil in his time.

"Now we don't want to have to unload the wagon," Marcus told them. "So follow my directions closely."

In a remarkably short period of time, Marcus had assisted the pregnant Carmelita to rise and accompany her husband out of the way of the legionnaires. They then unhitched the team of horses, lifted the corner of the wagon and removed the broken axle. Marcus wished he had something to set the corner down on so that his men could rest, but they were in a great plain with no tree stumps or even a helpful rocky outcropping in the immediate area. So he rotated the legionnaires bearing the weight of the wagon while two of their number climbed underneath the bed and repaired the broken axle mounting. They then quickly remounted the two wheels and hitched the horses up again. In a very short time the wagon was fixed and ready to roll.

"Marvelous," Alberto cried clapping his hands together. "Your men are simply amazing. I could not follow the speech you gave to inspire them, but the results do in fact speak for themselves, don't they?"

His wife stretched up on the tips of her toes to whisper in his ear. "But, of course, how could I forget such a thing? He reached for his purse. How may I compensate you and your men for your labors this afternoon in the very heat of the day?"

Marcus had been thinking about that. He didn't like acting like a merchant. Calidus was good at such things but Calidus wasn't a patrician either. So how could he handle this affair without compromising his sense of honor?

"That won't be difficult at all, Señor Alberto. Anyone who's been around the legion very long knows that the best way to thank these men is to treat them to a round of beer when we reach Fort Prime tomorrow."

"It shall be done!" Alberto announced with a flourish of his hand but he was unable to leave it without further embellishment. "And never has a round of drinks been more gallantly earned than that we shall deliver tomorrow night."

Marcus translated the complement—and the promise of beer—to the legionnaires who immediately let forth with a cheer.

Carmelita smiled up at her grinning husband before returning her attention to Marcus. "And you, good Tribune, how may we show our appreciation for your gallant rescue in our time of need?"

Marcus had to keep himself from laughing at the flowery speech. It was disturbingly reminiscent of his half-brother's letters and he began to wonder if perhaps everyone in the Jeweled Hills spoke in this fashion.

"I'm woefully ignorant regarding the customs of your people, but would it be possible for you to have me to dinner when we reach your home. Señora Carmelita mentioned earlier that her father lives in the city of Amatista. By coincidence I am traveling there to visit my brother. I'm sure we could find some night when the three of us are free to—"

"Wonderful!" Alberto exclaimed. "We must make it so. What a lovely coincidence that you are traveling to our beautiful city. It is the gateway in the southeast funneling the treasures of the Jeweled Hills to the lower regions of the Jeweled Coast. And now, with all of this piracy, it may play an even larger role if this overland route is to become ever more popular."

"I am confused by that," Marcus confessed. "Amatista is in the southern portion of the Jeweled Hills with only a couple of other minor city states between it and us."

"Only Topacio, really," Alberto corrected him. "There are other cities like Granate and Morganita, but it is only through Topacio's territory that we will have to pass."

"So my question is: Why isn't this overland route more popular? You said people are only turning to it now because of the pirates. But if this road ends up in your backyard, so to speak, why isn't it more heavily used?"

"Oh, I see why you're confused now," Alberto said. "I hope you will not be offended when I say that it is obvious that you have only a limited familiarity with commerce."

"That is true," Marcus agreed, "and no, I'm not the slightest bit insulted. Please, explain the preference for the sea to me if you can."

"But of course," the Gente said. "There are two reasons why we prefer the sea route even though it forces us to pay the tariffs on goods passing through the cities of the Jeweled Coast. The first is cost, as any merchant would know. It is always much more expensive to travel overland than it is by water. The costs can be twenty-five, fifty, even one hundred times more expensive to move goods by wagon than by ship. The final amount depends on the bulk of the goods being transported and how long it takes them to arrive. Only the smallest of goods—say a pocketful of gemstones—might be cheaper traveling overland."

He waited for Marcus to nod that he understood before continuing.

"This first reason would be true just about anywhere in the world. The second one is specific to the two routes in question. Until recently, the overland route was considered to be much more dangerous than the coastal passage, and that was before this savage shaman, Teetonka, started rallying the tribes and swearing to drive all the whites off the Sea of Grass."

"Excuse me," Marcus interrupted. "Did you say this Teetonka is *rallying the tribes*?" He wondered why the official back in the governor's office in Dona hadn't mentioned this when he told Marcus of the savages. It was obviously an important development which—if true—greatly increased the danger of the overland route.

"Yes, he has been trying to gather support to *purge the grass* for several years now with only modest success, but I am told he raids caravans to prove that the whites—and especially your Aquilan legions—are vulnerable."

Marcus relaxed a little. That didn't sound so bad after all. "So the overland route was more dangerous until the pirates starting acting up."

"Yes, the individual cities of the Jeweled Coast had treaties with the so called Trevilian Federation through which they paid the pirates off. There were always a few unexplained attacks, but in the past few months a pirate feeding frenzy has started making the Sea of Grass look safe by comparison."

Marcus nodded again. "That makes a lot of sense. Thank you for explaining it to me."

"Not at all," Alberto said. "We are happy to in some small way begin to repay our debt to you."

"If I may also ask a question?" Carmelita asked.

"Of course," Marcus responded.

"Will you share the name of your brother in Amatista? It is possible that Alberto and I are familiar with him."

"He's Juan Pablo Cazador."

Both Alberto and Carmelita frowned slightly.

"What is it?"

Both Gente immediately grimaced in embarrassment. "Please accept my apologies," Alberto said. "I did not mean to give you the impression that something is wrong. We are, of course, familiar with your brother, as you must have expected."

Marcus shook his head. "Quite the opposite—I never dreamed you would know him. Amatista is a sizable city and it seemed an unlikely chance that you would have even heard his name."

"Surely, Tribune, you know your brother is a very wealthy man," Carmelita asked him. "And he has often served as an official of the Gota government."

"*Very* wealthy?" Marcus repeated.

"Oh, yes," Alberto assured him. "In addition to his many business interests, your brother heads the Association—a group of important Gota and Gente families that control the silk monopoly."

Marcus tried to remember if his brother had even written about owning businesses. Land? Yes! He had farms and coal mines—the rock that burned. But actual businesses like a merchant would run? That possibility had never really occurred to him.

"I don't really know anything about my brother's businesses," Marcus told them. He tried to keep the disapproval off his face. "A monopoly does sound lucrative."

"Amatista is the largest center of silk production outside of the Qing Empire," Alberto told him.

"The Qing do not like the loss of their monopoly," Carmelita added. "Many think that they are behind the disasters that struck the businesses in Diamonte and Aquamarina."

Both of those were cities of the Jeweled Coast, Marcus knew. The Coast, in general, was far wealthier than the inland cities.

"Your brother basically built the Amatista industry on his own," Alberto admitted with grudging respect. "He found financial backers, coaxed the experts out of Aquamarina after the fires ravaged the growing silk district and found supporters among the Gota and Gente to establish the trade."

"His mother is so proud of him," Carmelita said, her eyes shining with sudden happiness. "All her life she has had to pretend not to hear the whispers about her half-Aquilan son, but he proved to be the perfect man to build this new enterprise. The Gota liked the Aquilan half of him and when he brought them on board for their political support, he was also able to raise a lot of capital among the Gente dons and señors."

As they warmed to the topic, Marcus could see that both Alberto and Carmelita admired Juan Pablo for his accomplishments. "So why did you frown when I mentioned his name?"

Rather than look embarrassed and try to pretend Marcus had misunderstood his expression, Alberto let loose with a sharp Gente curse. "It is the damn Qing refugees! They are everywhere in Amatista now because of Señor Juan Pablo. First he debased himself by marrying a Qing woman when he already had a perfectly respectable señora for his wife. But the business required him to marry again to convince the Qing to abscond from Aquamarina and resettle in Amatista and he abandoned all propriety as if he were a Gota barbarian. Then he encouraged thousands—it may be tens of thousands now—to follow them to our city and its hinterland to work in the silk factories."

"They are disgusting," Carmelita agreed. "They work for such a small pittance that the Gota prefer to hire them over proper Gente families."

Marcus had heard arguments like this before. When Aquila had first begun to expand it had brought tens of thousands of slaves home to do the sort of work that no Aquilan should have to. But the result was not universal happiness as the number of poor in Aquila and its territories blossomed forcing the government to eliminate the property requirement for legion service and to divert hundreds of thousands of denari from other projects to feed the poor. It was popular to this day to grumble about the situation, but the loudest complaints came from wealthy slaveholders unhappy that their taxes were going to feed the poor. He wondered how many Qing servants Alberto and Carmelita employed in their home.

But there was still at least one portion of the story that Marcus failed to understand. "You described the Qing as refugees?"

"Yes," Alberto said, "there were always a few of them around, but the situation got much worse forty years ago when the Qing Empire invaded Ttang across the Bottomless Sea. This caused hordes of the Ttang to flee their country in rickety little boats to end up in the cities of the Jeweled Coast. Mostly they stayed there for the first couple of decades, but since your brother established the silk trade in Amatista far too many have relocated to our home."

"As if it were not bad enough," Carmelita added, "that we have to put up with the Gota lording it over us in our own city, now we have these *vermin* everywhere as well."

The conversation had taken a decidedly unpleasant turn for Marcus. It was not that he could not understand the frustrations of the Gente couple, but why could they not see that their problems were ultimately of their own making? The Gente were infamously divided among themselves, remembering insults given three hundred years before and so conscious of status that they could barely unite to run their city-states much less the whole of the Jeweled Hills and the Jeweled Coast.

Their internal divisions were so bad that they had infected the Gota with their malaise. In the years following their conquest, the Gota had been united under a single thegn but today every major city claimed one.

He glanced toward the caravan which continued to pull away from them. "Well, we better catch up with the others. If you wouldn't mind, Señor Alberto, I will assign one of the legionnaires to ride with you and give you pointers on the fine art of driving a large wagon like this. A gentleman such as yourself has probably never had the opportunity before."

"Again you are most generous with us," Alberto told him. "I do not know what my wife and I would have done had you not been willing to lend us your aid."

"It has been my pleasure," Marcus assured him. At the very least, he mused, it was educational. Juan Pablo was evidently far more important than Marcus had realized. He wondered what trouble could cause such a man to reach out to his half-brother in Aquila for assistance.

He pointed at one of the men whose banter during the replacement of the broken axle had revealed that he had plenty of experience driving wagons and carts and jerked his thumb toward the front of the wagon. Then he scooped up the rest of his borrowed legionnaires and led them back to their Green Vigil.

Day Four
The Men Are Sharp and Well-Trained

Fort Prime was a typical Aquilan castrum with a deep ditch surrounding the exterior with the dirt thrown inward to build an earthen wall. Had they not been in the middle of a treeless prairie a wooden palisade would have fortified the square perimeter. Inside a wide street bisected the castrum and in the center could be found the headquarters of the commanding officer, the supply warehouse, a forum for business and a parade ground for reviewing the troops. Tents lined the street to either side of the central buildings laid out by cohort and hand. In short, Prime was laid out exactly like every other castrum Marcus had ever seen.

He noted with approval the crisp, watchful, movements of the Prime legionnaires. This was not a post which took its responsibilities lightly. The men on duty all wore their armor including their shields and while an appropriate number kept an eye on the wagons rolling in through the gates, the posted watchmen kept their eyes out on the plains where they belonged. No one gave the appearance of having forgotten that they were in the legion. It was a welcome return to normality for Marcus after his years stationed under the lax command of Praetor Castor in the Fire Islands.

The wagons were directed to begin pulling off the road to the west of the central street with legionnaires directing the traffic with a skill and efficiency that suggested they had done this many times before. As Marcus' wagon drew closer, he could see that there were far fewer tents than he had expected—there were no more than two hundred men posted in a fort large enough to support an entire legion. Understaffing was a perpetual problem in the military, but this seemed particularly light given the reports of active raiding by the local savages.

Kuno turned the wagon when their turn came and parked where directed. Then he jumped off the wagon and with Calidus' help began to unhitch the team.

Marcus caught Severus' eye. "Let's take a look around. I like the look of these legionnaires but something about this setup is troubling me."

"Could it be," Severus asked, "that you're wondering how two hands can hold a castrum this large?"

"Something like that," Marcus agreed.

****

"The men are sharp and well-trained," Severus conceded.

"I agree," Marcus said, "but there aren't enough of them to hold the outer perimeter. A whole phalanx could do it, but not one small cohort—I don't care how good they are."

He turned in place on the top of the earthen wall to examine the rest of the battlements. Legionnaires had been posted at regular intervals so they could see what was coming, but especially with their numbers distracted by the caravan, there simply weren't enough to respond to a significant attack.

Marcus pointed at the buildings at the center of the castrum. "Whoever is in charge here needs to fortify that. Throw up an inner wall that surrounds the praetorium, the quaestorim, the forum and the parade ground."

"That would take a huge set of balls," Severus noted. "Can you imagine the storm he'd kick up back in Dona, or even in the Senate in Aquila, if he let savages pillage the wagons of the caravan while he and his men hid behind an inner wall?"

Marcus couldn't care less about political storms and Severus knew it, but he played out the argument to see if there was something important he was missing. "The goods might be lost, but an inner wall would be the only chance to make sure all those civilians survive if the savages attack in force."

"How big a force are you thinking of?" Severus asked as he watched a red vigil stride toward them from the direction of the wagons

Marcus shrugged. "All it would take is two or three hundred men to rush the wall in the front and this cohort would have nothing left to defend against any number coming over the walls to the side and rear. It's too big to defend."

"That's how I see it too," Severus admitted. "Are you going to tell that to the officer in charge of this place?"

Marcus rolled his eyes at his old friend, "Only if he asks."

A Red Vigil called out to them from a hundred feet away, but did not stop advancing on their position. "I am looking for Tribune Marcus Venandus and Black Vigil Severus Lupus."

"We are they," Marcus admitted.

The Vigil came to a sharp halt and saluted crisply. "Tribune Marcus, it is my pleasure to invite you to dine tonight with Tribune Lucanus."

Marcus returned the salute, pressing his fist to his heart. "I would be honored."

The man addressed Severus. "Black Vigil, the vigils of Fort Prime would be most pleased if you would join them in the mess tonight. There will be stories to be told, Vigil, and we always want to learn what we can of the road."

Severus nodded without verbally answering.

The Red Vigil clearly understood the taciturn way of the blacks and pivoted back to face Marcus. "Tribune Lucanus has charged me to seek out members of the caravan who it would be proper to invite to his table. I've already extended an invitation to the Gota lord and the Caravan Master and his son. Would the Tribune care to recommend others who should merit an invitation?"

Marcus considered the request for a moment. He had made a point of introducing himself to most of the principals traveling with the caravan. There were seven major merchants, a dozen families, and a motley assortment of men who had personal reasons for risking the overland route to go north. "Only two others come to mind. One is a student magus traveling north. He would certainly be flattered by an invitation and he might know some people in common with your own magus."

The Red Vigil nodded.

"As for the other, there is a Gente man traveling with his very pregnant wife. I suspect they would both benefit greatly from a properly cooked meal. It would be a kindness to invite them, but I doubt seriously that they would expect it."

Again the officer nodded before asking for the three names and informing him that dinner would be served at the praetorium at sunset.

****

The first person Marcus saw as he entered the praetorium was Apprentice Magus Seneca Liberus who stood just inside the door looking around as if trying to figure out who it would be appropriate for him to approach. Marcus clapped him stoutly on the shoulder and the poor man nearly leaped out of his shoes.

"What!"

He whirled around, saw Marcus, and flushed with embarrassment. "Oh, excuse me, Tribune. You snuck up on me. I—normally I have a sense for people moving about me. It has to do with their spirits and—"

Marcus cut him off when he started to babble. "I think your stomach is the problem. It senses the chance to have a real dinner for the first time since we left Dona and that's all that you can think about."

Seneca clearly wasn't certain if Marcus was being serious or not. "I…guess that it's, Sir."

"Come on," Marcus said, "let's go meet the Tribune and his officers."

The younger man gratefully followed after Marcus as he walked deeper into the room and discovered that the legionnaires he was seeking were not yet present. No one else was really mixing yet. In addition to Master Burkhard and his son, there were all of the major merchants in the caravan—a fact that surprised Marcus somewhat, but shouldn't have. Half the reason for this gathering was to let the Tribune learn what was happening in Dona and elsewhere in the south and traders always made it their business to know what was going on in the world. Many of the merchants were southerners of some sort, the others were Gente from the Jeweled Hills and the two groups were standing on opposite sides of the room.

The Gota, Lord Evorik, stood with two women looking disdainfully upon his traveling companions. Where the Gente were dark of hair and features with their manicured mustaches and close-trimmed beards, the Gota had wild shocks of long red hair that screamed *barbarian* by contrast. The observation intrigued Marcus and he tried to figure out why he drew such a conclusion.

Both groups dressed in the same expensive silks, although the merchants added elaborately embroidered vests to their attire. Both groups wore copious numbers of jewels adorning their clothing—either topazes or amethysts, presumably depending on their city of origin. Both also wore rings with a variety of precious stones all in all making what to an Aquilan's taste was a crude display of wealth. The only true difference between the lord and the Gente men was that he wore thick bands of gold on his wrists and even his upper arms, where they wore thinner bands on their wrists alone. Were a couple of armlets enough to mark him a barbarian, or was it the hard look in his eyes with which he stared down the merchants in the room?

The guests stirred when Alberto and Carmelita entered the room behind Marcus and Seneca. Marcus met their eyes and nodded, but did not retrace his steps to speak with them. He was planning to approach the Gota lord first as he was obviously the ranking civilian in the room, but before he could finish acting on his intention, a man wearing the sash of a tribune—thick red band bordered on one side by a thin green line and on the other by a thin black one—entered the room. The magus walking beside him wore a sash with three stars. Behind them came two lesser tribunes to round out the party.

"Welcome!" The Tribune greeted them. "Welcome to Fort Prime. I am Tribune Lucanus. This is Magus Jocasta, my cohort wizard. And these are my Lesser Tribunes, Brennius and Caius. I thank you all for joining me tonight and look forward to speaking with each of you. The food will be out shortly. In the meantime," he snagged a cup of wine off a tray carried by a servant, or more likely, a slave. "Enjoy the wine and your night off from the trail."

He waited patiently while the few guests such as Marcus and Seneca who did not yet have drinks received them, and then the whole company indulged together to officially start the evening.

"She's beautiful," Seneca breathed even as Tribune Lucanus started across the floor in their direction.

Marcus glanced at Carmelita before he realized that Seneca was staring at the magus. "A word of advice," he offered, even though he was fairly certain the young man would prove unable to follow it. "Never get involved in a romance with your superiors."

Seneca turned to him in confusion. "But I'm not in the legion."

"You're still a student," Marcus reminded him. "Every full magus is your better."

He broke off as the Magus and Tribune reached them. "You must be Tribune Marcus," Lucanus said. "I've heard rumors of the campaign in the Fire Islands—legions of skeletons rising from their graves." He said it as if he half expected Marcus to deny the story.

"It did get rather dicey," Marcus admitted. "I'd be happy to share the whole tale over dinner if you're truly interested. But first, may I present a student traveling with our caravan to continue his studies in the north."

Suddenly shy, he had to subtly push the young wizard in the small of the back to get him to step forward, "Seneca Liberus of the Collegium Magicae in Aquila."

"I am an alumna of that school myself," Magus Jocasta informed them. "You must tell me everything that's been happening there these past years. I am simply starved for proper gossip."

She stepped aside with Seneca leaving the two tribunes alone together.

"I certainly would like to hear your story," Lucanus picked up the earlier line of conversation.

"Excellent," Marcus agreed, "because I would like to hear from you all about these savages on the Sea of Grass."

"Just let me meet the rest of my guests and get them seated at the table," Lucanus suggested. "Then we can talk all night if need be."

****

"Mule piss!" Lord Evorik exclaimed. "I know those tiny horses of theirs are fast and their arrows certainly are a nuisance, but no Sea of Grass savage can stand up to a company of Gota cavalry. Why my twenty warriors alone are sufficient to ensure the safety of the entire caravan, even without Master Burkhard's guards."

The Gota lord and his two wives, Marcus had learned, were traveling home to the city of Topacio after a diplomatic mission to Dona. He was, like many barbarians, a pompous and overbearing character, but based on the hard steel in his glare, Marcus was willing to bet he could back up at least half of what he was saying.

The conversation between Marcus, Evorik and Lucanus was in Aquilan, as this was a Republic fort. Marcus sat on the left of the Tribune while the Gota lord sat on his right with his two wives speaking quietly together beside him. They spoke Gente, which Marcus found particularly interesting. The conquerors had in some ways become the conquered.

"The savages like to attack out of a dust cloud," Lucanus picked up his explanation. "Their shaman have some minor gifts in this regard. Unfortunately, that isn't as much help to the defender as you might think because the wind is constantly picking up on these plains which makes dust all too common."

"The wagons also generate a lot of dust," Marcus observed. "We might as well be setting signal fires wherever we go."

Lucanus nodded sympathetically. "So to get back to the problem at Fort Segundus, the savages employed their hit and run tactics and the Great Tribune sent out a cohort to punish them. The savages charge in on their ponies firing arrows, but a solid legion shield wall is usually able to protect the men from such an attack while the second file readies its pilum. We carry four with us here as it is the principle method of spoiling a savage attack. That's why we have so many wagonloads of pilum in your caravan. Each fort is in constant need of resupply."

"Get on with the attack," Evorik demanded. "We're warriors, not clerks. You can waste time talking about resupply when you're in bed with your wives."

At least one of the Gente among the merchants could follow their conversation because he frowned in disgust at the Gota's statement.

"So normally it only takes a couple of well-thrown volleys of pilum to scare the savages off, but this time was different. They kept circling the cohort, forcing them to form a square. Then they shot high into the air so that their arrows came down inside the square where the shields were not protecting the men. Quickly the men ran out of pilum and there was nothing they could do to strike back—the cowards wouldn't come within reach of their swords. So the Lesser Tribune detailed a dozen men to break out and try to alert Fort Segundus to their peril.

"The men succeeded in escaping, but it appears now that letting them go was part of the savages' plan. They have a new leader and he's a wily devil. He let the fort send out reinforcements then revealed he had about a thousand more savages in his army. Even then, the phalanx could have handled the situation without too much trouble, but this Teetonka is also a powerful shaman and he broke our ranks with lightning—opening the way for his savages to swarm the legion."

He let that comment sit with them a moment before continuing. "It got bad then, but they still couldn't break us. We killed three or maybe four savages for every legionnaire they pulled down and in the end we routed them. The savages fled completely broken."

Evorik grunted in approval and slammed the table with his open palm.

"The threat is completely ended?" Marcus prompted.

"The remnants have gone back to their more typical raiding," Lucanus hedged. "In the aftermath of the battle, the Great Tribune ordered the other cohort stationed at Fort Prime to reinforce the legion at Fort Segundus until more permanent reinforcements arrive. These greens traveling with you are a good chunk of the new men. So we advise caravans to be cautious on the trail, but no, the major threat is definitely ended."

"That is good!" Evorik proclaimed with another open-palmed smack of the table. "I have always said that your legionnaires are tough men for infantry—not as dangerous as proper Gota cavalry, but tough men just the same."

Lucanus nodded politely while Marcus decided not to counter the man's argument with cold hard legion logic. Instead he kept the conversation on the topic that really mattered. "And the caravans are totally back to normal?"

The Tribune shrugged. "As normal as they get. The ones from the south are longer than we usually get while the ones from the north have become more erratic."

"What precisely does that mean?" Marcus asked.

"It's the difference between the way things are done in the provinces of Aquila and the way they are done in the rest of the world," Lucanus explained. "Caravans leave Aquilan territory quite regularly, but in the north the Gente don't think that way. So sometimes you get two or three coming south in a week, and sometimes you go two or three weeks without seeing any."

Marcus did not like the sound of this. "And it's been two or three weeks since anyone has come south?"

Lucanus nodded.

"You should not look so worried," Evorik told Marcus. "The Tribune, here, is quite correct. The Gente—they are shit! All that they worry about is the last time they bathed and which perfume shall they lather themselves in today."

Now that Marcus thought about it, Alberto and the other Gente men did smell quite a bit like expensive whores.

"I would feel better," Marcus admitted, "if we had fresh news of the trail ahead of us. It never hurts to know what your enemies have been up to. When was the last time you had a report from Fort Segundus?"

"The reports come with each caravan," Lucanus explained. "I will send one with Master Burkhard when you leave in the morning. Again it is nothing to be concerned about."

Marcus forced himself to sit back in his chair and relax. No matter how little he liked what he was hearing, there was absolutely nothing he could do about it—at least not until he could talk to young Seneca

Day Five
An Issue of Purity

"Did you enjoy your evening last night, Magus?" Marcus asked, promoting the young wizard with friendly politeness.

"What?" the young wizard asked, spinning around in surprise. "Oh, it's you, Tribune." He breathed a sigh of relief. "I don't know how you keep catching me by surprise. It's not supposed to be so easy to sneak up on a magus—even a magus-in-training such as myself."

Marcus couldn't help smiling. "My apologies, Magus, I didn't mean to startle you. I was just curious if you'd enjoyed the dinner party last night."

They'd gotten their earliest start yet this morning, rolling out of Fort Prime just as the sun had begun to peak over the horizon. Marcus gave the credit to Lucanus' legionnaires rather than to Caravan Master Burkhard. The legionnaires had made certain that everyone was up and ready an hour before dawn and had not accepted any excuses. As a result, everyone was tired. The stopover in Fort Prime had been a welcome break from the monotony of the trail but it had not been much of a rest.

Exhaustion, however, didn't stop Seneca from bubbling with enthusiasm at the mention of the dinner party. "I did, indeed! Magus Jocasta is an impressive—not to mention beautiful—woman."

"I'm sure she is," Marcus agreed. He wondered if the young man's little bout of puppy love had been as obvious to the seasoned Magus as it was to everyone else. He'd followed the woman around all evening and seemed surprised when it had been pointed out to him that it was time to get some sleep as the caravan would be leaving at dawn. All the way back to the wagons the young man had waxed eloquently about the older woman's abilities and accomplishments, with frequent reminders of her physical beauty thrown in between the other compliments.

Marcus decided to come to the point of his visit. "I wish to plunder your magical knowledge, if you can spare me a little of your time this evening."

Seneca brightened with excitement. "Of course, Tribune, how may the Collegium Magicae be of service to you?"

"I'm concerned about the trail ahead," Marcus explained. "I don't know how much you heard about this in Fort Prime, but there has been rather a lot of trouble with the savages in recent months and—"

"Oh, yes, Magus Jocasta told me all about it," Seneca gushed. "The legion at Fort Segundus really kicked their scrawny posteriors. Despite being greatly outnumbered, they broke the backs of the attacking raiders and sent them scurrying back across the plains."

It was that term *raider* that was causing Marcus his concern. Everything he'd been able to learn about the savages suggested that fighting a set piece battle against the legion was out of character for them. They were, apparently, masters of the hit and run attack—darting in on their fast little horses, firing off a flight of arrows, and racing away again before coming back from another direction to start their attack anew. Charging in to fight hand to hand was something they did *after* a foe had been fatally weakened. So Marcus wondered, had the legion really broken them, or had their leader, Teetonka, been smart enough to realize that he had erred in his judgment and called off the attack before he lost more men. Lucanus was certainly convinced that the legion had crushed all opposition, but it troubled Marcus tremendously that no caravan had come south in the past three weeks. That strongly suggested that a significant force of savages was still in the area.

"I'm wondering if you have advanced sufficiently in your training to have been taught the fine art of farseeing?" Marcus asked him.

"Oh, yes!" Seneca assured him. "I'm actually quite adept at the procedures. It's an important skill and one of the basic competencies required to graduate from the collegium."

"Excellent! I want you to take a look at the trail between here and Fort Segundus to see if you can find any caravans traveling toward us." He would also like the young man to look for savages, but they would presumably be harder to find so he started with the more straightforward task.

Seneca's enthusiasm drained away. "All the way to Fort Segundus?"

"Is that too far?"

"Maybe, I've never tried something far away, but well, I could try. When did you want me to do this?"

"Now."

"Right now?"

"It needs to be done before nightfall, doesn't it?" Marcus asked.

"Well, yes, but—I don't have the usual tools to help me with such a spell. I know it looks simple to outsiders, but it really is a complex working of energies."

Marcus didn't have any idea how farseeing worked, but it was a truism among officers of the legion that magi always made their spells sound much more difficult to cast than they really were. "I've seen a magus cast a farseeing in a cup of canteen water," he lied. "Can you really not pull something together to give us a look down the trail?"

Seneca thought for a moment. "I guess I can try. I need a bowl of pure metal. We used gold in the collegium, but silver or even copper are supposed to work nearly as well."

Marcus had anticipated this need and pulled out a silver cup his first sweetheart had given him when he left to join the legion. Her parents had married her to a Senator more than twice her age the next year, but he'd kept the cup as a memento of that first great love. He offered it to Seneca for the spell. "Will this do?"

Seneca examined the cup carefully, glancing up at Marcus when he found the initials M and V beneath the cup. He probably thought they stood for Marcus Venandus, but they were really for Marcus and Vesta. She'd been just careful enough not to want to create any incriminating evidence of their love in case their plans to marry each other didn't work out.

"How pure is the silver?" the young would-be magus asked.

"I don't know," Marcus conceded, "but I think it's pretty pure."

Seneca shrugged. "Let's give it a try. I'll also need a handful of salt and a few drops of oil."

"I can get them," Marcus told him, but the younger man had already risen.

"No need, I have a few supplies in my baggage."

He went to the wagon carrying his goods and climbed inside, appearing a few minutes later with a flask and a pouch. "So to be clear, you want me to summon a spirit to show me the trail ahead."

"A bird's eye view, if you can," Marcus told him. "Fly the bird forward and look for anything that isn't long blades of grass."

"That sounds simple enough," Seneca agreed. He sat down cross-legged and placed the cup in front of him, then looked up in alarm. "I forgot the water."

Marcus chuckled and pulled a water bag off the side of the wagon. "Will this do?"

"We should probably boil the water first to purify it, but we're running out of daylight so I guess it will have to do."

The student's comments reinforced Marcus' opinion that much of what wizards insisted upon was purely for show. He watched Seneca pull a handful of salt out of the pouch and then fling it into the air while he mumbled a few archaic-sounding words.

"What did you do that for?" Marcus asked.

The young man glanced reproachfully at him. "You do know that I am not permitted to reveal secrets of magery to the uninitiated, don't you?"

"That's not a secret of magery," Marcus countered. "You just threw salt in the air."

"It is so a secret," the student magus protested.

Marcus laughed. "What you really mean is that no one has told you why you throw the salt. You just know it's part of the ceremony."

Seneca squared his shoulders. "For your information, salt is a purifying agent. When I scatter it about me, the salt draws remnant magic out of the air, making it easier to cast my spell without the possibility of contamination."

"Interesting," Marcus mused. "Could you use it to disrupt a spell? Throw salt at a caster to suck his magic away?"

"No, salt is not that strong. It's just—wait a minute! I told you I can't talk about this."

Marcus suppressed a smile. "My lips are sealed."

Seneca pointed a finger at him. "No more questions! Agreed?"

"No more questions about the process at least."

"Good! Now be quiet so I can concentrate."

The young would-be magus bent over the cup and said a few words. It almost looked like he was praying. Then he filled the cup from the water bag, picked up his flask of oil and dripped a single drop onto the surface of the water.

"Now all I have to do is infuse my power in the drop of oil and…"

Marcus leaned closer, wondering if he would be able to see anything in the water.

A cloud of steam erupted from the silver cup, hitting both Seneca and Marcus in the face and blowing them over backward as if they'd been hit by a very strong wind.

A flash of pain flared momentarily on Marcus' face leaving behind only an annoying tingling feeling when it was gone.

"What happened?" he asked.

Seneca rolled onto his hands and knees, his face looking sunburnt after the explosion of steam. "I don't know. I thought I did everything right. I-I don't know why things keep going wrong. Maybe the cup wasn't pure enough or—I just don't know."

Marcus placed his hands firmly on the young man's shoulders. "Seneca, it's all right. No one was harmed. You tried to help me and it didn't work out. That's all that happened."

"I just don't understand why I can't get it right!"

Tears started to well in the young man's eyes and Marcus did not want to deal with a crying young magus. "Just wait a minute!" he said. "Think it through with me. You were trying to do a spell in the field without your proper equipment. This was not a classroom exercise. Of course it was more difficult. But we can learn from our mistakes, can't we? It's not all bad if we learn something, right?"

Seneca began to calm down. "I guess that makes sense."

"Of course, it does," Marcus told him. "Now think about what you did tonight and see if you can figure out anything we could do better if we decide to repeat this experiment tomorrow night."

"Repeat it tomorrow?" Seneca asked as if he couldn't believe Marcus had said the words. "You'd trust me to try this again?"

"Of course, I would—as long as you think you know how to make it work next time."

Marcus bent down and recovered the cup. He turned it over in his hands, examining it for damage. "Good, I was worried that little explosion might have broken it."

Seneca's eyes grew wide. "That's not just a cup is it? I thought you had it engraved with your initials in case someone tried to steal it from you, but that's not how you got it, is it?"

"No, it was a gift," Marcus told him.

"From someone who thinks you're very special, right?"

Marcus nodded. "Yes, that's right." There was no way he was going to tell this boy it came from his first love.

Seneca's shoulders drooped. "That's what went wrong."

"I don't understand," Marcus admitted.

"I thought it was just a cup, but whoever gave you that must have truly loved you. Was it your mother? Love is a form of magic all its own and it can interfere with a spell—especially if you're not prepared for it."

"Yes, this was a gift of love," Marcus confirmed. He was irrationally annoyed with himself for not having known this cup would disrupt the farseeing.

"That's what went wrong," Seneca said again.

Marcus forced himself to put on a pleased expression. "You see, already we're making progress. You didn't do things wrong you just didn't have all the necessary facts. Now eat something and get some sleep. Dawn comes early on the Sea of Grass."

Day Six
Armor Up

The wind began to pick up from the typical arid breeze that chaffed the skin but caused few other problems, to a gusty, dust kicking, annoyance which stung the eyes and set Marcus' teeth on edge. The direction of the wind had changed as well, no longer blowing primarily from the north but steadily from the northeast, precisely the direction that the caravan was traveling.

The Gente merchants in their caravan wrapped brightly colored silk kerchiefs around their faces to protect their noses and mouths from the assault of grit. Lord Evorik, his wives and his twenty Gota horsemen wrapped long silk scarves around their faces—although why they were wearing scarves in this weather Marcus could not understand. Whatever the reason, the scarves provided better protection than the kerchiefs and Marcus devoutly wished that he owned one. Lacking an article of cloth designed for the purpose, he took out his oldest tunic and cut four strips of protection from it, handing the extras to Severus, Calidus and the driver, Kuno.

The cloth helped, but it didn't calm the sense of uneasiness growing inside Marcus. He found himself straying far off to the side of the caravan where he could look forward and backward along its length, except the wind had picked up so much dust that he could only see maybe twenty or twenty-five wagons ahead and behind—the worst such visibility they had endured since they had begun this journey.

When he returned to his own wagon he found Severus and Calidus both waiting for him. "Well?" the Black Vigil asked.

"Well what?"

"You're acting like you think we're in danger," Severus told him.

"I am, aren't I?" Marcus told him. He looked up and down the line again. He was a man who trusted his intuition, but he had never had the second sight. What was it about this storm that was making him so uncomfortable and why had his skin started to prickle the moment the wind had shifted direction?

"You're thinking about the fact that we've all three been told by our different sources that the savages like to attack out of the dust," Severus told him.

Marcus nodded. "That and the fact that their shamans are adept at minor weather magic—mostly building winds to cover their movements."

"So why are you hesitating?" Severus asked. "Are you afraid of looking foolish if you're wrong?"

Marcus shrugged. The idea sounded preposterous to him. "Armor up—I'd always rather look foolish than be dead."

Calidus smiled. "You can always call it a drill, Tribune." He climbed into the wagon and started handing down pieces of armor: breastplates, grieves, and helmets. With the ease of long practice, each man slipped into his gear without falling behind the slowly moving wagon. When they were armored, Calidus handed down their swords and pilum before finally giving them the massive shields. Then he hopped down beside them ready for action.

Beside them, still driving the wagon, the Donan driver, Kuno, watched all of this with growing apprehension. "Stay steady!" Marcus informed him. "This may just prove to be a dust storm, but if it isn't, I'll have the legionnaires ready and we'll give the savages a reception they can't be expecting."

"You're armed?" Severus asked the practical question after Marcus' little speech.

The driver reached under the seat and pulled out a hatchet. "I've got my axe."

"You'll do fine," the Black Vigil told him but the man's eyes still darted back and forth as if he expected a savage to pop out and attack him at any time.

Marcus had no more time for him. Together with Severus and Calidus, he jogged up the wagon train at a pace slightly faster than the traditional double-time. His sense of urgency grew with the prickling of his skin—so much so that he didn't care about the stares and the shouted questions they received from the merchants as they passed. The only man he took note of was Lord Evorik, the Gota from Topacio, who had twenty horsemen under his command. The man was mounted as he always seemed to be, but rode easily beside the wagon with his two wives. Marcus slowed their pace to match that of his horse.

"Is there trouble, Tribune?"

"I don't like this storm," Marcus told him.

"You're thinking of the other Tribune's tales, aren't you?" the Gota teased. "A little dust and the savages must be attacking."

"It looks like a good time to drill the men."

Evorik laughed outright. "Maybe you're right. At the very least it will be more interesting than watching my wagons' wheels go around."

He turned toward his wives. "Hildurara, Riciberga, keep your knives handy. Fulgus may be smiling upon us and giving us a little excitement to break up this journey."

Both women reached into their dresses and pulled out sharp, dangerous-looking, little blades.

Evorik laughed again. "I'll round up my men and meet you by your legionnaires."

Without another word, he kicked his horse and raced up the line.

Marcus and his companions immediately increased their pace to reach the legionnaires whom Burkhard had begun placing near the front of the caravan, even as Marcus and his wagon had been assigned an extra dusty place in the rear. They found them walking in clumps in a stretched-out line reminiscent of how they'd marched before Severus had gotten his hands on them.

The older man ground his teeth but said nothing at the sight, but Calidus was not as circumspect. "I guess this proves that breeding is not enough to make a good officer."

"Is young Phanes that high born?" Marcus asked.

"His father is a cousin of Urbanus Kimon," Calidus explained naming an influential senator who was an on-again, off-again, ally of Marcus' father. A very pragmatic man, Urbanus liked to keep his options open and had supported the call to exile Marcus while the events in the Fire Islands were investigated, rather than let him be recalled for a show trial and executed for other men's crimes.

"And you're only now sharing this with me why?" Marcus asked. Much as he hated to admit it, he probably owed the Green Vigil something to repay Urbanus back for his mild support.

Calidus winked and grinned. "I figure a boy with those connections wouldn't be out here on the edge of nowhere for his first assignment if he wasn't a fuck up. Therefore you were already paying back Urbanus by trying to knock some sense into his thick head."

They were close enough now that Marcus could see that Phanes had ignored his suggestion and gone back to letting his legionnaires march without wearing their armor and weapons. Beside him, Severus ground his teeth even harder.

"Tribune?" he asked as the three men stopped beside the rear legion supply wagon.

"Go get them, Black Vigil!"

The older man almost smiled, before bellowing loudly enough to be heard from one end of the caravan to the other. "All legionnaires assemble for inspection! I want you standing here in front of the Tribune ready for war in two minutes and Sol Invictus help the man among you who dares to disappoint me!"

For a moment every one of the green legionnaires froze in place and then chaos erupted among them as they sprinted for the wagons which held their equipment.

Marcus watched with a small measure of amusement. "Not bad, Black Vigil, one afternoon under your gentle command and you have them jumping like seasoned troops."

"They're not a bad lot," Severus whispered. "Just need someone who knows what he's doing to tell them what's what."

"Speaking of not knowing what he's doing," Calidus said.

Green Vigil Phanes Kimon charged up to them, his face red with rage. "This is too much, Tribune Marcus! These men are under *my* command. You cannot—"

"Effective immediately," Marcus called out in his best parade voice, "I am taking command of this hand for the duration of the emergency."

"Taking command?" the younger officer repeated. "No you are—"

"Calidus!"

Without further instruction, Marcus' adjutant stepped beside the Green Vigil and placed a firm hand on his shoulder.

"Don't make me relieve you!" Marcus snapped in a quieter voice. "You can't be so blind as to not realize what's happening here. The plains are alive with unrest and this storm fits the pattern of savage attacks perfectly."

"What savages?" Phanes demanded. "They were all killed. You can't—"

"What the hell is going on here?" Gernot, the caravan master's son shouted as he raced up to them on horseback. "You've stopped the caravan. What the hell do you think you're doing?"

Marcus looked around and saw that the young man was correct. Many of the wagons had stopped and drivers and merchants were coming toward them to learn what was going on."

"I asked you a question!" Gernot screamed as he reached out and tried to grab hold of Marcus.

Calidus stepped away from Phanes, caught hold of one of Gernot's legs and pulled him off his horse. "You stay there and be quiet! The Tribune does not have time for your childishness right now."

Marcus needed to finish taking control of the situation. "You merchants and drivers, listen up!" His voice boomed out across the plain. "I need you to get back in your wagons and start them moving again. The legion is deploying in case the savages use this storm to cover an attack."

"The Gota too!" Lord Evorik announced as he rode up with his twenty men.

Fear and uncertainty were the predominant expressions on the faces of the merchants and Marcus had no time for them. "Move!" he commanded.

"What is going on here?" Caravan Master Burkhard demanded.

The last thing Marcus needed was another delay but Burkhard also commanded twenty guards on horseback. "We're preparing to fight off an attack by the savages. The storm—"

"What attack? Didn't you hear what Tribune Lucanus said? The Great Tribune in charge of Fort Segundus defeated the savages. They're broken. We have nothing to fear from them!"

"That is *not* what he said!" Lord Evorik insisted.

The damn prickling on Marcus's flesh was maddeningly strong. The wind roared and the dust was so thick they could only see twenty or thirty feet ahead. "We don't have time for this," Marcus told them. "Severus, form the men three deep. First rank has shield and sword. Second and third has shield and pilum. First rank blocks arrows; second and third will throw on my command."

"Which side do you think they'll come from," Evorik asked.

"They're already dead!" Burkhard insisted.

"The wind was coming from the north and switched to blowing directly into our faces from the northeast. I think that if they were coming from the north, they wouldn't have changed the wind."

"Changed the wind? Are you mad?"

"So you think they'll come from the south?" a merchant asked, clearly confused by what he was hearing.

"That's not how you would do it, is it?" Marcus asked the Gota lord.

Evorik considered for a moment. "No, I'd come in from there." He pointed to a spot a little bit further east than the direction the caravan was traveling. "I'd hit the first wagons to block the trail then ride down both sides of the wagons killing horses and men to cause maximum chaos."

"Then we'll gamble that that's the way they'll come in." He raised his voice. "The legion will advance double-time. Green Vigil, join the first rank. Calidus, take the second. Severus, take the third!"

Despite expressions demonstrating their uncertainty, the legionnaires scrambled to do as they were told.

"I hate being the reserve!" Evorik grumbled.

"You're men are the only ones with the speed to react if we guess wrong on this. And I'm counting on you to know when to hit their flanks if we succeed in stopping them."

The Gota lord hefted his spear meaningfully. "We'll be there!"

Marcus saluted the foreign lord—an uncommon courtesy, but if he was right and the savages really were coming, the survival of the caravan might well depend on Evorik and his warriors. Then he ran to catch up with his men. They continued to look left and right at each other as if they couldn't quite believe this was happening. A few of the braver ones twisted about to look at Marcus striding behind them. It was happening too fast and he had to do something to bolster their confidence or he'd lose them when—*if* he reminded himself because he really didn't know for certain that they were coming—the savages attacked.

"I see you looking behind you and I know what you're thinking!" His voice boomed against the wind to reach all of his men. "There's supposed to be a red band and a black band behind us."

Men nodded, proving that a great deal of their uncertainty derived from the lack of support if things went badly. "Well green is all we have for infantry, but that doesn't worry me. You know why?"

None of the greens answered him, but dependable Severus and Calidus shouted out: "Why Tribune?"

"Because I know something about the red and the black that you have all forgotten." He only paused for effect, but Calidus broke the silence by shouting: "What is that, Tribune?"

"They were all *green* once. Every man of the red and the black has stood where you are now, nervous before his first battle, wondering if he has what it takes to stand his ground. And they did stand, because like you they had their training and they had capable, experienced officers to tell them what to do. And what's more because they knew deep in their hearts that legionnaires of Aquila do not run. For hundreds of years we have stood our ground and *broken* our enemies. And you men, still green today, will do the same. You will stand your lines. You will throw your pilum on command and then you will charge in and slay our startled enemies in the finest traditions of beloved Aquila. And when we march in to Fort Segundus, you will hold your heads high knowing you are blooded legionnaires of the Republic."

A spontaneous cheer rose up from a dozen voices and was quickly joined by the rest of the men.

Marcus waited for it to die down before shouting. "The legion will now march!"

Immediately the green soldiers reduced their speed to the traditional walking pace of the legion.

"Black Vigil, align the hand for pilum throwing at no more than thirty feet." If he expected to launch his barrage at one hundred feet, he wouldn't have had to adjust his men's positions. The second and third ranks could have simply thrown their missiles above the heads of those in front of them. But at thirty feet they would be effectively throwing the pilum on a straight line and that meant they needed a space between the shields.

"The hand will spread out to arm length!" Severus bellowed.

The men did as they were commanded—a little bit sloppily but quickly enough.

"All pilum throwers move one pace to the right!" Severus ordered.

This happened more readily.

And now we wait, Marcus thought to himself. It was the hardest time in any military action, made doubly so by the fact he didn't know if he'd guessed right. His gut told him the change in the wind had to preface an attack, but honestly, the wind does change direction on occasion and he didn't like the thought of having to face the gleeful scorn of Burkhard and Gernot if he proved to be wrong.

But he wasn't wrong! The change was too rapid. The circumstances too perfect for a surprise attack. The—

Shapes appeared out of the dust cutting in toward the front of the caravan just as Evorik had predicted.

"Second rank, ready pilum!" Marcus shouted.

Both the second and third ranks immediately lifted their weapons, worrying Marcus that his third rank might be about to accidentally cut down his second.

"Second rank, throw!"

Twenty-seven pilum flashed out into the emerging line of horsemen, striking perhaps four of the animals and one man.

The savages shrieked in shock, pain and rage and a dozen arrows darted from their tiny bows only to glance harmlessly off the first rank's raised shields.

"Second rank one step to the left!" Marcus ordered and since the third rank already had their weapons ready, he followed up with the command, "Third rank, throw!"

Twenty-seven more pilum flashed out into the much closer raiders. What was more, these men had had two critical seconds longer to pick their targets out of the dust. Ten horses and riders tumbled to the ground and Marcus wasted no time in shouting his next instructions. "Now we kill them, boys! Charge! Charge! Kill them all!"

With a great shout, Marcus' under-strength hand drew their swords and charged into their first battle, screaming as much from fear as from rage and excitement. The savages were still completely surprised by the unexpected readiness of the defense. They continued to ride closer on their ponies, a few shooting arrows with incredible rapidity from their small bows, and then Marcus' legionnaires were among them, hacking at the legs of men and horse alike while the savages tried to retreat and regroup. They couldn't ride closer to the wagons, there was no room to maneuver there, so they tried to turn east and ran smack into Lord Evorik's twenty cavalry men, legs wrapped tightly around their horses' stomachs while they jabbed expertly with their long spears.

Adding to the confusion, more savages continued to ride in, not able to see the disaster striking their brothers because of the very same cloud of dust that had shielded them from view as they approached. Marcus' green legionnaires met and killed them, while others turned into the jumble of pony riders being slaughtered by Evorik's men.

The screams of pain and the sounds of swords hacking bodies combined to make the terror almost a palpable thing. And then suddenly the savages were gone, Evorik's men were riding in pursuit and Marcus' young legionnaires were cheering their very first victory.

****

"To victory!" Marcus toasted Lord Evorik and his men and with a mighty cheer they downed their cups of wine.

Immediately after order had been restored to the caravan and the Gota leader had returned to announce that the savages would not be returning tonight, Marcus had broken out two amphorae of his wine, giving one to the green band legionnaires to be enjoyed under the watchful eyes of Severus and Calidus, and making a present of the other to Lord Evorik in recognition of the role he and his men had played in the battle. In addition to boosting the general morale, it made Marcus feel better about transporting the wine in the first place. He wasn't some lowly merchant. He was a military commander carting supplies critical to the well-being of his army.

Lord Evorik wiped his mouth on his sleeve. "This is good! Not like that shit you Aquilans served me in Dona. This drink has bite!"

Actually, Marcus was willing to bet it was roughly the same vintage, but apparently no one had ever told the Gota you were supposed to dilute the product of the grape with water before serving it. That meant the beverage they were drinking was roughly twice as strong as what Aquilan society deemed proper, but Marcus was a legionnaire and had cheated and drank the stronger stuff more than a time or two. "I'm glad you like it, Lord Evorik," he assured him.

Instead of answering, the Gota refilled his cup and lifted it high over his head. "Death to the savages with their piss-ant little bows!"

"Death! Death!" his men shouted.

Everyone drank another round then cycled past the amphora to refill his cup of wine. At this rate, it was likely that they would finish the vessel before the night was over. Marcus decided that it was not in the interests of the caravan to get these warriors too drunk. He would not offer a second amphora this evening.

Evidently Evorik was thinking along the same lines. "That shithead, Burkhard, should be bringing us wine and begging our pardons. We saved his entire caravan. He didn't even throw his twenty guards into the fight. And yet he hides like a coward from the men who saved his ass."

That was an unusually long speech for Evorik and evidence that he was truly angry with the Caravan Master. "He's hiding because we embarrassed him in front of the whole caravan."

"He's hiding because he's a *coward!*" Evorik growled.

"Well, maybe, but think of it this way. Both he and his son tried to stop us from taking actions that broke a savage attack into pieces before it wounded a single one of the men in his care or damaged a single wagon. That has to hurt. He looks like a fool—"

"He *is* a fool!" Evorik insisted.

"But he's also the man who knows the trails from here to Topacio—your home in the Jeweled Hills."

"He's not the only one," Evorik said. Marcus expected the lord to point out that he had already traveled this route once when he came south on his diplomatic mission, but he didn't. "Burkhard relies on a half-breed scout called Mataskah to help him choose the trail. I'll bet we could buy him if we needed to. Burkhard's not the sort of man who inspires loyalty."

"To what end?" Marcus wanted to know. "We're still all going the same way to the same place. So what's the point of hiring the scout away from the Caravan Master?"

Evorik scowled. "I don't know, but I don't like Burkhard and I want to know what my options are if he turns coward again and deserts us."

Day Seven
How Bad Do You Think It Is?

"I tell you it was a fluke!" Caravan Master Burkhard shouted. He was surrounded by close to twenty frightened and angry Dona and Gente merchants and backed only by about five of his guards. "The Aquilans broke the savages weeks ago." He glared at Marcus as if somehow his predicament was the Tribune's fault. "This attack was a fluke!"

"Then where did the savages come from last night?" one of the older Gente asked.

Catching sight of Marcus, Señor Alberto called out to him. "Tribune Marcus, you were the one who saved the caravan last night. What do you say? Is it safe to continue?"

Marcus had been approached by a half dozen Gente last night with a similar question. He decided to try to put an end to this sort of talk right now. "I have to admit that I'm confused by this gathering. When you paid to join this caravan, did not Caravan Master Burkhard tell you that part of what you were paying for was protection from the savages on the trail?"

The gathered only stared at him, neither agreeing nor disagreeing with his statement.

"And did not many of you bring a man or two along as added protection?" Marcus pressed them. "The truth is that raids by savages have always been a danger to anyone traveling on the Sea of Grass. Aquila has tried to reduce this danger by establishing forts on the trail, but they've only reduced it."

"But the legions broke the savages," somebody shouted.

Obviously not, Marcus wanted to tell them, but that was not the way to build morale. "Two months ago the savages gathered in unusual numbers and tried to destroy the legionnaires stationed at Fort Segundus. They failed and were beaten quite badly. But that doesn't mean they were *broken*. Last night shows us they were not. At the very least, they have returned to raiding caravans."

"So what do we do?" Someone asked.

"You have two choices," Marcus told him. "You can go forward with the caravan or you can attempt to return to Dona on your own."

"On our own?" several voices cried out.

"Yes, Caravan Master Burkhard agreed to take us north. I doubt very much that one small raid will change his mind on that, will it Caravan Master?"

The Caravan Master seemed relieved that Marcus was succeeding in calming his customers, but his son, Gernot, continued to fume beside him. Burkhard stepped forward. "Yes, Tribune, we will continue to travel north. We should reach Fort Segundus tomorrow. Anyone who absolutely wants to return to the south would be well advised to travel that far with us and wait for a caravan traveling in the opposite direction. It is not safe to travel the Sea of Grass alone."

"That makes good sense," Marcus agreed. "We'll learn a lot more about the trail ahead of us when we reach Segundus."

Grumbling unhappily, the merchants began to return to their wagons. After they departed, Burkhard approached Marcus. "That was good of you. You could have turned them on me and taken control of the caravan there if you'd wanted to."

And why would I want to do that? Marcus wondered. What he said was, "You made a major mistake last night. It would have cost you nothing to mobilize your men to support me. If I were wrong, you shrug it off and say *that was a good drill*. But I wasn't wrong and your men stood by with dumb expressions on their faces while Lord Evorik and I saved your livelihood." He glared hard at the older man. "Don't let it happen again! And rein in your son before he gets himself hurt acting stupid."

Without waiting for a response, Marcus continued up the caravan to check on his legionnaires.

****

"What is that?" Evorik asked squinting into the morning sun at a strange shape on the horizon. It was casting a shadow which made it harder to identify, but that was what was strange. It was casting a shadow but was nowhere near the Sturm Mountains to the east or the jagged cliffs of the Jeweled Hills still at least two hundred miles to the north of them.

Marcus lowered his hand from his brow and looked up at the Gota lord riding—because Gota always rode—beside the walking Tribune. "I can't see it clearly. I suppose we'll find out soon enough. How far away do you think it is?"

"Difficult to tell," Evorik muttered before looking over his shoulder away from Marcus. "Richimar, Odoacer, go find out what that thing is and don't get yourselves killed." Both men kicked the side of their horses and took off without ceremony. The Gota rode on fancy saddles with elaborate decorations sometimes etched with silver and gold, but as far as Marcus could see they gave no more control of the animals than did the savages' blankets. They held on by squeezing the horse's middle with their legs and guided the noble beasts with the subtlest of pressure on the reins.

"They'll tell us soon enough," Evorik stated the obvious.

Marcus just continued to walk. That was what legionnaires did. They walked without tiring for league after league at a speed that often shocked their enemies. The mobility of the legions—their amazing endurance in trekking across the land—was almost as important to their victories as their discipline and skill in battle.

The shape—whatever it turned out to be—was still fairly far away because the two Gota rode for several minutes before pulling up and circling the thing. One of them caught something on the end of his spear and lifted it to his hand. Then the two kicked their horses and galloped back.

By the time they returned trailing a long piece of silk a dozen or more of the merchants had gathered beside Marcus and Evorik with Brunhard and his son once more pushing to the front on their horses.

"It's a fucking wagon!" the Gota with the piece of silk exclaimed. Marcus was pretty sure that this one was Odoacer, although with their full beards he found it a little hard to tell the northern barbarians apart.

"And it's not the only one," Richimar announced. "There's a whole string of them—probably a whole caravan."

Merchants groaned and muttered to themselves in fear.

"They didn't even steal all the cargo," Odoacer added. "It's like the damn savages don't know what's valuable."

Greed flickered into the expressions of many of the men who'd been worrying only moments before. Marcus grimaced, his disgust for their lust for profits overcoming his normally ironclad self-control. Not one of them appeared to have any real brains. Their wagons were full. They couldn't transport this cargo anyway no matter how valuable it might prove to be. And speaking of value…the savages were out to make war so this ability of their leaders to stop their warriors from plundering the caravan was an ominous sign of the enemy's discipline—not proof of their alleged idiocy.

Evorik glanced down at Marcus, meeting his eyes. He too understood what the report really meant. Marcus gave a slight jerk of his head back in the direction they had come to get a sense of the man's disposition toward their journey. The Gota lord gave his head the barest of side-to-side shakes. Marcus nodded.

"How bad do you think it is?" Caravan Master Burkhard asked.

Marcus studied him trying to understand his game. Burkhard had to be a hard man to make this trip again and again, but the Tribune guessed that the savages did not usually attack a caravan. That meant that the journey was like a game of chance—perhaps the dice rolled snake eyes, but it was more likely that you got lucky sevens. And generally speaking the savages probably were interested in plunder, content to cut off and break a few wagons before retreating. Do enough damage and the caravan would be forced to leave some goods behind. Therefore this determination to destroy everything and leave the booty on the plains must be especially troubling.

"I don't see how this changes anything," Marcus told him aware that the side conversations had just ended as merchants strained to hear what he was saying. "It really gives us little more information. We knew there were hostile savages out here—yesterday we killed a number of them. Possibly we killed the same group that attacked this caravan. If we want to know the real score in this area, we have to push on to Fort Segundus."

Burkhard nodded glumly but the merchants, unlike this morning, seemed excited for the chance to push on.

Marcus wondered how much time they would lose plundering the remains of the unlucky caravan ahead of them.

****

The wagons had definitely been traveling south and some of them, poor fools, had tried to run for it as if the heavy and ponderous land-ships had any chance of outpacing the quick-footed ponies of the savages. The remnants of the carcasses of horses still strapped into their harnesses showed the preferred method of keeping the wagons from escaping. Kill even one of the animals pulling the burden and you stop the wagon in its tracks.

Most, but by no means all, of the wagons had tipped over, some splintering as they crashed and some looking as if they'd be ready to roll if you pushed them back onto their wheels. All of them had had their cargo pulled out and broken open—which suggested some limited plundering had occurred as men searched for light, portable, goods to steal. Not necessarily a sign of poor discipline—Marcus would let his own men plunder what they could carry under similar circumstances—but further evidence of how committed the savages were to purging foreigners from the plains.

"Not enough bodies," Evorik noted. "That's a bad sign. The savages like to torture prisoners to see how tough they are. It brings credit to the captor if he takes a strong man."

Marcus began to weigh the pros and cons of giving his green legionnaires this information—assuming someone hadn't already told them back in Fort Prime. On the one hand, the sort of fear the thought of being tortured to death instilled was a powerful motivator to keep fighting, but it also could undermine morale and weaken discipline. Then he realized that there was no way to keep the information from them. If they didn't know already, someone would have overheard Evorik's comment and the news would be up and down the length of the caravan faster than a bird flies.

Merchants jumped off their wagons to begin sorting through the remains of the cargo.

"We'd better put a stop to that," Marcus suggested. "Let's find Burkhard. He's still supposed to be in charge. I want to keep pushing toward the protection of Fort Segundus. We don't know there aren't other raiders out here in addition to the ones we bloodied yesterday."

Evorik grunted and together the two men went to find the caravan master.

Day Eight
Might As Well Let the Savages Kill Us

It was late the next day before the caravan reached the remains of Fort Segundus. Despite Marcus' best efforts, he had not been able to convince the Donatan and Gente merchants to stop pillaging the remains of their unfortunate brethren. They'd lost half a day and rolled out with badly overloaded wagons which advanced at a crawl as the horses strained against this new and unnecessary weight. And Burkhard had only shrugged and let it happen. He had to know how stupid the merchants were being. Perhaps he thought they would come to their senses and throw off the extra burden the next day on the trail, but if that was his hope it proved futile. And instead of pushing on and reaching Fort Segundus a couple of hours after dark, they reached it near dusk on the eighth day on the trail.

It was not a reassuring sight.

The gate had been torn down or more accurately, blasted apart like a great oak splintered by lightning. And the dead—the dead legionnaires were everywhere—laying where they had fallen. Still wearing their armor, some with weapons in or near their hands, the only things missing from them were their heads. These formed irregular ranks in the middle of the long central street that bisected the castrum. Planted on pilum, most of the legionnaires still wore their helmets which made the grotesque scene all the eerier.

"They must have really respected these men to treat them with such honor," Evorik observed.

"Honor?" Marcus snapped. "We mount the severed heads of criminals after we crucify them. We don't *honor* our enemies by desecrating their bodies."

"Nor do we," Evorik assured him before shrugging. "But they are savages, remember? You can't expect civilized behavior from them."

Both the praetorium, the headquarters of the castrum, and the quaestorium, the central supply warehouse, had been burnt down to the ground as had the tents of the legionnaires. Other than that and the busted gate, the castrum was pretty much intact, if Marcus had sufficient men to defend such a long stretch of wall.

Clearly stunned by the devastation, it took a surprisingly long time for the first merchant to approach Marcus with a question that properly should have gone to Caravan Master Burkhard. "Tribune, the savages have destroyed the legion at Fort Segundus. What are we going to do?"

Fortunately, Marcus had had time to think up an appropriate response. "First we're going to eat dinner and then gather to sort through our options. Go spread the word. I want every wagon owner to meet at the fort's old forum in an hour. We'll give every man a chance to speak if he wants it and then we'll decide what we're going to do."

It would be easier if these men were legionnaires and required to follow orders, but they were civilians so he'd treat them like voters back in the Republic and try to guide them to a sensible conclusion.

****

An hour into the debate, Marcus came to the firm conclusion that he definitely preferred the military's way of doing things. He'd heard the expression *like herding cats* numerous times and now he understood exactly what it meant. Civilians were idiots. They seemed unable to come to terms with the simple choices that confronted them. They could go forward or go back. There was no other option.

Some of them didn't even seem to be able to grasp the fundamental problem. The savages had united under this shaman, Teetonka, and were determined to drive all the foreigners off the plains. They had killed the better part of a full phalanx of the legion—hundreds of well-trained men. And to all appearances they had serious magical power reinforcing their attacks—not just dust storms to conceal their movements but lightning strong enough to blow open the gates of Fort Segundus and let them ride their ponies inside. Normally under these circumstances, Marcus would be arguing for a retreat. He had seventy-seven green legionnaires—not nearly enough to succeed where a whole phalanx had failed. Yet, he'd been exiled and really couldn't be certain of his reception if he returned to the Republic without permission. The governor of Dona might be willing to accommodate a reasonable delay or he might place Marcus in chains to be shipped back to Aquila and possibly executed.

He abruptly realized that conversation had ground to a halt and everyone was looking at him. Rather than admit that he didn't know what they had asked him, Marcus got to his feet and strode into the center of the circle.

"All of this talk is wasted," he told them. "There are two choices—and you know what they are. Onward toward Fort Tertium where we may find an army of savages laying siege to the legionnaires there."

That suggestion caused an eruption of protests and groans as if a great many of the merchants truly hadn't considered this very likely possibility.

"The second option is to return to Dona and wait for either Aquila or the Jeweled Cities to put a force together to either reopen the Sea of Grass or the shipping lanes. Neither of those things is likely to happen quickly."

"But you think it's safer to go back?"

Marcus resisted the urge to roll his eyes. "Safer, but not safe," he told them. "Right now there is likely no safe place anywhere on the Sea of Grass."

Other merchants started to ask questions, but Marcus cut them off. "Now before you all decide what you're going to do, you need to ask Master Burkhard what he's going to do. Because it makes a substantial difference if he's going to move on toward Tertium or back toward Prime."

"He will go forward!" a Gente merchant named Adán Nacio announced. He was evidently an important man for other merchants looked to him to decide what they would do. "He has taken money to lead us north and he will lead us."

"That's not exactly accurate," Marcus corrected him. "We've paid him to use his best judgment to guide us—and if the Caravan Master says it's too dangerous to proceed north he has a responsibility to guide the wagons back to the south."

"He must—"

"I will continue to Topacio," Burkhard interrupted. "Will you be going with me, Tribune?"

"I believe so," Marcus said. "I have business in Amatista and I can't get there by going south."

"Does that mean the legionnaires will go north with you?"

Marcus nodded. "It's my intention to turn these legionnaires over to the commander of the next fort we reach. They were supposed to come here to Segundus but that is obviously not possible so I will surrender them to the authority of the next fort commander we meet."

"That means they won't be with us for the entire trail," someone complained.

"That's correct," Marcus said without further explanation.

The men didn't like that and began to mutter among themselves. Marcus decided to go ahead and enrage them. "While we're on the topic of the legionnaires, I'd like to make an observation. Almost all of you overloaded your wagons when we found the remains of that south-bound caravan. Your speed has been cut in half, or worse, and your horses are exhausted from pulling your new loads. This is not sustainable—especially in the military circumstances we find ourselves in. Speed is your best friend now. I advise you to drop all of your newly acquired goods and a quarter of what you have carried from Dona. The legion is willing to keep to the pace of the wagons only if the caravan makes a good-faith effort to keep up with the legion."

"You can't do that!" was shouted by a dozen different men.

Marcus let them voice their anger for several moments before calmly stating. "Yes, I can. The best hope this caravan has of survival is to reach Fort Tertium. The dust that the wagons kick up makes it impossible to move with stealth. So if we are to move forward, the only thing we can do to reduce our disadvantage is to lighten our loads and move faster. Caravan Master, how far is it to Tertium?"

"Four or five days at normal wagon speed," Burkhard said. "At this speed? Assuming the horses can hold up under the heavy load, it could be nine or ten days."

"And that's impossible if the army that destroyed Segundus is still out there," Marcus told them. We need to turn four or five days into three to have any chance at all of slipping past. Even then, all we're really likely to accomplish is to have the savages come after us with fewer men than they would like, but we'll take any advantage we can craft."

"We can't leave our goods behind!" several men protested.

Burkhard finally took on some of the leadership of the meeting. "Yes, you can. The Tribune is right. We need speed if we're to accomplish this, because after we reach Tertium it's still another four or five days to Fort Quartus." He glanced at Marcus. "It's the salt pan. We're winding our way around it and all of that territory is open to savage attack. A couple of days past Fort Quartus and we start to get into territory that Lord Evorik's people patrol and the savages are less likely to hit us there. If they're going to raid the north, the towns make richer targets."

"They don't like to face real cavalry!" Evorik bellowed. "But I don't believe we'll make it to Fort Quartus by the route you've laid out. We're going to reach Fort Tertium and find an army camped around it and our slow moving wagons will be easy prey for the savages."

"Then you think we should return home?" Burkhard's son asked as if he couldn't believe his ears. "My father says—"

"I think we should take our third option," Evorik cut him off, "and go directly north through the salt pan."

"The salt pan!" This idea got people even more excited.

"It's impossible!"

"Too dangerous!"

"Might as well let the savages kill us!"

"Lord Evorik," Burkhard said. "I realize you are a brave man and so tend to minimize the dangers, but there is no way across the salt pans. Men who try get swallowed up in the ground or simply die of thirst before they reach the other side."

"Miners go there," Evorik reminded him. The pans were, in point of fact, the primary source of salt for the entire region.

"They go to the edges, my Lord, but no one goes through the salt pans. It's just not possible."

"Your scout, Mataskah, says otherwise," Evorik argued.

"The half breed?" Burkhard asked as if he couldn't believe Evorik would bring *him* into the argument.

"Yes, the half breed, he says he knows the way across the pan and can get us there in one and a half days. Then it's just another day to Fort Quartus which would surprise the savages and let the Tribune here warn the Aquilans of what we think is happening at Tertium. I could then ride ahead to alert Topacio and rally a few hundred cavalry to join up with the legion and put down this savage menace once and for all."

"No!" Burkhard shouted. "I will risk my life traveling to Fort Tertium, but crossing the salt pan is not a risk. It's certain death and I will not do it!"

"Let's hear from the savage!" someone called from the back.

"From Mataskah? He can barely speak," Burkhard countered. "Don't you understand, he's one of them!"

"I speak!" the half breed scout passed to the center of the group from the outskirts where he had been sitting in silence. "I Mataskah. I live my life in

Grass Sea. I no work for Oyáte. Teetonka hate men like me. Say I too white to live in Grass Sea."

The gathered men quieted as they listened to the scout.

"I travel twice through salt to north when I young man," Mataskah continued. "Master Burkhard right! It hard trail, very dangerous, very thirsty, but no Oyáte. Why they go where no man can live?"

"Your wagons are too heavy for the salt pan," Burkhard pleaded in a much quieter voice. "You'd have to drop half your weight even to try and if you get stuck, what will you do for water. This is not a plan. This is trading a possible death in battle for certain suicide."

"I'm of a mind to try it," Evorik stated. "Any who want to can come with me, but I'm ready to see home again and I don't think I'll do that traveling towards Tertium."

Anguished pleas and cries greeted these words, but Evorik withstood them without weakening. "I am not some fucking caravan guard fighting for his wages. I have no responsibility to any of you. But I'm also a generous man. Any who dare the salt pan with me will be under my protection so long as they lighten their wagons as the Tribune suggested."

He looked at Marcus. "What say you, Tribune? Will you come with me or with Burkhard?"

"You make a good case for the salt pan," Marcus told him, "but I haven't made my mind up yet." In truth, he did not like the appearance of abandoning these men, but he very much liked the thought of getting the jump on the savages and bypassing Fort Tertium and warning Quartus of what was happening. "I'll decide by morning." He let his glance play meaningfully across the gathered merchants. "You will help me make my decision by seriously lightening your loads."

He walked out while the men were still protesting and went to check on his own wagon.

****

"Tribune?"

Marcus looked up to find Señor Alberto and his very pregnant wife slowly approaching his wagon just as he was about to climb under it to go to sleep. Severus had taken to sleeping with the legionnaires to keep the young fool, Phanes, from undoing all of his work to turn the greens into a disciplined fighting force.

Marcus immediately came forward to offer his hand to Alberto. "Señor, Señora, what a pleasure it is to see you again. How can I help you?"

A spasm of pain momentarily twisted Carmelita's face and a tendril of dread touched Marcus' soul.

"But where are my manners?" he asked. "Come closer to the wagon. We will have a cup of wine and the Señora can sit."

Without waiting for a response he went to the back of a wagon and lifted off of it a short wooden chest with some of his personal things within it. Carrying it back to the two Gente, he placed it on the ground and watched with approval as Alberto tenderly helped his young wife to sit. Then he busied himself pouring three cups of wine, diluting the concentrate as was the Aquilan practice, with an equal part of water.

"Here, drink this," he said to Carmelita and waited patiently while she sipped the wine.

"It is very fine," she said with a slight smile. "You, Tribune, have been very good to us."

"It is why we have come," Alberto said. "It seems a poor reward to you after your earlier generosity but we continue to need your help."

"I am quite certain that my father will reward you tenfold for your kindnesses," Carmelita added with a hint of urgency—as if she feared that Marcus had grown tired of the couple and would turn them away.

"What seems to be the problem?" Marcus asked.

"As we indicated before," Alberto began, "my father-in-law engaged in a contract which will break him if he defaults. It seemed a simple matter at the time, but then the pirates increased their activity and the savages began their marauding and well—we are almost out of time."

Marcus sat down on the ground and made a gesture for Alberto to continue. "Tell me about the contract."

"Lord Totila is the cousin of the Thegn of Amatista."

"He is a cruel and notorious miser!" Carmelita added.

"His scandalous daughter—"

"Whom reputable women would not even sit at the same table with," Carmelita cut in.

"Is marrying the son of Thegn Hathus of Granate—"

"His third wife, the—" A spasm of pain cut off the word that Marcus was fairly certain would have been *whore*.

"It is an important political alliance for Amatista. Relations with Granate and Morganita have been especially tense these past years. It is hoped that this marriage alliance will not only lower that tension, but strengthen Amatista's ties to Granate at the expense of Morganita. So it is important that the wedding be a spectacular celebration—a marvel to be spoken of for decades to come."

Marcus didn't see that they were making any progress. "And the contract?"

"In his youth, Lord Totila traveled the world and in one of your own provinces called Vitrum he saw the most amazing creations of a glass so pure it looks like crystal. There were elaborate lamps which hung from the ceiling and reflected the light through pieces cut to look like precious stones. There were mirrors so finely constructed that you can see your reflection as perfectly as others look at you. And there were cups crafted from glass to make it appear you were drinking from gemstones."

"Very expensive trinkets," Marcus observed. Since before Vitrum had been brought into the Republic, senators and the leaders of the patricians had vied with one another to see who could lay the most impressive table and the *crystals* of the northern province were among the most prized utensils.

"I see you know more than military affairs," Alberto told him. "It is a thegn's ransom, or at least a princess'."

"And that—oh!" Carmelita broke off as she touched her stomach, then valiantly continued her speech. "And that *miser* would pay no money up front and warned my father that if he failed to deliver the glassware on time he would confiscate all his estate for causing Amatista such embarrassment."

"Oh, I see," Marcus said. "And you're trying to carry the cargo back to Amatista in time for the—wait a minute! Where are your guards! If your wagon is full of Vitrum crystal—why don't you have any guards?"

"We've lost them," Carmelita said. "We started out with six guards nineteen months ago and—"

"You've been gone nineteen months? When is this wedding supposed to take place?"

"In the Jeweled Hills," Alberto explained, "women cannot marry until they turn sixteen. On the coast they are more liberal and permit their fifteen year olds to marry."

Marcus almost asked what a *fourteen* year old could have done to merit such derision from Carmelita, but it was late and he needed to understand why they had come to him. "So you lost your guards how?"

"Two to illness, two were murdered, and two simply disappeared. Maybe they were bribed to leave," Alberto shrugged, "and maybe they were killed. It has been a difficult time. We do not know for certain who is trying to keep us from returning—my father-in-law's rivals or enemies of Amatista. There have been many attempts to sabotage us. I realize that your impression of my worth is lowered by my difficulties in this caravan, but I am not unskilled with a blade and I have proved that several times on this venture."

Marcus tried to bring the conversation to the point. "So you've got a wagon packed with Vitrum crystal and…"

"Not just crystal cups," Carmelita interjected. "We have the beautiful full length mirror and two of the hanging lamps—they call them chandeliers."

"And…"

"We can't leave any of it behind as you have suggested," Alberto complained. "I admit that I suffered a moment of greed and collected even more goods from those unfortunates we passed on our way here. I have already thrown it to the side of the road, but as for the rest—I cannot leave it behind or my father-in-law will be ruined."

Normally, Marcus would have believed Alberto to be exaggerating his problem, but disappointing the cousin of a ruling thegn was obviously courting disaster.

Marcus stood. "Excuse me a moment, please."

He walked up the line of wagons until he found a small group centered around Calidus—all of them drinking Marcus' wine.

The moment Calidus caught sight of him he excused himself from the men he was laughing with and hurried to Marcus' side. "Tribune?"

"How full is our wagon? You told me we could carry twelve thousand pounds. Are we carrying that much? And if not, how much room do we have in the wagon?"

Calidus scratched his head. "The wagon is full, but light. I doubt we are carrying more than nine thousand pounds—even with your *personal* baggage."

"Good! Come with me."

Without explaining further, Marcus led Calidus back to Señor Alberto and his wife. "This is my adjutant, Red Vigil Calidus," Marcus introduced him. "When we finish speaking, he will fetch twelve legionnaires and bring them to your wagon. They will then transport a quarter of your load to my wagon and I will leave behind one fourth of my wine cellar to make room for it."

Alberto shook his head in horror even while Carmelita touched her heart in appreciation.

"But Tribune," the Gente merchant protested, "you cannot leave your wine. It is uncivilized."

"I suspect that very little will actually be left behind, although tomorrow there is going to be a lot of hung over legionnaires, Gota warriors and caravan guards."

"But Tribune," Alberto objected again.

"I will hear no more protests!" Marcus told them. "Your mission is clearly of grave importance—much more so than the comforts that my wine cellar provides."

"You are a most generous man, Tribune," Carmelita announced. "And while I realize that a man of your station probably pays no attention to such things, I want you to know that my father will thank you for this gesture by filling your cellar with the finest wines available in the Jeweled Hills. Your palate will not suffer from your kind—oh!" She broke off and touched her stomach again, then would have fallen from her seat if not for the speed with which Alberto and Marcus leapt to catch her.

"Oh, Alberto," she whispered. "I am so sorry! But I think the baby is coming."

****

"Have you made up your mind yet?" Evorik asked as he—unusually for him—walked up beside Marcus. It was an hour before dawn and Carmelita's agonized screams proved she had not yet had the baby.

The Gota grimaced. "That woman's screams could rip the shit from a man's bowels. Why can't the baby get the idea and come out already?"

Marcus slapped a comradely hand upon the man's shoulder. "It was kind of you to let your wives help her with the delivery."

"Kind? Do you know any Gota women?"

"No, I don't," Marcus confessed, "other than your two wives that is."

"And to them you have not yet spoken a dozen words," Evorik reminded him. "I will tell you something that may help you when you come to the Jeweled Hills. No one *lets* a Gota woman do anything she has decided to do. You just get out of the way or prepare to fight to keep her knife out of you." He laughed as if this was the funniest observation in the whole world.

"Perhaps I've met a Gota woman after all," Marcus told him in the same spirit of jest. "My last mistress tried to gut me when she figured out I was leading my men out to kill the damn witchdoctor she worshipped."

Evorik's laughter bellowed forth even louder. "I hope you whipped her well as she deserved."

"I didn't get the chance," Marcus told him. "The skeletons her witchdoctor raised killed her before I got back from the campaign."

"Oh, this is the tale you told at dinner—the one in the Fire Islands," Evorik realized.

"That's right. We didn't talk about what the skeletons did to the rest of the island. They didn't seem to be able to tell the difference between those people who supported Kekipi and those who opposed him. They just murdered everyone."

"That is one of the things I hate about magos," Evorik agreed. "Their magic—it so often hurts everybody. Take this dust storm the savage shaman raised. Yes, it hid them from us, but it also hid us from them—if you take my meaning."

"That is one of the keys to beating them," Marcus said. "We must learn the weaknesses in their magic and their tactics and turn those vulnerabilities against them."

"Do all Aquilans make things so complicated?" Evorik asked. "I say you just lead enough horsemen into battle to be sure you kill them all. It's like hitting a walnut with a blacksmith's hammer. You smash them to pieces."

"And if we don't have enough horsemen?"

"Well, there is that," Evorik agreed.

The woman screamed again, a high-pitched, agonizing shriek of pure agony.

"Is that normal?" Marcus asked.

Evorik shrugged. "I don't know. I don't have any children yet. If I did, they'd be with me."

"I see."

The two men lapsed into silence for a while, waiting to see if a baby's first cries would break the night, but the next sound was another of Carmelita's screams.

"So have you decided?" Evorik asked. "Which route will you take in the morning?"

"Well I'm not going south again—that's for certain," Marcus said.

"Yes, I heard about your difficulties there. Why is it so often among you so-called *civilized* people that men who cannot fight have the power to determine the fates of those who can?"

Marcus didn't know and didn't want to talk about his exile.

"As for the trip north, I admit that I'm tempted by your shortcut across the salt pan, but I don't like the idea of abandoning our fellow travelers. While I have no technical responsibility to them, let's face it, if they are attacked again without my legionnaires and your cavalry it will not go well for them."

"Sad, yes, but they are responsible for their own choices."

Marcus nodded. In essence, he agreed with what Evorik was saying, but he still felt bad about not shielding the travelers.

"Then there is the pregnant woman. She and her husband are in danger of being left here alone and I don't see them surviving that even if the savages do not return."

"I see," Evorik said, but it was obvious to Marcus that he did not understand.

"So here is what I suggest. We take a day to let the woman have her child and recover part of her strength, and then we go north by way of your short cut. Anyone from the caravan who wishes to journey with us will be allowed to do so. But if they wish to take the traditional route or to return to the south, we permit that as well."

The Gota lord nodded. "You make good sense, Tribune, but I want to make one change to your plan. I'm told that the sun bouncing off the white salt can be blinding, so I want to make the journey across the pan at night.

There's a good moon and the savages are much less likely to notice our dust cloud at night than they are during the day."

Marcus considered this suggestion, rolling it around in his mind. Traveling at night was usually considered more dangerous, but… "If your scout agrees, I'll bring my men as well."

"It is settled then. Let us celebrate our decision with more of your fine wine. I think we will want to fill all the amphorae we can with water in case this shortcut is not as easy as our guide suggests."

That made a lot of sense to Marcus. In fact, he might well dump out a few more amphorae of wine to build a strong reserve. It would be a shame to waste it, but it wasn't as if he were a merchant depending on the profit he would get from selling the drink.

Day Nine
It's Risky

The prickling sensation returned the moment dawn began to brighten the horizon. It started on the back of Marcus' neck as he leaned over the small camp fire watching Calidus cook breakfast. The meat was some kind of snake indigenous to the plains, not that Marcus really cared. He was a legionnaire. He could eat anything.

He touched the back of his neck and immediately looked around. There was no wind at the moment—a rarity on the Sea of Grass—and thus no dust cloud to hide an enemy attack, but that didn't matter. He ran for the walls of the fort as the prickling feeling extended down his shoulders and onto his arms. The fort was large and it took him three minutes to reach the wall—a huge dirt mound looking down into a ditch that surrounded the fort. The sentries he'd had Severus post over the night were still in position and doing their jobs. "Do you see anything?" he asked them.

The two greens saluted. "No, Tribune! The plains are quiet."

He stared out at the Sea of Grass ahead of them and confirmed that they were correct. Then he sent each of them to circumnavigate the fort and check with the other sentries.

Waiting for their return seemed to take an interminably long time but commanders had to get used to waiting while their orders were carried out so Marcus occupied his time by watching the terrain for enemy activity while he thought about what the prickling sensation might mean.

The first time he felt it had been when Seneca's farseeing spell had gone awry. The steam had made his flesh react like this, just as the dust storm had. Was it some new sensitivity to danger he was experiencing or just a bad case of nerves?

He looked back into the castrum where a nervous Burkhard was finally succeeding in getting the merchants moving—not that he had convinced most to lighten their wagons. Marcus wondered how many of those merchants would change their mind about following the Caravan Master when they learned the legion was not going with them.

The prickling intensified for a moment, then receded again, not disappearing but becoming a mere irritant. He needed to figure out what the sensation meant. Was he making the right decision in taking Evorik's shortcut or the wrong one?

It took several minutes but the legionnaires returned to him to report that no one could see any savages in any direction. Slightly mollified, Marcus thanked them and returned to the caravan where Burkhard had begun shouting questions at Severus. The moment he saw Marcus, he turned his attention on him. "What do you mean you're going through the salt pan? Last night we agreed that you would accompany the caravan to Tertium."

Marcus shook his head. "That's not what we agreed, Caravan Master. What we agreed was that if I took the trail to Tertium, the wagons would have to seriously lighten their loads. Most of these merchants did not even discard their excess cargo. They have little chance of making it to the next fort even if the legion goes with you. So it is of no matter at all to you that we will not be in your company but taking our own path, because in all likelihood you are dead either way. You can't make enough speed with wagons that heavy."

Señor Adán Nacio stepped out of the crowd to confront Marcus. "You are only a military man and cannot be expected to understand the complex ways of commerce, but there is a tremendous amount of money to be made here. We will all," he gestured toward the other merchants, "happily cut you in for a bonus of say two percent of the net value of our wares if you will see us through to the Jeweled Hills."

A touch of human greed gnawed at Marcus, but no self-respecting patrician of Aquila ever let himself appear to be motivated by the pursuit of wealth. "I'm sure you think that's a generous offer and maybe it is, but money is of no use to the dead. And I do not believe that you are likely to reach the Jeweled Hills. Lord Evorik's alternative comes with a different set of dangers, but to my mind also offers the best chance of success."

"Perhaps three percent would be a better figure," Adán suggested as if Marcus hadn't spoken.

Marcus waved his hand dismissively at the comment and walked away.

Before he'd traveled fifty feet, Calidus called out to him. "Tribune!"

Marcus turned and found the young would-be magus, Seneca Liberus, hurrying along beside his adjutant.

"This young scholar," Calidus said, "asked me to help him find you. Apparently he couldn't hear your voice putting those merchants into their places."

Seneca blushed. "I'm...I'm sorry to interrupt, Tribune. But I listened to what you said last night and I'd like to take the shortcut across the salt pan with you, but..." He clenched and unclenched his fists helplessly.

"But..." Marcus prompted him.

"But Señor Joquin refuses to go that way and my things are in his wagon."

Marcus sighed. "How much baggage are you bringing?"

"Just a chest of clothes and a crate of books."

Marcus cringed—books were always heavy—and looked to Calidus.

"We'll make room for him Tribune, but it might cost you another amphora of wine."

"Fine," Marcus agreed. "Calidus, detail a couple of legionnaires to help him move, but do it quickly, Burkhard's ready to start his wagons rolling."

"Oh thank you, Tribune!" Seneca gushed and ran off much faster than the adjutant to recover his things from the Gente merchant's wagon.

As wagons began to move toward the broken gates of the castrum, other merchants—mostly Gente—approached Marcus about joining their venture across the salt pan. Ahead of them, he saw Severus arguing with Burkhard's son, Gernot. He finally grabbed the boy by the scruff of his neck and pulled him to the side while legionnaires forced five wagons—all presumably carrying legion supplies—out of the caravan. All in all, it looked like Marcus and Evorik would be leading maybe fifteen wagons. All of the others were moving on toward Fort Tertium at a glacial crawl.

Dust had begun to cover the fort from the moving wagons when Alberto ran up to Marcus carrying a large clay jug. "Tribune! Tribune! You must share a drink with me. My Carmelita, she has given birth to a boy."

Marcus smiled. For the first time since the sun had come up he began to feel good. "That's great, Señor. Congratulations!"

Alberto pulled the stopper out of his jug and tipped the light brown liquid into his mouth. "Whew!" he said wiping his lips on his shirt sleeve. "That is strong. I bought this brandy in Dona to celebrate this occasion. Please, please, have a drink with me."

Marcus accepted the jug and took a long pull. Alberto was right. This was strong stuff—the sort of drink that put hair on your chest if you didn't have it there already.

"What are you going to name the lad," he asked.

A huge grin split Alberto's face. "We will name him Gaspar after my father-in-law and Marcus after you."

"After me?" Marcus asked with genuine surprise.

"Yes, Tribune, after *you*! Without you, our journey would have ended that first day on the Sea of Grass, and without you, we would have been killed by savages and forced to leave behind our cargo so that my father-in-law would be ruined. You are our savior and we will remember your courage and your generous spirit every time we speak our son's name."

Marcus felt a surprising tightness in his throat and for a moment couldn't speak. Then he clapped Alberto on the back again and said, "Thank you! You just be sure to take excellent care of my little namesake. Now I know you're excited, but—"

He broke off for a second as the prickling sensation suddenly returned, then cut off again.

He looked around. What was going on? Why the sudden stop and start to the—

The dust thinned above him as he looked up and he felt the pins and needles directly on his face. Then the light breeze pushed another thick cloud of dust overhead and the sensation departed again.

Why would the sensation appear and disappear with the sunlight? It didn't make any sense, did it?

"Tribune? Are you all right?"

"Yes, yes," he lied. "I'm perfect this morning. Now what I want you to do is go back to your wife and make certain she is as comfortable as can be. It's going to be a long hard journey for her and we need to help her regain her strength."

"Of course, Tribune," Alberto said and continued to assure Marcus that he would take the most excellent care of Carmelita and the infant, Gaspar Marcus, all the way back to the wagon.

****

The last wagon had pulled out of Fort Segundus and had already disappeared from view—not because of its great distance, but because of the billowing cloud of dust kicked up by more than eighty wagons, and three hundred twenty horses making their way across the overly dry plains. It had taken nearly two hours to get them all through the broken gates and Marcus hadn't felt the strange prickling sensation for most of that time. The more he considered the abruptness with which the pins and needles sensation began and ended, the more it bothered him—especially once he remembered that the cloud of steam released by Seneca's spoiled farseeing spell had not been the first time he'd experienced the strange feeling.

Some half-a-year previously in the Fire Islands, Marcus had been soaked with a disgusting magical goo that erupted from the broken star-shaped pendant worn by the rebel witchdoctor, Kekipi, The same goo had killed three of his legionnaires, but in Marcus it had only caused a minute or more of intense pain reminiscent of the far weaker feeling of pins and needles he had been experiencing here in the Sea of Grass. He didn't want there to be a connection between the two sensations, but the fact remained that it was a similar kind of pain.

Had the goo changed him? And if so, what did this feeling mean? At the time of the attack on the caravan he had wondered if it were some sort of warning signal—a sixth sense. But if it was warning him of something now he couldn't figure out what that was.

He continued to stare after the wagons. He could hear the noise they made rolling across the Sea of Grass, the bouncing and creaking of the wagons and the neighing of the horses punctuated by an occasional sharp shout from a man. They were all dead. And if they died too soon, those who had stayed behind in Fort Segundus would be killed as well. They really didn't have the numbers to defend themselves against a serious attack.

He continued to weigh the problem in his mind. If the savages had moved on from here to attack Fort Tertium then it was highly probable that their leader would have left someone to watch the old fort. That someone could have been a simple scout lying flat on the plains a couple of miles away with no realistic chance of ever being discovered, but it seemed more likely that it would be a shaman with the savages equivalent of a farseeing spell. That way Teetonka could receive very detailed knowledge of what was happening at Fort Segundus without actually risking even one of his men.

He looked at his supposition again and decided it was sound, if hypothetical.

He took his line of reasoning a step farther. A shaman was a very valuable resource. He wouldn't want to leave him all alone in case an Aquila magus managed to spot him and the legions succeeded in boxing him in. So the easiest thing to do was to detach one of the smaller tribes rallying to his totem and set them as bodyguards for the shaman. If a significant force were to arrive, the tribe could send messengers ahead to warn Teetonka. If a weaker force—say a large caravan with a score of guards plus some Gota warriors and roughly a hand of legionnaires were to arrive, they could harass the new force while waiting for modest reinforcements. But if that force were to split itself in two…

Marcus jumped to his feet and ran in search of Seneca, Evorik and Severus.

****

"It's all speculation," Evorik pointed out. "We don't know anyone's been watching us at all and we certainly don't know how strong their numbers are if they are watching."

"Absolutely true," Marcus agreed before turning to Seneca. "Did Magus Jocasta tell you if the shaman have mastered farseeing magic?"

Seneca slowly nodded his head. "They remove their spirits from their bodies and place them into birds of prey like hawks or eagles. Apparently it is a very difficult skill to master, although I'd like to give it a try."

"How far away can they be and keep control of the animal?" Marcus interrupted.

"I asked her the very same thing," Seneca said. The similarity in the workings of his and Marcus' minds clearly excited him.

"And she said?"

"It varies with the strength of the shaman, but something like eight to ten miles was the best most can master."

"That's not very far on horseback," Evorik mused, "and they'd see us coming so we couldn't surprise them."

"That is where I think you're wrong," Marcus told him.

Evorik frowned. "How so?"

"It all has to do with how they're looking for us. Tell me Seneca, how do you defeat a farseeing?"

"Well there's a spell for short term blockage and wards that can be set up to block an area permanently. Fort Segundus had primitive ones set up—nothing truly permanent—but the savages destroyed them. Would you like me to show you the remains?"

"Not right now," Marcus told him. "So how would you defeat a farseeing, or a hawk-seeing in this case, if you didn't have access to your spell?"

Seneca stared at him as if he couldn't believe the Tribune could have asked him something so foolish. "You can't do that. It takes magic to defeat magic."

Marcus smiled at him. "Seneca, this is your lucky day, because I'm going to teach you a mystery of the legions. Just remember you owe me a lesson when I come to claim it."

"I don't think—"

"Lord Evorik, you probably already know this, but please bear with me as I instruct this young man." In point of fact, he had no idea if Evorik knew what he was going to tell Seneca, but he wanted to give the Gota lord cover if he needed it.

"Seneca, there are two major ways to defeat a farseeing. The first, as you have suggested, is by magic, but that often does not help the legions because our enemies know something is amiss by the big blank spot in their vision."

Evorik chuckled. Severus, Black Vigil that he was, stood silent as if he'd heard everything before and was patiently waiting for the lesser souls to catch up with him.

"The second way is much cleverer, because it uses camouflage to either hide subjects from the watcher's view or to disguise the subject so that the magus misinterprets what his magic reveals to him. It's this latter course that I plan to use today. Whether our shaman is using traditional farseeing or a hawk, he can't see us so long as we use the dust cloud as cover when we move."

Evorik's eyes twinkled while Seneca's mouth opened in a great big, "Ohhhhhhh."

Then Seneca shut his mouth and frowned for a moment. "But why would we be moving in the dust cloud? The wagons are traveling northeast. We want to head straight north and we're not going until tomorrow anyway."

"Wrong on all accounts," Marcus told him. "Now the first thing we have to do—and it needs to be very fast—is to get every merchant and driver who stayed with us dressed up to look like legionnaires in case the dust clears and the shaman sends his bird back to check on us again."

"Dressed like—"

"Then my legionnaires, Lord Evorik and our *scout* are going to slowly follow after the caravan. If my hypothesis is correct, the savages will attack them four or maybe six miles out from this castrum. Once the wagons are destroyed they can come on to Fort Segundus and take us down, or maybe wait until we hit the road."

"But if we trail behind the wagons and counterattack when they begin their raid..." Evorik said.

"We have a chance to do enough damage to them that they won't feel strong enough to attack again on their own," Marcus finished for him.

"It's risky," Severus noted, "but really not a bad risk. If the savages aren't there, we can just return. If they are there in greater force than you've guessed, well, we might as well die out there as back here."

"But if I'm right, we not only kill a bunch of savages, we save the lives of a lot of merchants and make it damn unlikely that there will be any hostiles remaining in the area strong enough to chase us into the salt pan," Marcus finished.

"So what do we have to lose?" Evorik asked.

"Only this—if I'm wrong and the savages are out there but ignoring the wagon to come at us first, we won't be here to fight them and everyone we leave behind is likely to be dead."

Seneca audibly swallowed. "Am I going to be one of the men you leave behind?"

"Yes," Marcus told him. "I can't risk you in the field in these conditions." Then he gave the young man something to hang his courage on to. "You are the Acting Magus of this auxiliary unit. Call us the Seventy-Seven, because I have seventy-seven men plus officers and allied cavalry."

The young man's eyes widened with surprise before his lips turned upward in delight. He stood up and saluted. "Yes, Tribune, I will not let you down!"

"I know you won't, Seneca, but remember—today, at least, I do not need you casting spells for me. I need you to use your brains to help me make it look like there are legionnaires in this camp."

"Are we in agreement?" Marcus asked Evorik.

The Gota lord nodded.

"Then let's get moving. The whole plan falls apart if the damn savages attack before we're in position."

****

Walking behind more than eighty wagons while trying to stay in the cloud of dust they kicked up was the very definition of *unpleasant* conditions. Despite the strip of cloth he'd used to cover his mouth, Marcus could taste the grit of the plains on his tongue and knew that every other man behind him could say the same. Evorik wore a perpetual scowl when Marcus could see him well enough to make out his expression, but the Gota prided themselves on their toughness and he did not whine or complain. Only Mataskah, the half-breed scout, suffered with more stoicism, but then, he'd lived out here in the Sea of Grass his entire life and so was probably more accustomed to these conditions.

Marcus had insisted the scout accompany them for two reasons. First, he knew the territory and that might prove useful if things went differently than the Tribune planned. But far more importantly, there was no way to know if the scout was truly loyal to them. He *said* that Teetonka would kill him for his white blood, but no one in the caravan really knew if that was true. If Marcus had left him behind, Mataskah could have ridden around them and warned the other savages of the Tribune's plans and that would definitely be bad.

"Waiting," Evorik grumbled, "is a shit job. Cavalry is meant to dash in and seize the glory."

"There will be no glory to have if we move too soon," Marcus reminded him. "But if I'm right, you're going to have a drinking tale to make your fellows envious for the rest of your life."

Marcus thought he was right. His skin had been prickling for twenty minutes now which suggested to him that a magical dust storm had kicked up in front of the wagons to conceal the approach of the savages.

The barbarian lord smiled at the thought of battle. "Yes, that will be good! I—"

The high-pitched battle cry of the savages which they'd been warned about at Fort Prime erupted into the night. Marcus' surprise counterattack had preempted this shock tactic during their first battle, but his plan this second time involved moving in after the attack had begun. He'd weighed this decision hard in his mind and decided that it was necessary. First, he wanted to catch a large number of the savages in his attack and that required him to pull them in from their hit and run tactics and get them to commit to battle. Second, he believed that the merchants were too focused on the profits their goods would bring in the north to honestly evaluate the dangers in their chosen course of action. By letting the savages attack the caravan now, he increased the chance that the survivors would make a more sensible choice.

It was a hard decision, but when coupled with his need to decisively blunt this savage offensive, it seemed the only option that could accomplish all of his goals.

"Double-time!" he shouted and as one man, legionnaires who were already readying their weapons and squaring their shields moved to the mile-eating pace.

Evorik and his men kept up without orders. "We really have to get you all some horses," the Gota happily told Marcus. "You move far too slowly on your own feet."

"It's all in the timing," Marcus reminded him. Ahead of them the screams and shouts of Gente and Dona merchants joined the war cries of the savages. The natives would be sweeping down the column, leaping from their horses onto the wagons, attacking with bow and axe, and losing their sense of the larger battlefield—

Ahead of him the rear wagon appeared and Marcus instantly revised his initial plan when he realized that horsemen were still approaching on either side.

"Form ranks," he shouted, "one man deep. Pilum out! Throw on my order then kill the bastards straight up the line!"

Men scrambled and Evorik shouted orders to get his cavalry out of the coming line of attack.

The savages swooped their ponies around the last wagon and started to turn to go up the other side without ever realizing there was an organized force of men stepping out of the dust in front of them."

"Throw pilums!" Marcus shouted, hurling his own as he said the words.

Eighty-one pilums launched into a dozen or so riders more or less at the same time.

Nine horses and five men went down and Lord Evorik bellowed, "Charge!"

The twenty Gota horsemen swept through the Aquilan line and butchered the startled savages with swift jabs of their spears.

Evorik barely even slowed down.

Within a dozen rapid heartbeats he was leading his men up the line of wagons searching for more horsemen to fight.

This was not the time for slow formations.

"Break ranks and charge! Find the bastards! Kill them all!" Marcus shouted and with a roar of fury and excitement his green legionnaires sprinted forward looking for more savages to fight. They found them everywhere—knocked from their ponies by the Gota sweeping ahead of them, or on their feet fighting merchants dagger to dagger or hatchet to sword. And the dust storm which was such an important component of the savage battle strategy proved again to be a double-edged weapon, for while it concealed the raiders on their approach it also hid from them the falling blade of the counterattack. After all, they expected to hear screams and shouts and it was remarkably hard to tell a man's bellow of fury from a shriek of pain and rage.

Marcus' legionnaires were green, but they stayed clustered in groups of friends as they fought the scattered savages they encountered. And three swords against one hatchet usually made a quick end to things. By the end of the battle, Marcus suffered only seven wounded men and no fatal casualties while Lord Evorik lost only one man dead when an arrow unluckily hit the warrior in the left eye.

The merchants, drivers and caravan guards had done less well. They had more than forty men injured and fifteen more straight up killed. And their casualties could have been much worse if the savages hadn't put so much of their effort into killing at least one horse per wagon to make certain they crippled the caravan's advance.

As to the savages? They'd killed more than seventy with Marcus' little trick and while many had escaped, Marcus didn't think they'd return without significant reinforcements.

Calidus and two legionnaires dragged a struggling savage across the plain to Marcus.

"What have we here?" Marcus asked. He'd given orders to kill the wounded among the savages. Normally they would have crucified them as a warning to others, but there were no big trees out here on the plains—really no trees at all.

"I think he's the chief or something," Calidus said. "He's the only one wearing this feathered cloak."

"Feathered cloak?" Marcus repeated. Calidus had succeeded in getting his full attention and he stepped forward to examine the prisoner. The cloak was indeed made of feathers—hawk feathers if Marcus was not mistaken—and the Tribune's fingers prickled as he touched the thing.

Unable to punch or kick Marcus, the savage spit at him to show his defiance.

Clasping the cloak around the man's neck was a bird's skull—again in all likelihood a hawk's. At his belt was a flint dagger—not steel like most of the savages wore. This one might well have been crafted by the man's own hands. Marcus drew the blade and again the tingling of his skin that had begun with the dust storm intensified.

"This is all magic, isn't it?" he muttered.

The man also wore jewelry—a topaz rock secured to his wrist with a leather strap and a piece of quartz hanging far down from his neck so that it bounced against his heart.

"Strip him!" Marcus ordered. "Remove the jewelry as well as the loin cloth. Then take him over there somewhere and slit his throat. I think you've caught the shaman who's been keeping track of us and I don't want to take any chances with him."

The men did as Marcus asked. While they executed the savage, Marcus squatted down and touched the ground next to the cloak.

He felt nothing special.

He touched the cloak and the pins and needles feeling immediately surfaced on his fingertips. He tried the back of his hand and got the same result. He then repeated the experiment with every item the shaman had owned. Was it magic he was detecting rather than danger? How was this possible?

Leaving the items on the ground he turned in time to see Calidus raise his sword and hack at the shaman's neck. It took three good blows before the head fell to the ground. Immediately the force of the wind diminished and with it the prickling sensation quickly died away.

"It is magic," Marcus muttered. "Why can I—"

He caught the movement from the corner of his eyes and turned in time to catch the Caravan Master's son, Gernot, charging him with a dagger.

Stepping to the side at the last moment, he dodged the blow and drove a solid right fist hard into the young man's mouth. The lower lip split and Gernot staggered back a step. Without hesitation, Marcus moved in and hit the young hothead again, making him drop his knife and knocking him to the ground.

"My mistress fought better than you," Marcus spat the words. "What the hell is this all about?"

"My father may die because of you!" Gernot raged.

He tried to get back to his feet but by this time, Calidus and the two legionnaires had run back over and immobilized the young man.

"What did I do to his father?" Marcus asked Calidus.

"I don't know, Sir. I haven't seen the Caravan Master since we rescued the wagons."

"The savages shot him in the neck!" Gernot screamed. Furious tears formed in his eyes.

"And that is my fault how?"

"You should have been here to protect him, but you took all the legionnaires away, you coward!"

"Are you really this stupid?" Marcus asked him. "I *paid* you to journey with this caravan. Your father owed *me* protection yet I have bailed him out of two battles. And those legion wagons also *paid* to come in this caravan. The legionnaires were not here to fight, but to travel. It's *you* and *your father* who let everyone down. How dare you blame me for your failures?"

"He's dying!" Gernot shouted.

"And if he lives, you will owe me his life!" Marcus snapped. "Now get up! You've tried to cheat me once and now you've tried to kill me. I'm done overlooking your stupidity because of your youth. Get up and get out of my sight!"

He turned to find his adjutant. "Calidus, I'm sick and tired of these *merchants*. Grab some legionnaires and get these wagons moving again. I want them all back in Fort Segundus before nightfall. Start by taking horses from the wagons of dead men to fill out the teams. When that's not enough force them to throw out cargo until their horses can pull the wagons."

An idea came to him. "And make sure you mark which wagons got an extra horse because I'm confiscating those animals. When we get back to Segundus we'll put them with wagons trying to go north with us across the salt pan. Anyone who's going back south can make do with only three horses."

Calidus saluted and left to carry out his orders.

Marcus looked around him, not caring that his unhappiness showed on his face.

It was going to be a long day.

****

By the time that Marcus led the caravan back to Fort Segundus, he'd begun to really regret not finding the time to sleep the night before. To complicate the problem, he didn't know how much rest he could squeeze in tonight either. Chaos reigned among the merchant wagons and he was going to have to get them organized—figure out who was going forward with him and who was going back to Dona if they were to have any chance of leaving again at dawn. His initial hope of starting for the salt pan under cover of darkness was now totally gone. With the shaman dead, it probably wouldn't matter anyway, but he would have felt better if the caravan was miles away before the sun came up over the horizon. So instead of sleeping like he needed to, he arbitrated disputes between merchants and his legionnaires, forbid men with overloaded wagons from joining the northern party, and generally put out of his mind anyone who insisted that they were turning around and heading south.

"I am worried, my friend," Lord Evorik announced as he stepped up beside him. "You are forcing all of these merchants to leave much of their goods behind and three percent of those goods are our plunder from these nasty skirmishes."

"Please tell me you're joking," Marcus responded. The truth was, he didn't know the Gota well enough to know if this was a serious complaint or not.

"Of course, I am!" Evorik insisted. "It does my heart good to see these merchants sweating over their lost profits." He paused to shrug. "On the other hand, they do owe us three percent of their cargo."

"We're not merchants," Marcus reminded him.

"No, we are *warriors*," Evorik agreed. "But warriors deserve to be rewarded for their deeds and these merchants have promised us a measly three percent. Honestly, we should take one-fifth, but that will probably upset my half-brother because he'll have to spend an afternoon listening to them whine about their lost sceattas and I like Alaric so I don't want to upset him."

"Alaric?" Marcus didn't even try to conceal his surprise. "Are you saying your brother is Alaric, Thegn of Topacio?"

"Half-brother," Evorik corrected him. "Why do you think he made me ambassador?"

"I never thought about it," Marcus answered. He really ought to pay more attention to such details.

"I think you said that you were going to Amatista," Evorik prompted. "You know, my second wife, Riciberga, is from there."

"Daughter of the thegn?" Marcus ventured half-seriously.

The Gota shrugged, "Cousin. Her brother is an important man—an asshole named Totila."

Connections clicked in Marcus' mind. "The man whose daughter is marrying the son of the Thegn of Granate?"

"Very good," Evorik complimented him on his knowledge. Then he added, "I think it's a bad sign. Riciberga's cousin better start watching out for himself."

"Meaning?" Marcus asked although he thought he knew.

"Totila is building relationships with Amatista's neighbors. A bond with me is one thing—I'm only the half-brother of the thegn and I have a great many half-brothers." He smiled. "It is a natural consequence of having so many wives. But marrying his daughter to the actual son of a thegn? That suggests ambition." His smile turned cruel. "I wonder if Totila has forgotten that Hathus of Granate is ambitious too. Every thegn wants to be Great Thegn and rule the other cities just like every son wants to cut his brothers out of their inheritance."

"I remember reading once that you Gota don't practice primogeniture like some kingdoms do. It's one of the things our peoples have in common," Marcus noted.

"That is correct," Evorik told him. "Inheritance can be very complicated. I have heard that you Aquilans just write down what you want to happen and store the will in your Temple of the Virgins." He laughed as if he couldn't imagine something more foolish. "That works for our common people—the Gente and the lesser Gota—but for thegns…" He shrugged. "Why should a son let a piece of paper decide his future?"

"Perhaps its lucky we don't have thegns," Marcus reminded him.

"I do not understand how your government works," Evorik admitted. "You cycle men in and out of your consulships and your other offices every year. I would get dizzy if I cared enough to try and follow it. Why do you put up with it?"

Explaining the complexities of Aquilan history to foreigners was rarely worth the effort. So Marcus contented himself with saying. "We had a very bad experience with kings about three centuries ago. So we got rid of them. And if the system appears complicated on the outside, well, it works for us."

"Indeed it does. You've conquered three-fifths of the southern continent and have a toe hold on the coast of this one. Only the Qing are larger than your Republic."

"We only came this far north because Dona stopped trading with us and began to supply our enemies. Trade is important, even if it's done by merchants. I would think that the Senate will be furious with these pirates and savages and will be seeking an alliance with your people to reopen travel between your Jeweled Cities and our provinces."

"Yes, I see that too. In fact, I am bringing letters from the Governor of Dona asking what we can do to help keep the trade routes open. I think we will mobilize some cavalry to push the savages back on the plains, but the pirates, they are a problem for the Jeweled Coast."

Marcus thought about that for a moment. The great problem of the Jeweled Cities was that they could not unite for a common purpose. Everyone was always looking for a chance to cut down his neighbor. That did not bode well for their chances of taking down the pirates which meant Aquila would probably have to do it. And without the border states of the

Trevilian Federation—those same pirate states—it was quite possible that Aquila would set about turning the Jeweled Coast into a new province or two. They would be very wealthy prizes and legionnaires and their praetors liked loot.

He wondered if Evorik and the other Gota understood that midterm danger?

It was time to get to work. "I should be—"

"Tribune," Evorik started speaking at precisely the same time. "You've never said—"

Both men broke off.

"Please continue," Marcus, told him. "I was just going to say I have details to worry about."

"As do I," Evorik agreed. "I was just wondering…I heard about your problems at home and your need to leave the Republic for a time, but why did you choose the Jeweled Hills?"

"Oh, that?" Marcus made a dismissive gesture. "I have a brother—a half-brother to be precise—on the side of my remarkably *polygamous* father." He chuckled. "He only marries one woman at a time, but he's gone through quite a few of them. So I decided to take him up on a longstanding invitation and visit him." That wasn't the actual truth but it was close enough to be believable—and Marcus didn't want to share his brother's secrets no matter how much he was coming to like this man. "Before starting this journey," he concluded, "I didn't actually know any other people outside the Republic."

"So that explains it," Evorik said, but he didn't actually look convinced by Marcus' explanation. "Do you mind telling me who your brother is? Perhaps I have heard of him."

"You probably have," Marcus agreed. "Señor Alberto tells me he's quite well known. His name is Juan Pablo Cazador."

"You're the brother of Señor Juan Pablo Cazador?" Evorik asked with the same shock of surprise with which Marcus had greeted the news that the Gota's brother was a thegn.

"Half-brother," Marcus corrected him with a smile.

"You know who he is, of course," Evorik said.

"Not as clearly as you northerners think I should," Marcus admitted. "I've been corresponding with him since I was eight years old. We write each other a letter every year or two, but I've come to realize on the journey that he really never told me much in his—just the sort of stuff a young man and then a young legionnaire would be interested in. Which cities had gone to war and which of his race horses were winning that year—that sort of thing. It wasn't until I met Señor Alberto in this caravan that I learned he was a prominent merchant heavily involved in Amatista's silk trade." Marcus couldn't help frowning. He hadn't realized how much he'd looked up to Juan Pablo or how much it hurt to have a hero tarnished by involving himself in commerce.

"He's more than *involved* with the silk," Evorik told him. "He's pretty much responsible for the whole industry now—at least those parts outside of Qing. I wonder if you appreciate just how difficult this task was? His birth made him uniquely qualified for the undertaking but it was still a monumental accomplishment. His Gente blood gave him access to the señors—the merchants among the Gente—whom he needed for their business connections and their wealth. But his Aquila blood let him interact with the Gota—you know we view you as practically our equals. You're head and shoulders above the Gente scum. So the Gota of Amatista were willing to deal with Señor Juan Pablo when they would never have considered doing so with the Gente. But none of that would have mattered if he hadn't had the big brass balls to court and marry the Qing woman, Kang Sujean. He risked his own status to elevate hers and this convinced the Qing in Aquamarina that Señor Juan Pablo's respect for them was no ploy. So they agreed to abandon that city where they had had so much trouble and move to Amatista.

"It still took years to put it all together. There were many problems." He laughed. "To hear the Señor talk about it, building the silk industry was even more complicated than fighting a war. He had to build buildings to house his silk worms and great manufactories to spin the threads into cloth and dye the silk. He had to convince Gota lords and Gente dons to start growing mulberry to feed his little spinner. When the Gente refused to work side-by-side with the Qing, he had to build up a Qing labor force which further angered the Gente because it cost them their jobs in the manufactories." Evorik laughed again. "Can you imagine those fools? They thought he would dismiss the only people who knew how to make the silk!"

He wiped water from his eyes before continuing. "And that was just the beginning—there were floods and fires and assassination attempts and—but Juan Pablo will want to tell you all of this himself. What is important is that your brother persevered and built an empire that has enriched a great many people more than himself. All of Amatista has benefited from his brilliance as have we in Topacio who are allied with their interests. Many Gota like myself have planted the mulberry bushes on our hills to harvest the leaves for his hungry little silk worms. Who would have thought that this otherwise useless land could produce such a profit? You will see. Wealth springs up wherever he goes."

Evorik's unusually long speech helped to restore some of Juan Pablo's luster in Marcus' eyes. That he was still a merchant was disappointing, but their father had abandoned him to his wife's mercantile family so what else could he do? But discovering a new way to profit from the land—that was what patricians' did—so long as others did the actual work. That was an admirable activity, even if the rest of it was rather base.

"Your mind has gone somewhere else, Tribune," Evorik noticed. "What are you thinking?"

Marcus shook his head. "Just wondering how it is that Juan Pablo and I could exchange so many letters and yet I seem to know nothing about him."

"Is that not for the best?" Evorik asked him. "Now you will have the honor of getting to know him as a man."

Day Ten
Why Is It Buzzing?

The wagons rolled at dawn and Marcus still had not managed to get any sleep. There had simply been too many important details to see to as he finally had to personally check each wagon that had decided to go north to make certain they had lowered their weight as he'd ordered. Señor Adán Nacio had been especially indignant at Marcus' insistence, but Marcus didn't really care. Assuming the older man's anger survived the rough trail ahead of them, what influence could the merchant really have over him? It wasn't like he was going to Amatista to live permanently, and even if he did, by all accounts Juan Pablo would be able to shield Marcus. So he stood at the broken gates of Fort Segundus and watched Lord Evorik ride forth with the half-breed scout, Mataskah and turn sharply north toward the salt pan that had scared nearly half of their surviving caravan into abandoning the journey and turning south. Once out the gate, Lord Evorik sent several of his men ahead to scout the path while Marcus and his legionnaires made certain that all the other wagons traveling with them got onto the trail.

All told, about sixty wagons chose to make the journey northward. Despite their endless stream of grumbled complaints, the merchants had figured out that this might well be the last caravan to reach the north in a long time. This meant the goods they carried might well bring prices two or three times higher than they would have in normal times and the greed for profits gave the men courage they might not normally have. When Marcus found himself wondering just how much he thought Calidus might be able to get for his wine, he had four more amphorae of them dumped out and filled with water in case their calculation of the time required to cross the salt pan proved badly short. Each wagon was carrying sufficient water for three days.

When the last wagon rolled through the broken gate, Marcus left a detail of men under Calidus to guard the rear and strode forward to join Evorik in the front. It was the best time of day for marching. The air was not yet hot and even though he was *very* tired, he still had a spring in his step as he nodded to Alberto and Carmelita with their new baby snuggled in her arms. She nodded back, looking as tired as he felt, but far happier.

"Seneca," Marcus greeted the young man as he walked past the wagon.

Startled, the student wizard dropped the small book he was writing in. "Oh, it's you, Tribune. How do you keep sneaking up on me like that?"

"I think you were so involved in your writing that an elephant could have snuck up on you," Marcus told him. He tried to pass on his way but the young man jumped to the ground and began to walk beside him. "Is it true, Tribune, that the salt pan resulted from a great battle between magi centuries ago?"

Marcus wondered how anyone thought he could be an authority on such things. "I don't know," he told him, "but I certainly hope not. The salt pan stretches for hundreds of miles and I hate to think that even an army of magi has that kind of power."

Undeterred, Seneca asked another question. "Are there really great sinkholes on the pan? I've read that they look like solid ground but are really only covered by a thin crust that will swallow a man whole as if he never existed."

"Someone mentioned as much to me," Marcus admitted, "but I've never been here and I don't know."

"What about magic?" Seneca pressed him. "Since salt can soak the stray threads of magic from the air, I've been wondering if there will be enough left to work spells?"

"You're asking me? I thought you were the one studying to be a magus."

"Yes, but—"

"Seneca, I have not had any sleep for two full days. I'm tired and I'm grouchy and I'm trying not to bite your head off but it's really hard to restrain myself. Can you please ask someone else all of these questions?"

Seneca started to say something, thought better of it, apologized and went back to the wagon.

Marcus continued up the line toward Evorik. He wanted to see what he had gotten himself and his men into.

****

The salt pan first appeared as a white scar across the Sea of Grass that contrasted starkly with the yellow-brown color of the plain. Over the course of the next hour, the scar grew until it formed a white sea on the horizon bordered by a grassy beach. The pan was slightly lower than the plains leading up to it, making Marcus wonder if once upon a time this had been a shallow lake or sea. Whatever it had been, it was a land of death now, covered so thickly in salt that nothing could grow for miles and miles ahead of them.

As he took his first step forward into the salt, three things happened that gave Marcus pause. First, the ground crunched in a disconcerting manner, not quite like sand. This was like no terrain he had ever tread before. Second, the temperature of the air around him jumped at least ten degrees as the sunlight reflected off the white surface and back up into the faces of Marcus and the other travelers. Finally, and apparently noticeable only to himself, the pins and needles feeling returned to him, stronger than he had felt it since entering the Sea of Grass.

There's something about walking across salt that automatically makes a man thirsty and Marcus immediately began to worry that he had made a terrible miscalculation in coming this way. But rather than give into his fears and insist they turn back he halted the caravan and altered his legionnaires' accoutrements. "All armor off and in the wagons, including shields. If we have to fight in a hurry, grab only your shields. I'll tell you if you have time to don the rest of your gear, but the heat in this pan is such I do not want you carrying more weight than you have to."

After the armor was stored back in the wagons, Marcus divided his men into four groups and set them at different parts of the caravan to help keep the wagons moving if anyone had trouble. He cautioned them against drinking too much water and reminded them that their stores had to last two days. He was very glad he'd poured out the amphorae of wine to carry more water, only wishing he'd dumped even more.

They trudged on, wrapping cloth across their mouths and noses to cut down on the salt dust stinging their eyes and making them miserable. Evorik's people proved worth their weight in gold, not only working with the half-breed scout to find their trail, but teaching the drivers how to preserve the strength of their horses by sponging the salt grime out of their nostrils.

By noon, the suffering had become intense and the heat was still rising, but as the merchants' complaints grew Mataskhah the scout only encouraged them to move faster—constantly worried that they were not making enough progress to get across the pan in his promised day and a half.

Their path was not directly north as Marcus had expected, but it meandered a bit, first northeast and then northwest, the scout altering their directions based upon sign he alone could read.

By midafternoon, Marcus began to stagger from the dual impact of the heat and his exhaustion. The constant prickling of his skin made him itch as if he had a bad case of poison ivy. And his brain began to shut down so that he could barely think about more than putting one foot in front of the other. He didn't even realize he had fallen until one of the legionnaires was trying to drown him with a cup of water.

"Easy there, Tribune," the man told him. "You're not drinking enough. You can't make it in this heat if you don't drink enough."

Marcus coughed and sputtered when the hot liquid touched his lips but this time, at least, he didn't waste the whole mouthful.

Severus came *running* from further down the line of wagons. "Damn it, Sir!" he cursed with unusual disregard for Marcus' rank. "I told you to get some rest. Two nights without sleep and you think you can walk the salt pan. Didn't I train you better than this?"

While Severus worked himself into a good rage, Marcus stopped listening to him. Lying here on the ground he *heard* something—more with his body than with his ears—something his boots had kept his feet from noticing when he was walking across this patch of salty desert.

"Give me that cup!" Severus told the legionnaire who was trying to help Marcus. Then the Black Vigil put his hand firmly on the back of Marcus' head and held the cup to his lips. "Drink this *now!*" he told the Tribune.

Marcus covered the hand holding the cup with his own shaky fingers. "Do you hear it, Severus? It's buzzing."

The furrows of concern etched into the older man's brow deepened dramatically.

"Drink this—"

"The ground, Severus, why is it buzzing?"

Severus lowered his voice to barely a whisper. "You're going to scare the men, Tribune. They're just a bunch of green banders. You have to stop talking like this."

"But I can hear it," Marcus whispered before passing out again.

Day Eleven
We're Surrounded by Sinkholes

"Tribune? Please get up. We have a serious problem…Tribune? I know you're sick but…it's bad, Sir. Please! Marcus?"

Marcus slowly came to his senses wondering where he was that someone would be using his given name. He opened his eyes to find the blurry face of Severus Lupus staring down at him, but with the darkness all around them, he couldn't recall exactly where they might be.

Behind Severus a face he was coming to know quite well pressed close to take a look at him. Seneca Liberus was full of his youth and evidently a great deal of fear and concern. The whole dirty business came back to him—the Fire Islands, his exile, his brother's letter, the long sea voyage and this interminable trip across the Sea of Grass.

He remembered the buzzing in the earth when he had fallen upon it. He couldn't hear it anymore and resolved not to ask about it at this time.

He sat up with a great deal of difficulty and realized he was in his wagon, pressed up against the amphorae of water and wine. "Wh…" He tried to ask a question but his mouth was too parched to make the sounds.

"Water," Severus demanded and moments later someone pressed a cup into his hand that he in turn held to Marcus' lips. The liquid was cool, even cold, like the night air. He took a couple of swallows, licked his cracked lips with his swollen tongue, and drank again.

"You ought to give him wine," the familiar voice of Lord Evorik complained. "That will get him moving again."

Marcus could feel his strength slowly growing and carefully took the cup from Severus. "What happened?" His voice was still rough, but he could form the words.

"Heat sickness, Tribune, you'd had no sleep in two days and the heat of the salt pan overwhelmed you."

That was not what Marcus had meant, but rather than explain that he asked, "And what's happened since?"

"My gold wasn't enough," Evorik growled in a whisper. "That flea-ridden asshole of a scout has run off on us and I lost two good men."

While the most likely meaning of the Gota lord's words was that the scout had murdered the cavalry men, that didn't seem like a plausible explanation. He took another sip of water before asking, "How?"

"We're surrounded by sinkholes," Severus explained. "We're really in a very narrow channel surrounded by the things. When Seneca here went looking for the scout to add a note to his journal, he couldn't find him so he asked Lord Evorik who started a search that quickly spread outside the caravan where two of his men blundered into sinkholes. The ground just broke open and swallowed them up before we could do anything."

"And?"

"We need to figure out what we're going to do before all the merchants get up."

"I don't know if we can find our way back," Evorik admitted. "The damn scout moved us east and west enough that it would be difficult to retrace our trail and any mistake might drop into another damned sinkhole."

"We also have a problem with water," Severus said. "You might have drunk too little, but everyone else has drunk too much. I estimate that most of the wagons in the caravan will run out this afternoon. We have to be out of the salt pan by nightfall or we're going to start losing people to the heat as well as the terrain."

"Help me out of the wagon," Marcus said. He didn't like asking for such aid, but his limbs were still weak. "I'm going to need some breakfast while we look this over, and I'm afraid I'm going to have to drink more of our store of water."

With the Black Vigil's help, he climbed out of the wagon and looked around. The moment his feet touched the salt the pins-and-needles feeling which had never quite gone away intensified mightily. Interested, he tested the connection to the salt by crouching down and touching the ground with his bare hand. Not only did the pins-and-needles feeling further intensify, but a low buzzing filled his ears as if the earth itself were humming to him.

He lifted the hand and the sound stopped.

What was going on inside of him?

Rising he asked to be shown the place where they'd lost the first of Evorik's men. It was one hundred yards to the west of the caravan and he could still make out the ripples in the salt where a horseman had once ridden. "How big is the sinkhole?" he asked.

"We don't know," Evorik admitted. "How do you test such a thing? But I lost my other man on the other side of the wagons. It's bad." After a moment he added, "Hate to lose the animal too. That was a mighty fine horse he was riding."

Marcus wasn't certain how to respond to that, so he didn't. "Someone bring a rope so if I put a foot wrong I don't end up like these two poor Gota."

When the rope had been brought, Marcus tied a bowline around his waist. Then he set about trying to figure out how Mataskah had been able to tell the surface of the sinkhole from the rest of the terrain. He tried to keep a few feet back from the camouflaged hole, but within ten steps realized just how impossible that was going to be. Without warning, the ground cracked beneath him and he sank over his head into the salt as if it were quicksand.

The rope went tight beneath his armpits and just as his body prepared to scream in horror he was breaking back across the surface and being dragged back to solid ground. He lay there panting on his back, trying to push back the horror of drowning in salt. His eyes burned because he hadn't closed them quickly enough and his skin felt parched and—wait a minute. His skin wasn't prickling as he had become used too.

He sat up and rubbed at his flesh, knocking a thick layer of clinging salt off of him. Why wasn't it prick—

"Tribune?"

"Give me a moment, Severus."

As Marcus cleaned his flesh the sensation slowly returned. But that didn't make any sense, did it? The salt had intensified the feeling. His body should be on fire with the pain of a million needles poking deep inside him, yet the sinkhole didn't feel that way at all.

He rubbed his fingers on his chest to make certain they were clean and touched a part of the earth that was not covered in spillage from the sinkhole. The tingling sensation returned with a vengeance, as did the buzzing sound. So why wasn't the salt of the sinkhole making his flesh react this way?

He checked that the rope was still around his waist. "Keep a firm grip on this, all right?"

Then he got to his hands and knees and slowly retraced his path to the edge of the sinkhole. He didn't need to see the ripples from his near disaster. He could have found it with his eyes closed because not only did the prickling sensation ease as he approached it, but the buzzing sound began to diminish a good foot and a half before that.

He got to his feet, crouching, and shuffled forward along the edge of the sinkhole, successfully finding the contours of the deadly trap. It was hard going. He couldn't walk straight, but he was able to figure out the line between safety and disaster...

Could he lead a caravan this way?

"What are you seeing, Tribune?" Evorik asked him. "I can tell no difference between the trap and the safe ground."

"I'm not sure I can put it into words," Marcus said.

He straightened up, his back cracking with relief as he stopped crouching over. Straining mightily he could still hear ever so faintly the buzzing sound. Stepping back away from the sinkhole it became ever so slightly louder. Moving forward, he discovered that at the very edge of disaster it disappeared.

"This is going to be an awful lot of work," Marcus told them, "but if there's a path through this, I think I can find it. What we're going to have to do is keep me secured with a rope like this in case I mess up and fall into another of these sinks. Then we're going to have to mobilize the legionnaires to mark the trail as I uncover it so that none of our wagons fall in. And we're going to have to accept the fact that we might move a couple of miles in one direction and have to turn around and retrace our steps. The only question I have is do we want to continue trying to go north, or do we want to try and make our way back to Fort Segundus."

"North," Evorik answered without hesitation. "There is no safety in returning. That bastard scout obviously lied to us. We can only expect to find more savages waiting if we try to go south."

"Besides, we really might be within half a day of the northern edge of the pan," Severus noted. "We need to get out of this place before nightfall. I agree, going south is not an option unless you can't find a path to the north."

"I don't understand how you're finding the sinkholes at all," Evorik added. "We only woke you because as the leader of the legionnaires your men insisted that you assist me in deciding what to do. I didn't think you would have such a hopeful solution."

"Hope is good, but let's not get over confident," Marcus said. "We've got a long way to go and no idea how truly bad it's going to get."

****

It went from bad to worse before dawn began to light the horizon. Marcus found the edges of the western sinkhole, but fell in twice more in the process. It seemed that any time he tried to push the pace he missed the telltale signs that told him where the border with danger lay. In two hours time, he discovered an extremely narrow path that appeared to lie between the two sinkholes and was ready to start exploring how far it went. Over the protests of Lord Evorik, he recommended that the caravan not start moving at dawn, but give him a chance to explore the extent of the lane of safety ahead of them.

It was a good thing he did.

Half a mile upward, the lane disappeared and he and the legionnaires helping him had to walk back and start all over again. By then the caravan was awake and the merchants frightened and angry.

Marcus let Severus and Evorik handle them—far from a diplomatic solution but the weight of all of these lives was firmly on his shoulder and he had no energy for their nonsense. He backtracked the caravan for a mile and a half before he found a direction that gave him more hope. He sent two of the men back to get the merchants moving and began charting a course northwest around the sinkholes and hopefully toward salvation.

The weather was damnably hot and he—like the rest of them—was drinking too much water. Why hadn't he poured out all of the wine and filled those amphorae from the spring at Fort Segundus? It would have been easy to do. Why hadn't he seen it was necessary? And why was he wasting his time now on these recriminations when he needed to focus on finding a path to safety?

By noon he had led the caravan two miles to the northwest and was as exhausted as he ever remembered feeling. Calidus kept food in his belly and insisted he take short breaks to recover his strength, but with the heat of the day upon them there was no recovering to be had. The strong sun, combined with the salty air, sacked the energy from his bones with the moisture from his lips and skin.

He pressed on.

By mid-afternoon they had moved only one more mile and he was fast losing any hope of getting them out of here. He'd had to backtrack again, losing precious progress and was now passing the narrowest of bridges of good solid land. Matsahkah didn't have to be waiting with more savages. He had to figure that none of them could emerge from the pan without him.

Even more disturbing than the heat and the parched air was the way in which Marcus' whole body came to yearn for that strange buzzing song. The sound that had disturbed him so much the night before had become their lifeline and he snatched at any scrap of the strange music. The sinkholes were an abomination of silence by comparison as if something far beneath him had sucked all the music—all the strange prickly sensation—out of the salt above it leaving only dead hollow crystal grains to trouble the surface.

His legs were ready to give out again within an hour of sunset and he called a halt, finally forced to accept his limits. "We'll take a brief break, say two hours. Let everyone eat something and rest. Then when the moon's up, we'll start forward again. We're pretty much out of water so we'll push on through the night and try and get out of this ghastly place."

The merchants were too exhausted and too frightened to argue with him, which really was a bad sign. For his part, Marcus crawled under his wagon and lost consciousness moments after his head touched the ground—lulled instantly to sleep by the strangely beautiful music within the salt.

****

This time it was Calidus who woke him. "Tribune, the moon is up."

He woke more quickly than he had that morning. After a drink of water and a bite of food, he met with his legionnaires again and resumed picking out their path from amid the many dangers of the salt pan. The brief rest had not exactly revitalized him, but it had helped, and as the night deepened and the heat fell, Marcus began to gain more confidence. They encountered fewer sinkholes and the horses, strengthened by the cooler temperatures, found the stamina to increase the pace behind him. After midnight they encountered no additional sinkholes at all and an hour before dawn Marcus stepped off the salt and back onto the Sea of Grass.

Day Twelve
Beautiful and Awe Inspiring

"We're still nearly out of water," Calidus noted.

The whole caravan had rested until noon with many merchants foolishly drinking the last of their reserves as if they believed escaping the salt pan resolved all of their problems.

"Lord Evorik," Marcus addressed the Gota, "we're getting closer to your territory. I don't know this terrain at all. Can you find us water?"

"Fort Quartus is probably the nearest source," Evorik told him. "You see that jagged peak there?" He pointed at a noteworthy crag rising above the hills to the north. "My home in Topacio is about ten miles north of the Tooth, as we call it. The city is five miles further north from there. Two good days journey south of that—three or four at the pace of these wagons—is your Fort Quartus. Say sixty miles short of those hills and I make that to be only thirty or forty miles from where we are now. We're well west of it. If we had more water, I would suggest we head straight for the Tooth and forget this last fort, but we can't do that. It's going to be too hard to get there without losing people as it is."

Marcus nodded. "We really should drop more cargo, but I doubt that the merchants will agree this close to their destination. "So let's gather them up together and tell them what we aim to do."

****

The members of the caravan might be exhausted and dirty after their crossing of the salt pan, but they were in no way cowed by their grueling experience. Quite the opposite, they gave off an aura of invincibility and the sort of confidence that said: *You've given us your worst and we're still fighting.* Marcus' green legionnaires acted the same. None of them were happy with what they'd just endured but surviving it had pulled them together and toughened them much in the way that battle hardened veterans. They'd learned a lot about themselves and their commander in the past days and they were not going to be beaten by another forty measly miles.

"So that's where we stand," Marcus summed up. "Lord Evorik estimates it is at most another forty miles to Fort Quartus and fresh water. I laid in a few more amphorae than most of you did so we have enough to give the horses a small drink and wet our own mouths, but there is no denying that it's going to be a hard journey."

"If we travel again through the night as we did to escape the salt," Señor Adán suggested, "we can avoid the parching heat of the day and be close to our destination by sunrise."

"Lord Evorik?" Marcus turned to the Gota. "You and your men will be scouting the trail. What do you think?"

"Damn fine idea!" Evorik agreed offering a rare complement to the Gente merchant. "Let's be blunt. Staying still means death to us now. So let's push as long and hard as we can so we can reach Fort Quartus."

In a rare moment of total unanimity, the meeting broke up and the men went to prepare their wagons. Legionnaires brought the last of Marcus' water around to help revitalize the strength of the horses. Marcus looked at the remaining wine in his wagon and whimsically noted that if it came to dying of thirst they could do it drunk and happy.

Then they hit the trail and started pounding out the grueling miles. The salt pan had left all of them burnt out and exhausted, but there was something uplifting about having the feel of grass beneath their feet again. Like the rest of the caravan, Marcus couldn't help feeling that they had just about won.

****

Marcus noticed with satisfaction a team of legionnaires quickly and efficiently repairing a broken wagon wheel. They barely needed to be told to go to the merchant's aid, waiting only for Green Vigil Phanes to reluctantly agree that it was needed before springing into action. They'd come a long way from that first time he had mobilized them to help Señor Alberto and his wife.

From his observation as well, the water supply, while desperate, was not totally used up. He'd carefully marked the wagons that appeared to have husbanded at least a slight reserve against the needs of the entire caravan. He'd learned from Calidus that he had a slight reserve as well which he had reluctantly decided to mix with wine at a ratio of five parts water to one part wine, just to stretch it out a little farther. Starting with his legionnaires, he'd give that out to anyone who was primarily walking. It would only be a mouthful apiece but that was a hell of a lot better than nothing. If only they weren't traveling so slowly. He didn't know what they were going to do if they walked all night and still hadn't found Fort Quartus. Eventually horses and men were going to start to drop as he had done in the salt pan and that was the beginning of the end for all of them.

****

Calidus poured the last cup of extremely thin wine from the amphorae and handed it to Marcus. "And your drink, Tribune."

Marcus accepted the cup. All of his legionnaires and a handful of the merchants had all had a single cup of the water/wine mixture and now he suspected the caravan truly had used up all its reserves. They'd break out the wine if they needed to, but Marcus knew that that was a genuine signal that the end was upon them. While the wine would wet the mouth and bring some small comfort, it didn't truly help a man who was dying of thirst. He didn't understand why this was the case, but legion lore insisted it was true.

He put the cup to his lips and then thought of the young mother, Carmelita, trying to feed her baby with no water in her. "Thank you, Calidus, I think I'll savor the drink while I make my inspection of the wagons."

Calidus' frown told Marcus he wasn't fooled, but like a good adjutant, he accepted his superior's decisions even when he disagreed with them.

The sun was setting and deep shadows were stretching across the plain behind the wagons. Soon the heat would start to lift and the horses and men would gain a little second wind to help them in this final push toward salvation. He hoped it would be enough. It *had* to be enough. They had to reach Fort Quartus both to save themselves and to warn them of what had happened at Segundus.

Ahead of him, Alberto and Carmelita's wagon loomed into view. If he was being honest with himself, Marcus would have to admit that he was quite taken with the young señora. There was much to respect in the courage of the young woman, accompanying her husband into foreign lands to help him save her father's fortunes, and then attacking this difficult ride north in her extremely pregnant condition without a single complaint that he had yet heard. Everyone in the caravan liked the woman and he hoped that others had done as he was doing and put a little aside to help her and the new child.

As he reached the wagon, he saw Alberto checking the harness on his team of horses and Carmelita, already in her seat at the front of the wagon, holding little Gaspar Marcus Lope in her arms. "Hello," he greeted them.

Despite their obvious exhaustion, both husband and wife managed smiles for him.

"It is good to see you, Tribune," Alberto told him. "As you can see, we are ready for our final push. A few more miles and all will be well again."

"Absolutely right," Marcus told him. "Evorik tells me it's just a few more hours. In fact, he's a little surprised we can't already see the fort. Come dawn we should be within a mile or two of fresh water."

He held out the cup. "But in the meantime, Señora Carmelita, please accept the last cup of the legion water reserve for you and your son with our complements. It has been very slightly mixed with wine to stretch the water supply."

"Oh, Tribune Marcus," Carmelita protested. "I could not possibly accept. You and your legionnaires are walking while all I have to do is—"

"Feed my namesake," Marcus reminded her. "Please, it is not much, but we all want you to have it." He turned to Alberto for support. "Wouldn't you agree, Señor?"

"I absolutely do, Tribune," Alberto swore. "And what is more, you and your men have once more earned my eternal gratitude. To think of my Carmelita while all are in such distress."

Reluctantly Carmelita took the cup and drank the very weak wine. When she had finished she handed the cup back and forced a smile onto her face. "Thank you, Tribune, for Gaspar and me both."

Marcus just hoped it would be enough.

****

By midnight the temperature was much cooler, and the walking had become only difficult. The moon continued to give enough illumination to keep them moving forward although the amount of the horizon they could clearly see was much reduced. Evorik and his men mostly walked their horses, preserving the great beasts' strength as much as they could. Everyone was tired, everyone was grumpy, and the feeling of invincibility that had invigorated them when they escaped the salt pan was long gone. Life had become a drudgery of step after step after step and the hope represented by Fort Quartus seemed a very long way off.

An hour before dawn, hope returned to the caravan in the form of a far distant thunderstorm and the promise of rain that it brought with it. They saw the bolt of lightning first, a brilliant white flash crackling its jagged path out of the heavens and down to earth. Then, moments later, they heard a roll of thunder rumble across the plains. As if they were one body, every man and woman in the caravan, whether seated or walking, paused to look ahead, wondering if the awesome sight would be repeated and praying that it portended coming rain.

They waited more than a minute before the lightning returned, crackling straight down to earth before sending another wave of thunder to wash across the plains. A little cheer lifted from the wagons. The sight had been both beautiful and awe inspiring, and it was followed, if not quickly, by many more. At the rate of about one every ninety seconds, the heavens lit up in the glory of the bolts from heaven. Marcus knew intellectually that they did not want to endure such a storm, but like the others, the promise of rain water proved too much for him and he said a silent prayer to Sol Invictus that the clouds would move in their direction.

After about ten minutes of watching, Marcus remembered what they had to do and passed the word for the caravan to begin moving forward again.

****

When the predawn light finally began to brighten the horizon, the storm continued to rage in all its glory. They could see the clouds now, a surprisingly small patch of blackness on the distant horizon, as the lightning continued to jab at the earth.

Marcus had worked his way to the front of the caravan to better watch the celestial storm, but Evorik pulled his attention away from the show. Still leading his horse, he walked up beside Marcus. "Tribune, it galls me to say it, but I lost my way in the dark." He pointed to the northwest—away from the storm in the northeast. "We've come too far east. We've missed the fort and need to change direction. Walk up this low hill with me and I'll show you the bad news."

Marcus followed the Gota up a very shallow rise from which he could plainly see the earthen walls of what could only be Fort Quartus looming in the distance to the northwest. Evorik was completely correct. They'd come maybe six miles past the castrum and still had a ways north to go to reach it—say ten miles all in all.

He forced himself not to sigh. Ten miles was half a day's journey when the men and horses were fresh, but now? "I'll get the wagons turned," he decided. "I need you to take your horsemen and ride ahead to the fort. We need help. We'll give you extra water skins to carry and bring back full, as soon as you can. Warn the commander of the garrison about what we saw at Segundus and suspect is happening at Tertium. Then get him to send some men with more water to help us get this caravan inside the walls."

Evorik nodded seeing the sense of it and without hesitation mounted his horse. "We'll get these people water," he promised. "You just keep them going in the right direction." He started to swing his horse around, mouth opening to shout orders when he froze. His eyes squinted against the brightening horizon and he whispered, "Gods preserve us! I think the legion already knows about the savages."

Marcus turned to see what had captured the Gota's attention. The combination of the brightening horizon and the shallow hilltop revealed to his squinting eyes what could only be a battle unfolding perhaps thirty, or at most fifty, miles ahead of them to the northeast. Figures on horseback were the most readily discernible, swarming like ants around what Marcus' gut told him must be the Fort Quartus garrison. Even as he watched, a lightning bolt pounded hard into the middle of the confusing mass. He could readily imagine that another legionnaire—or more—had just died.

Rather than depress him, the sight of the horror firmed Marcus' resolve. His spine straightening despite his exhaustion, the Tribune turned to the Gota lord. "You better get moving. Tell whoever is left in the fort what's happening to their forces in the east and that we need help now! If the legion is dying out there, the savages will be at Quartus in at most another couple of days."

"Tribune…" Evorik started to object but the imperatives of the situation were so obvious that he didn't finish the thought. Twisting in his saddle, he called to his men. "Odoacer, Richimar, ride down the line of wagons collecting water skins. We're pushing ahead to Fort Quartus to get help."

Men in the caravan still driving their horse teams in the wrong direction, looked up at Evorik's words. They couldn't see the battle ahead, but that was only a matter of time. Eventually someone would notice. The best thing to do was to get them turned and making best speed toward Quartus.

Decision made, Marcus broke into a run back toward the wagons.

Day Thirteen
What's Wrong with the Fort?

Panic rippled down the length of the caravan.

"Yes, it's bad, boys!" Marcus admitted. "But we're still out ahead of it. If we get to the Fort we can shelter behind its walls while we wait for news of the battle and send for reinforcements from the Jeweled Hills. What we need to do now is move, move, *move!*"

It amazed him what a little adrenalin could do to counteract his thirst and exhaustion. The goal was in sight. Fort Quartus was only a few miles distant. Evorik's riders were already far out ahead. In a couple of hours time, he'd be racing back across the plains with bulging water skins to renew the strength of the horses while a hand or two of fresh legionnaires carried more water skins right behind him. The caravan was going to make it just as long as no new disasters slowed them down.

Swarms of horsemen—it was impossible to count numbers at this distance—were now branching outward from the main battle but to what purpose Marcus couldn't say for certain. The most likely explanation was that someone had tried to escape the horde of savages, but that would require cavalry on the legion side of the battle. Evorik had told him that detachments of Jeweled Hill cavalry often worked with the legion out of Fort Quartus but without getting substantially closer to the battle it was impossible to distinguish between Gota and savage riders.

Closer was not something Marcus wanted to be at this moment—certainly not until he had the wagons safely behind the walls of Fort Quartus.

A couple of the groups were heading in this general direction, but unless Marcus was badly misjudging the distance, he didn't think they could probably reach the caravan until very late in the day.

He forced the battle from his mind and refocused his attention on getting his people to safety.

****

By noon the distant battle was over and Marcus' gut told him the legion had not been triumphant. Swarms of horses still stood on the field and the thunder storm slowly began to dissipate.

It looked bad.

As for Marcus' own horses, they were dead on their feet and he'd actually had to cut seven of them out of their teams and leave them to walk behind or not as the inclination took them. He had expected Evorik to be back by now, and was very unhappy that he was not. They were still something like four miles away, but without fresh water, he didn't know if the animals could make it.

Whatever adrenalin had come with the realization the savages were already here in numbers had long since departed and forcing the body to take each new step forward was a trial for everyone.

Something appeared and disappeared in his vision, compelling Marcus to stop and concentrate on what he had seen. A dark shape appeared near the fort ahead of them—a dark shape followed by a string of others making pretty good progress coming back toward them.

Evorik?

Whether it was or wasn't the Gota lord, Marcus continued to encourage the caravan to roll forward.

****

"Here, take a sip of this, Tribune," Evorik told him.

"The horses have all had a drink?" Marcus asked.

"Not their fill by any pretense, but enough to keep them moving," the Gota assured him.

"And my men?"

"You're the last holdout," Evorik laughed. "You can drink without offending your pure Aquilan officer's conscience."

Marcus accepted the water skin and wet his cracked lips. Then he took a little more water and held it in his mouth, enjoying the feel of moisture return to his parched tongue. Finally he forced a couple of swallows down and tried to return the skin to Evorik.

"You keep that one," Evorik told him. "Fulgus knows there's little enough in it. But unlike your men, your work is only going to begin when we reach Fort Quartus."

"Tell me."

"The Great Tribune in charge of Fort Quartus got word of the siege of Tertium and requested reinforcements from Topacio. We've worked together in the past and sent about eight hundred cavalry to reinforce the

Great Tribune and together they marched on Tertium. That was three days ago, and like us, the Lesser Tribune left in charge of Quartus is…unhappy at the implications. He's got one under strength hand to hold the fort with and the malingerers of the garrison who claimed to be too sick to march out with the rest of the legionnaires."

That did look bad. It was, in fact, worse than the situation they'd found at Fort Prime. It was likely Marcus was going to have to do something drastic in Quartus if they were to have any chance of survival.

"First things first," he said. "We have to get the caravan to the fort. How is its water supply?"

"It's the only piece of good news," Evorik told him. "The fort is built on a low hill—really not a hill at all by my standards. A spring emerges from the hill and forms a little creek that meanders off into the plain. They've dug a well to the source of the spring inside the hill at the central plaza you Aquilans build into all of your forts. You won't die of thirst in there."

An idea began to spark in Marcus' mind. It wasn't enough to win the coming battle but it might help raise the odds of his success. "We have to get the caravan to Quartus. Did this Lesser Tribune—what's his name by the way?"

"Cyrus."

"Must be from one of the provinces," Marcus noted. "Did he send legionnaires to help us move the caravan?"

"No."

"No?"

"He said he needed all of his men to prepare the defense of Fort Quartus, if needed."

That was a decision Marcus personally regretted, but he could understand it. He already had a number of tasks he planned to put the men to as soon as they were able to work again. "And what are they working on?"

"Nothing!" Evorik's flat expression reinforced the word.

"Nothing?"

"They're standing on the walls waiting for word of how the battle went."

"And losing their only chance to prepare for it," Marcus said to himself. "Well I cannot let this stand. I need you and your men to return to Fort Quartus. Take Severus with you. Black Vigils hold a lot of weight in the legion. You tell *Lesser* Tribune Cyrus that *Tribune* Marcus Venandus orders him to have his men prepare food and water sufficient for this entire caravan. Furthermore, he is to move all barracks accommodations—those are tents I presume?"

Evorik nodded.

"Move them all to the forum and strip anything of use from the outer grounds. He also has to make the parade ground ready for all of these wagons. And I want to know what his supply situation is. How much food does he have? How many pilum? How many extra shields and sets of armor and swords. Praise be to Sol Invictus that we are carrying wagons full of supplies—especially pilum—because I think we're going to need them. Finally, I want all construction equipment inspected and ready for use when I arrive. If the battle went as badly as we both fear, we are not going to have much time to prepare our defenses—I refuse to let that idiot waste the little we have."

Evorik looked pleased. "I'll send my men back with another round of water, but I'd better stay and help Severus keep this hand in line."

Marcus agreed. "Unfortunately, you don't leave your best hand behind when you march off to battle. I think we're going to have to remind Lesser Tribune Cyrus of what it means to be a legionnaire."

****

When Marcus led his caravan into Fort Quartus, his exhausted greenband legionnaires marched in a credible column at the front and rear of the line of wagons. A very unhappy Lesser Tribune Cyrus, flanked by his own vigils, plus Severus and Evorik and a handful of the fort's legionnaires, stood before him in the mouth of the gates and saluted crisply in his perfectly clean uniform.

Marcus returned the gesture, pressing his clenched right fist against his heart. "Tribune Marcus Venandus taking command of Fort Quartus until the end of the present emergency!" he barked the order so that everyone within a thousand feet of him would hear it.

"We don't actually know that an emergency exists, Tribune," Cyrus protested.

Marcus couldn't fault him for not wanting to give up his command, but he absolutely did blame him for the piss-poor justification for keeping it.

"Black Vigil Severus!" he bellowed, even though his old friend was standing four feet away.

Severus saluted. "Tribune!"

"Did you brief Lesser Tribune Cyrus on the situation we discovered at Fort Segundus?"

"Yes, Tribune!"

"And did you brief Lesser Tribune Cyrus on the information related to us by Tribune Lucanus of Fort Prime?"

"Yes, Tribune!"

Cyrus began to cringe with each of Severus' confirmations.

"And did you brief Lesser Tribune Cyrus on the attacks made on the caravan during our journey both to Fort Segundus and on the trail to Fort Tertium?"

"Yes, Tribune!"

"And did you further brief Lesser Tribune Cyrus on the attempt by the half-breed scout, Mataskah, to destroy this body of legion reinforcements and the caravan carrying legion supplies?"

"Yes, Tribune!"

Cyrus' shoulders began to droop with the growing evidence of how serious their circumstances were.

"And did you also brief Lesser Tribune Cyrus on our theories regarding the situation at Fort Tertium—theories that were confirmed by the request for reinforcements sent by Fort Tertium to Fort Quartus?"

"Yes, Tribune!"

"But Great Tribune Rogatus led a substantial army, reinforced by eight hundred Gota horsemen, to Tertium and they must have defeated the savages on the plains because they are legionnaires."

Marcus lowered his voice. "Lesser Tribune, they were legionnaires at Fort Segundus too. We can die just like everyone else does, we're just a hell of a lot harder to kill."

"But..."

It was clear to Marcus that the Lesser Tribune simply had no idea what to do.

Marcus abruptly shifted his attention to Severus. "Has a meal been prepared?"

"Yes, Tribune."

"Good, get our men fed and let them rest until midnight. Then we'll get them to work strengthening the fortifications here at Quartus.

He turned back to Cyrus. "Lesser Tribune, your men need to get my wagons situated, the horses watered and fed, and a meal to the humans. All of that needs to be completed in two hours time and your men assembled—including the sick so long as they are not actually already dead—in the forum and ready for inspection. Unless Great Tribune Rogatus won a totally decisive victory at the Battle of the Thundercloud out there, we have to be prepared to defend Quartus against the savages."

Finally he turned to the Gota lord whom he'd come to depend on so much in these past few days. "Lord Evorik, my friend, I don't know how we would have come so far without the strength and courage of your men. I am afraid that I need to call upon you one more time."

The Gota lord scratched his red beard while he waited to hear Marcus' request.

"See to your horses and rest your men tonight. In the morning, we will need to send you north to Topacio with word of what has happened."

"It might be better to wait until some survivors of the battle reach us."

"I know, but if we wait too long and the savages arrive in numbers, we won't be able to get you out at all."

"My wives are still with the caravan," Evorik protested.

"Could you switch out two of your men so they can ride with you?" Marcus asked.

The Gota leader thought about that for a moment before reluctantly shaking his head. "No, they're fine horsewomen, but they couldn't keep up."

"Then you have my word that I and my legionnaires will die before we let even one of those savages within spitting distance of them," Marcus swore.

Evorik nodded gravely. "Then I'll go at dawn. Perhaps we'll be lucky and some of the survivors will reach us during the night."

Marcus thought that was a definite possibility. If someone was running from a savage horde that had just broken a phalanx of legionnaires and an army of Gota horsemen, they were unlikely to stop to sleep just because it was nighttime. "We can only hope that's the case."

"We'll wake an hour before dawn and leave as the new day first begins to brighten the horizon."

Marcus suppressed a grin. For a moment there, the Gota had sounded almost poetic enough to be one of the Gente.

"I'm depending on you, my friend."

"I'll bring the reinforcements," Evorik promised. "You just make certain that my wives are alive and waiting for me when I get here."

****

Marcus stalked the outer portions of the castrum checking the layout of the land one more time before enacting his defensive changes. Behind him, Seneca Liberus followed after him balancing a book, an ink bottle and a quill pen in his hands as he asked his never-ending stream of questions.

"So I don't understand what's wrong with the fort," he complained.

"Nothing is wrong with it," Marcus informed him. "It's a solid structure which in many ways is perfect for fighting the savages. The outer ditch and the steep earthen wall will keep them from riding their horses straight into the fort. The interval just inside the wall is wide enough to catch all the savages' arrows before they reach the legionnaires' encampment. There is also plenty of growing grass to feed our own draft horses and the larger steeds of our allies."

"Then why aren't you planning to use it?" Seneca asked. The question proved how bright the young man was. He had heard the various instructions Marcus had already given and seen the frown on his face when he inspected the wall and drawn the correct conclusion.

"Because it's too big," Marcus told him. "This fort was built to house two legions." That size was evidence to Marcus' mind that Aquila was looking ahead to the day they might want to incorporate the Jeweled Hills as a province. "We have less than two hands to defend it with. If the savages attack in the numbers we saw at the Battle of the Thundercloud, we will be swarmed and pulled down."

"I read something about weather magic back at the collegium," Seneca informed him. "It must take a great deal of power to form clouds and call lightning out in a barren plain like this. And it's hard to keep control of something so powerful—especially something as chaotic as the weather. I might be able to interfere with their shaman if they try such a feat here at Fort Quartus."

Marcus succeeded in keeping the smile off his face, but it was hard. The young man couldn't even manage a basic farseeing but he thought he could engage in weather magic. "I will leave the magical parts of this battle in your capable hands, Acting Magus. Advise me when you have evidence that the shaman is bringing magic into play and act as you deem best."

Seneca nodded solemnly and made a note in his book.

"Now if you will excuse me, I have to speak with Señor Adán Nacio."

Seneca simply followed after him."

****

"Señor," Marcus called out to the older gentleman—the oldest who was traveling with the caravan. Like the other Gente, he was dressed in a silk shirt and wore a wide-brimmed black hat. His vest was embroidered with silver thread in an aesthetically pleasing geometric fashion. His boots and pants were also very high quality and despite their many days on the trail he had kept his graying beard and mustache neatly trimmed. Everything about the man spoke of wealth, taste and respect.

"If I could have a moment of your time, I urgently need to speak with you about the defense of this fortress."

Adán's eyes flickered with surprise for a moment. While Marcus had always treated him with respect, he had never sought him out for advice and usually opposed the man's unsolicited suggestions. But he handed his half-eaten plate of food to one of his drivers and, still carrying his cup of water, stepped to the side with Marcus.

"I am making plans to defend this fortress from the savages if our fears are valid and it proves to be the case that Great Tribune Rogatus did not win a decisive victory."

"You mean to say, you fear that he and his boorish Gota allies were totally crushed by the savages this morning."

That was in fact exactly what Marcus had intended to say but one does not speculate verbally on so little evidence about disaster befalling superior officers. It was a crime within the legion often framed as mutiny or at least holding a defeatist attitude.

"If such a thing happened that is all the more reason to bolster our defenses."

In fact, most of the horsemen they could see had remained at the site of the battle throughout the day. They still couldn't make out any details so they could not dismiss the possibility that the legion and the Gota had won, but Marcus' gut told him the opposite had happened.

"What do you want with me?"

"I need an officer to help me corral the merchants and their drivers into helping first to build up our defenses and second to fight if it comes to that."

"An officer?"

Marcus could see that he had piqued the older man's interest. "Yes, to act under my command, but given primary charge of those among us who are not legionnaires or Gota. The Gente hold you in high regard, Señor Adán. I think they will take orders coming from you more readily than coming from an outsider like me."

Adán nodded, clearly pleased with the idea. "What rank were you thinking to give me?"

"It is my understanding that a man of the Gente given charge of a group of a couple of hundred soldiers holds the rank of capitán. We don't have that many men to put you in charge of, but I believe it a fitting rank."

From the sparkle in Adán's eyes, he agreed with Marcus, but the older man kept the enthusiasm out of his voice. "And what tasks do you fear my people will not want to carry out?"

Marcus got down to business. "We have to build a new wall within the fortress around the area we now occupy. The outer wall is too large to defend. It's going to take terrible grunt work because we need it finished by tomorrow night. If we get more time, we can strengthen it after that, but the basic wall, with a few innovations I am planning, needs to be done by this time tomorrow night."

Adán looked about him in amazement at Marcus' audacity. "I don't think such a thing can be done," he said. It was not an argument, just a simple statement of fact.

"If we want to live, it will have to be," Marcus told him. "And that means that every man and woman in the fort save Señora Carmelita and her new child, must dig and dig until their hands are raw and their hearts burst in their chests."

"The señors will not like that," Adán observed. "Such work is beneath their dignity."

"It doesn't get any less dignified than dying," Marcus reminded him.

Adán took a deep breath. "I agree. Fortunately for you, you have found in me a capitán up to the responsibility. I will get your civilians working."

"I suggest, Capitán, that like my legionnaires from the caravan, you give your new soldiers until midnight to rest."

Adán shook his head. "I will start cycling them through in shifts—two hours digging, followed by two hours rest. The first shift will not accomplish much, but it will show the others how seriously we regard this business."

"Excellent!" Marcus complemented him. "I will leave this part of the defense in your capable hands."

As he stalked off to find Lesser Tribune Cyrus, Seneca trailed after him still scribbling notes in his book.

****

Cyrus had been predictably horrified at the notion of putting an inner wall around his Great Tribune's headquarters, but Marcus had not found it difficult to bully him into line. His legionnaires—there were about a hundred of them when he added the malingerers to Cyrus's under-strength hand—were now hard at work digging the new trench—a task every legionnaire excelled at because fortifying every camp in enemy territory was among the most basic of legion activities. He didn't think that his three hundred men were likely to build the whole new wall in one day—the area was still too big, but if he got two days he would have a descent surprise for the savages when they returned.

To set up the second part of that surprise he was inspecting the creek with Severus, Calidus, and the now ever-present Seneca.

"I want to dam the creek so that the savages can't water their horses from it," Marcus told them.

"You what?"

"I want to try and flood all the ground between the outer and inner walls, including the ditch we're currently digging," Marcus explained. "I want to make a lake the savages would have to cross to get to us."

"That's…quite an idea," Calidus said. Marcus knew him well enough to understand that that was not a criticism. His adjutant was trying to figure out how to make his Tribune's vision a reality.

Severus greeted the idea with an unusual level of enthusiasm. "The savages are probably unfamiliar with large standing bodies of water. This could really weaken their resolve and buy us more time."

"Why wouldn't they just break open the damn and drain the water out again?" Seneca asked.

"They undoubtedly will do that," Marcus told him. "Which is why we are going to dam the creek in multiple places simultaneously. We're also going to dig a traditional earthen wall in reverse at the main gate—anything we can do to make it harder to drain this lake we're building. The idea here, Acting Magus, is to buy ourselves time. So we are creating multiple obstacles for the savages that they will have to overcome before they get to us. The lake itself is a double trap."

"Double?" Seneca asked.

"The first is the water," Calidus explained, "but the second, and probably greater obstacle, is the mud that we'll make of this plain if the water stands upon the ground long enough. I very much doubt that these savages have any experience with fighting in the mud. It weighs down both man and horse, tires them out faster, and makes them more vulnerable."

"We could also put traps beneath the surface of the water," Severus noted. "They would probably only be useful if the savages try to ride or run through the flooded castrum, but it would certainly encourage them to slow down."

"Good," Marcus agreed. "Keep thinking. Now how do we make this happen?"

"Tribune?" Seneca asked but then kept talking without waiting for permission. "When I was a lad, my family had a dam built on one of our creeks to create a small lake. I have seen this done. We will need big stones, but we will almost certainly find them as we dig the trench for the new walls. I could help you with this!"

Seneca met his officers' eyes and both men gave him a slight nod.

"Very well, Acting Magus, you are in charge of identifying the stones we need and getting them transported to the outlet of the creek at the outer wall. Use the legion wagon drivers to pull the big rocks. Calidus, find me backup sites to damn that creek after the outer wall is blocked. And figure out the best way to close down the front gate after we're through using it. I want this to slow the savages down for as long as possible. Understood?"

All three men saluted in acknowledgement of their orders.

"Good, then let's get to it." He started to turn away, but hesitated. "And officers, we can't have a repeat of what happened to me in the salt pan. Everyone gets at least four hours of sleep tonight!"

****

The first survivors of the Battle of the Thundercloud rode into Fort Quartus on dying horses a few hours before dawn. They were nine Gota cavalrymen—every single one of them injured and one certain to die. Marcus met them at the outer gates as he would meet every single returning legionnaire and warrior. He saluted as the men rode up to him but it was Evorik, roused from sleep at the news the Gota were approaching, who stepped forward and hailed the men. "Who do you ride under?"

"We serve Lord Thursimod who holds from Lord Ildefons, brother of the Thegn of Topacio."

Evorik growled low in his throat. "And how is my charming half-brother?"

"He is dead, Lord Evorik, killed in the first attack by the savages."

Evorik let loose the most creative string of curses Marcus had ever had the good fortune to hear. When he finished he strode forward to the Gota spokesman and said, "Did he die well?"

The man swallowed hard. "He did not die poorly, my Lord. A thousand of the savages had concealed themselves by lying flat on the prairie, hidden by the tall grass as we got an early start on the day's march. When they sprang up and let loose with their first dozen flights of arrows, the entire army was taken by surprise. Lord Ildefons was in the vanguard as was fitting, and by terrible misfortune, one of the arrows in that first flight took him in the eye."

Evorik cursed again. "May Fulgus rot these savages' balls! Did he have his sword drawn?"

The man flinched from the question, telling everyone what Evorik feared.

"Damn them all to the icy hells!"

"My Lord," a man called from the rear of the rank, "I did not see it myself, but I heard from one who did that Lord Ildefons was drawing his sword as he fell. He was fighting, my Lord. He did die in battle!"

"But if it was not actually drawn, the Halls of Fulgus will be closed to him!" Evorik yelled. "Rot these honorless savages! We will wipe them from the Sea of Grass!"

Marcus stepped forward. "Lord Evorik, I'm sorry your beloved brother—"

"Beloved?" Evorik turned on him. "I hated the conniving scum! But worthless as he was, he was ten times the man the best of these savages might be."

Thursimod's men didn't quite know whether to cheer or to protest the Gota lord's mixed complement.

Marcus cut through Evorik's talk. "I need to know everything that happened. I need to know how bad the situation is. Will you let these men tell me?"

Evorik glowered but did not object.

Marcus turned back to the leader. "Your name, Sir?"

"I am called Atta, Tribune."

"What happened? Not all the details, just the final summation."

"They surprised us, Tribune, and many fell in the first attack. We had started before dawn, to make haste to relieve Fort Tertium when at least a thousand savages sprang out of the grass with their bows and caught us totally unprepared. What was worse, they came with the storm behind them. Lightning fell within our ranks, killing men and horses, and while the army reeled in confusion many thousands more came mounted on their ponies. Hundreds fell in the first onslaught but Great Tribune Rogatus has steel in his soul and he rallied his legionnaires into a strong square, pulling the Topacio cavalry into the center of the square to regroup."

"You hid behind the infantry?" Evorik snapped as if he could not believe what he had heard.

Marcus stepped in to head off an argument. "It's a good strategy. We've used it quite effectively in the south. The cavalry readies itself while our foes waste their missile weapons on the shields of the legion. Then the riders sally forth to great glory and break the ranks of the enemies."

Atta nodded vigorously at Marcus' words as if to silently affirm that this was indeed the plan.

"Remember, Lord Evorik, that your half-brother was dead. There must have been great confusion among his officers as they struggled to rally their men."

He returned his attention to Atta. "But I'm guessing that by the time Great Tribune Rogatus was able to form square his own losses were too great and the savages were able to riddle the cavalry with arrows."

"There was a terrible loss of horses," Atta agreed, "and the arrows of the savages seemed endless. So Great Tribune Rogatus changed his strategy. He ordered my Lord Thursimod and the other surviving great men to lead a break out and warn both Fort Quartus and the Jeweled Hills that the savages were riding in unprecedented strength."

"And you did break out," Marcus stated the obvious.

"A few score, perhaps, and not all together," Atta agreed. "But not before we saw Great Tribune Rogatus struck by lightning and the legion's square begin to collapse."

Marcus frowned at the thought of all of those men dead.

"Many will have survived," Evorik reminded him. "They always do. The question is: How many will be able to reach you before the savages come in force."

Marcus nodded thoughtfully. "You are correct. This changes nothing except that it gives me a small cavalry force if you're willing to leave Warrior Atta with me when you leave to warn Topacio."

Evorik did not look pleased to be reminded he would be leaving soon. "What say you, Atta? Do you still have stomach for a fight? The Tribune is a good man, but he could use some experienced horsemen to bolster his infantry."

"Of course, Lord Evorik," Atta swore. "My men and I long for the day we water these plains with the blood of the savages."

"Then I think I'll get my men up now and we'll get started," Evorik announced.

Marcus did not think that was a good idea, but he did not want to directly counter the Gota lord's authority. "I'm sure your men will be up to it, Lord Evorik, but what about the horses? The trek across the salt pan was especially hard on them not to mention an additional day and a half with almost no water. Might it not be wiser to let them rest the full night before you make your last push for reinforcements?"

"Curse you, Tribune, for being right," Evorik snarled before stalking off into the darkness.

Marcus returned his attention to the Gota survivor. "Warrior Atta, I'm going to need your men to act as scouts tomorrow, looking for survivors and the enemy. Take your men to the center of camp. You'll find food and water there. Then get some rest. I'll need you back in the saddle a few hours after dawn."

Atta and his warriors nodded and went off to eat and get some sleep.

Even though there were still a million things to do, Marcus followed them. It was only going to get harder from here on out.

****

Still bleary eyed from fatigue, Marcus met Evorik and his men at dawn. The lord's two wives, Hilduara and Riciberga, had risen and come down to the gate to see their husband off, but other than that it was only Marcus and the two guards watching for enemy activity from the gate. He waited patiently while the lord made a quiet farewell to his women, then shook the Gota's hand. "We've come a long way together, Lord Evorik," Marcus told him. "I look forward to finishing our journey on your return."

"Just keep my women safe," Evorik grumbled. The idea of leaving now with the great battle coming clearly went against the grain, but he was a man used to wielding authority and being forced to view the whole battle and not just his small part in it. He understood why he, and only he, could bring the call for reinforcements. Aside from his personal influence, he was the half-brother of the Thegn of Topacio. No one else in the caravan had the hope of raising a substantial relief force as quickly as he.

Evorik mounted his horse. "A day and a half to the border and fresh mounts with another day to the city giving warning all the way. Then," he shrugged in frustration, "realistically, it will be no sooner than three days to raise a force and start back, but more likely we are talking five or even seven."

Seven would actually be fast for many kingdoms. Even with a professional standing army such as the legions it was very difficult to move the men from a peacetime to a wartime footing in a hurry. With the constant infighting of the Jeweled Hills and the need for the ruling Gota to respond quickly to any uprising of the Gente, it was possible that they would mobilize more quickly than most, but…

"Then two to three days to return. We'll push hard, but the horses have to be in shape to fight when we get here," Evorik finished.

"So eight to twelve days all told," Marcus summed up for him. It sounded long. Everything depended on when the savages came against them, or even if they came. It was possible that Tertium had not fallen yet and they would return to bring their force against that presumably sturdy fortress. But in his heart, Marcus didn't believe the fort still stood. The savages were coming here when they lucked out and caught the legion in the open. No, the battle was coming. It only remained to be seen how much of a hurry this Teetonka was in after what looked to be a crushing victory.

He would give his men time to loot the dead and the legion baggage train. He'd also want to rest his horses after the battle and give his wounded time to be treated. But after that, he would come in his thousands thinking to have a quick victory at Fort Quartus as he had evidently had against the better garrisoned fortresses of Segundus and Tertium. How would he react when he found things not to his expectations? Would he hold up and think the matter through or send his men against the fort in one mad rush to overwhelm them with their numbers? Both options held advantages and disadvantages for Marcus but both courses of action required the same response from him now.

In the hazy light of predawn he saluted Evorik and his men one more time as they rode out of Fort Quartus and headed north at a fast walk. His horses could not possibly be fully recovered from their journey across the salt pan and here they were depending on them to hold up under another arduous journey. Evorik's numbers were too hopeful, but again, right or wrong it had no impact on Marcus' duty.

He turned away as the rim of the sun broke the horizon to find Evorik's wives still standing next to him. "He's a strong and capable man," Marcus reminded them. "He will rally a relief force and return in record time."

Hilduara, the senior wife, nodded gravely. "Only a fool stands between Evorik and his goal."

Marcus hoped she was correct. The truth was that he really didn't know the Gota lord that well, although he continued to like what he learned of him.

"I was wondering, Lady Hilduara, if you and your sister wife would be willing to help in the defense. We are going to have many wounded if the savages come against us here and I was much impressed at your ability to help Señora Carmelita with her child birth. Would you be willing to organize a hospital for us here in Fort Quartus?"

Hilduara did not even look at Riciberga before agreeing. "You make good sense. We will get the Gente woman and assess our needs."

Decision made they turned to leave, but the guard on the gate interrupted them. "Tribune, I think you'd better see this."

Marcus stepped through the gate to find what the guard was looking at. Evorik and his men had made good time for such a short while, already more than a mile away, but in the distance a group of horsemen had clearly spotted them and were angling to cut the Gota off well before the hills.

"He's a strong man," Riciberga reminded everyone. "Woe be it to the savages that catch up to him."

"I make their numbers about even," Marcus said, "although their bows do give the savages an advantage."

"Evorik is a wily one," Hilduara said, "this will not stop him."

Marcus wished that he could be as certain.

Day Fourteen
Time Is Not Our Friend

Marcus found Seneca with the drivers of the legion wagons, using their horses to haul a very large stone up out of the trench the legionnaires and the civilians from the caravan were digging around the center of the castrum. It was a huge boulder and the horses strained mightily to lift it while a couple of red band legionnaires from the fort used their shovels to ease the stone's path out of the hole.

It took about fifteen minutes before they accomplished it. Now it was just a matter of moving the boulder a few hundred feet to the place where the creek cut through the outer wall.

"Good!" he complemented them. "Keep the stone moving. I want that creek damned before noon, understand? Earlier if you can manage it. It's going to take forever to fill this fort and make my lake."

Working legionnaires and Gente merchants alike paused in their shoveling to stare at him, doubtless wondering what he was talking about.

"And you men," Marcus addressed them. "Keep digging. This new wall is critical to our survival."

Capitán Adán moved in and brow beat civilian and legionnaire alike until they got back to work. Marcus offered him a grave nod of his head before moving on to find Calidus. "Originally I saw my barricade just inside the entrance to the fortress as a sort of reverse wall with the ditch facing toward us, rather than away. Now I think that may be too ambitious given our time restraints. Can you build me a thick mound maybe three or four feet high and at least six feet thick? That way, survivors coming into the fort can walk or ride up the mound on one side and down the mound on the other, but it will still keep any water flooding the outer fort from escaping out the gates."

Calidus nodded. "That sounds fairly simple and it solves the problem of finishing the wall while the savages gather outside the gate shooting arrows down upon us."

"Good! Take twenty men from the inner wall and get to it. Time is not our friend. If they don't take a day or two to recover after yesterday's battle, the savages could swoop down on us this morning or this afternoon."

"The inner wall is not going to be finished by this evening," Calidus told him.

"No, it's not," Marcus agreed. "But I think it will be finished sometime tomorrow. That will free more men up for other projects while the others deepen the ditch and strengthen the wall. Now get to it and don't let anyone slack off. Our lives are going to depend on the work we do in the next day or two."

Calidus saluted and strode off to do as he was told.

****

Marcus greeted another group of Gota horsemen—fifteen this time which was frankly much better than he had expected.

"Lots of men got away," their leader explained. "When the square collapsed there was chaos all around. The savages simply couldn't kill everyone fast enough. There are more men out there. We saw many on our way here."

"Could you find them again?" Marcus asked.

The Gota frowned.

"I know you and your horses are tired, but I *need* those men to hold this fortress until Lord Evorik returns with reinforcement from Topacio. Can you find them again?"

Lord Evorik's name seemed to strengthen the man's resolve. "Of course I can, Tribune. We will start out immediately."

"First I want you to go the inner fort, get a meal and some water, and change horses. Warrior Atta brought in a dozen or so riderless mounts when he went out on patrol this morning. He's back out there now, but there are fresher horses to be had than the ones you're riding."

The warrior nodded at the sense in Marcus' words. "We'll eat and drink in the saddle," he told him.

Marcus did not reject that idea. He needed those soldiers. "Take extra water skins as well. A drink will help speed those men back here."

Again the warrior showed his agreement with a quick nod of his head. He started to lead his men deeper into the fort, but Marcus stopped him. "I'm glad to have the strong warriors of the Gota to fight beside us. We suffered a defeat out there yesterday, but we are far from beaten."

Several of the men grinned at that, then kicked their heels into their horses' sides and rode off to get their food.

Marcus turned back to examine the plains to the east. After watching the group of horsemen heading north to cut off or possibly rendezvous with Evorik, he'd seen no more sign of the savages. Could those earlier horsemen be Gota also trying to reach home to rally reinforcements? From this distance there was really no way to tell. But every hour without the savages appearing made the fort a little stronger. Seneca and Severus had succeeded in blocking the little creek and the flooding of the fort—if it could truly be called that—had begun. Now Seneca was strengthening the dam, making it harder to take apart. His plan appeared to be working if they just had enough time.

****

In mid-afternoon, Marcus saw the first group of legionnaires arrive who did not get an assist from Gota horsemen. They were marching in formation. They'd lost their shields—an almost universally accepted symbol of cowardice—but their sheer sense of dignity defied this explanation. It was the spirit that Marcus so desperately needed in his defenses—a self-awareness that recognized that they had been beaten without admitting they had been broken or defeated.

"Legion halt!" the Red Vigil leading the twenty-seven precious legionnaires snapped the order and the entire line stopped immediately in front of Marcus and saluted.

Marcus returned the greeting.

"Red Vigil Honorius Cletus and legionnaires reporting for duty, Tribune!" the leader announced.

Marcus wondered what the man thought of the preparations he could see in front of him—a mound rising in front of the gates, a wall rising around the inner fort, a strange Tribune greeting him. If it troubled the man in any way he gave no hint of it in his expression.

"Welcome back to Fort Quartus, Red Vigil. You and your men are sorely needed. In a moment I'll send you to the inner fort to get a meal and four hours of sleep. I can't spare you anymore. We're expecting the savages to follow you home and we want to be ready to properly greet them."

One of the men in back, a black bander by his age, grinned at Marcus' tiny witticism and it did the Tribune's heart a world of good.

"What's your name, legionnaire?" he asked pointing at the man.

Surprised, the man barked it out without thinking. "Lysander, Tribune. I'm black band."

"You're also an Acting Black Vigil, Lysander," Marcus told him. "I need men with heart and men with experience and you look to have both. Now the rest of you men, go get some food while the two vigils here tell me how you escaped the savage horde."

Lysander's grin returned fierce and proud and he stepped up next to the Red Vigil while the men filed into the fort.

"Well?" Marcus prompted them. "Report!"

Red Vigil Honorius spoke first. "There was utter chaos when the square collapsed, Tribune, and the savages just couldn't kill all of us. I led what I could of my band out of the storm and we hid in a little gully until nightfall. I would have liked to have done more for the others, but there was no hope. There were thousands more of the savages than there were of us and there was just no way to hold the phalanx together after the square broke."

Marcus glanced at Lysander. "It was pretty much the same for us, Tribune. My vigils were dead but three of my mates and I got clear and we hid until nightfall when we commenced the run/walk to return and warn the fort. We caught sight of the Red Vigil here shortly after dawn and linked up with him as did several other small groups."

"How many more do you think escaped?" Marcus asked.

Both men paused to think for a moment. "Not hundreds," Lysander finally said. "But I wouldn't be surprised if there were dozens or more."

"I considered hiding again when the sun rose," the Red Vigil admitted. "If I'd done that, especially if we hadn't run/walked, I think I would have reached here sometime tomorrow."

That made a lot of sense to Marcus and the fact that these men had come here instead of trying for the comparatively greater safety of the Jeweled Hills told him these men were not cowards. They would still fight. But he needed more information.

"How about Fort Tertium? Do you have any idea if it's already fallen?"

The two men exchanged glances. "I don't know, but, it seems likely doesn't it," Lysander said. "Teetonka must have been coming here when he caught sight of us marching. He had too many men to have come here and still be laying siege to Tertium."

"And how many do you think he's coming with?" Marcus asked.

"At least five thousand," Honorius answered while Lysander said, "Five thousand."

It was unusual for two different people to make identical estimates so Marcus pressed them on it. "How did you come to that number? If they surprised you, there would have been little chance to count heads."

"We talked about it," the Red Vigil said. "I can't remember how we agreed to that count, but it's a hell of a lot of savages."

Marcus appreciated the clarification. "And when do you think they'll reach here?"

"I can't say," the Red Vigil admitted. "We did see a few small groups of scouts today but not the main army."

"They spent much of yesterday torturing people," Lysander added. "You could hear their screams deep into the night. If they've enough prisoners, we might gain a day or two to prepare while they have their fun."

"Hmmm," Marcus mused. "I hate to see any of our men suffer, but every hour they buy us will make us that much stronger." He gestured for them to enter the fort. "Come with me and I'll show you what we're doing. If you have any ideas as to how to make it better, sing out."

Together the three men climbed the still far too shallow mound before the gate. Calidus' men were hard at work growing the pile of earth and the teams dragging rocks in the wagons were bringing up another load.

Both of Marcus' new vigils looked confused by what they saw.

"You remember the creek that runs through the castrum over there?" he asked them.

Both men agreed that they did. "We've blocked it up so that it's overflowing. The water hasn't reached this far yet, but it will overnight. If we get enough time, it will flood the entire castrum short of that new wall we're building around the inner fort."

Lysander's eyes bulged with sudden appreciation. "Bet the savages have never seen anything like that before."

"That's probably too much to hope for," Marcus cautioned, "but it seems likely they will not have much experience assaulting islands."

"So they drain your little pond," Honorius said, "and that buys us what—a few hours?"

"I'm hoping for more than that," Marcus said. "I'm hoping they try and assault through the standing water—I doubt it will be that deep. I'm hoping they bring their ponies through that gate, over that mound—"

"And into the ditches to either side," Lysander cut in. His wolfish smile had returned to his face.

"And we're starting to add shallow ditches throughout the fort," Marcus explained, so that first charge is likely to cause a lot of chaos—"

"And the legion is good at taking advantage of chaos in our enemies' ranks," the Red Vigil started to understand the plan. "Oh, and the mud," he added with a grin every bit as nasty as the Acting Black Vigil's. "It's a small thing, but small things can make a big difference, especially when they're bound to be unfamiliar with them."

"By itself this is too small to win the day, but we have a large store of pilum, Marcus told them, "and we've been adding men all day. Our odds are improving rapidly."

"Tribune," Lysander offered, "there's a man that made it out with me whose father was a blacksmith. It's been years since he, himself, did any of the work, but there is a smithy in the fort and I wonder if he couldn't fashion us some caltrops. With the light moccasins the savages wear and a bit of water and mud to hide them, they might do a lot of damage if we placed them right before the ditch surrounding the inner wall or scattered them on the backside of that mound before the gate to make the savages veer into the pits."

Now it was Marcus' turn to flash a predator's grin. "Making that happen just became your first responsibility, Black Vigil. A surprise like that—it's what we need to win this thing. You see, they surprised your Great Tribune when they caught the legion in the field, and they may well have surprised Fort Segundus too. But—"

"They took Fort Segundus?" the Red Vigil interrupted him.

"Yes, and we think they took Tertium, don't we?"

Both men nodded.

"Those are big losses for the legions, but we're going to turn those victories into a disadvantage for the savages. They think they know what's coming, but they're wrong! I want them to come running in, charging over the walls—preferably at night and find themselves at least ankle deep in water, splashing their way toward our inner wall. Let them throw the gates open and bring in their horses. I want to hear the screams of man and beast as they step on our caltrops and fall into our pits, and slip in the mud. And then when they finally reach our inner defenses we're going to hack them into pieces—butcher the poor uncivilized bastards and keep killing them until they break and go running back outside the fort wondering what in the Gota's icy hell has just happened to them."

He stared each man hard in the eye. "And when they come back, we'll give them more of the same. And if they're too afraid of another straight up response, we'll let them drain our little lake and laugh at their cowardice. And when they finally come again, we'll kill them again, as many times as it takes, because you see, we have one more surprise in our bag. Lord Evorik, brother of the Thegn of Topacio, has gone to seek a relief force. He's left his two wives here under our protection so he could travel faster. All we have to do is hold on until the Gota come. So go up to the inner fort, get something to eat, and get a little rest. Then get to work helping us make these walls stronger so we can teach the savages what it really means to fight the legion!"

****

The creek had over-spilled its banks and was spreading onto the parched ground to either side with more gusto than Marcus had truly expected. He didn't know a lot about water. In his home in Aquila, creeks came out of the hills to meander ever downward until they ran into a river. Here the nearest hills were sixty miles distant and the water didn't flow from them but just seemed to bubble up from the ground. But it obviously came from a larger source because the engineers who had built the fort had not been satisfied with the spring. They had built the headquarters complex on a slight rise above the source of the creek and sunk a well through that hill to tap the body of water at its underground source which meant that the defenders would have a fresh source of water so long as the new wall held.

He watched the water spread for another minute, then walked on to check on the progress of his inner wall. He had gained eighty-five men today—a combination of Gota horsemen and legionnaires—and hoped to get more tonight and tomorrow. Every single one strengthened his defenses—especially the legionnaires trained to fight hand-to-hand on the ground. Already most of them were hard at work completing the new ditch which, with a little luck, would be filled with water before the savages arrived.

That ditch and the wall behind it were about three-quarters finished now and the men were exhausted. He'd keep pushing them until the line of defense was completed, then rest them in greater numbers to boost their fighting fitness. He'd keep working those not sleeping in part to keep them from thinking too much about what was coming, and in part because there was much that could still be done to strengthen this fortress. It was far too early to have genuine hope, but they'd come a long way. This would be no easy victory for the savages.

The horse team was dragging yet another boulder out of the ground. Where did a land so basically flat get so many rocks from? They'd drop this one in the creek bed, strengthening the dam. Slightly smaller and thus easier to transport boulders went into the mound walling off the fort's gate. There was so much to do yet, if only the savages gave them another day.

Marcus looked at the moon overhead, no longer full but still giving quite a bit of light. "Just one more day, Sol Invictus," he prayed. "Please give us one more day."

Day Fifteen
It Might Get Bloody

It was dawn before Calidus woke Marcus. That was three hours more sleep then he had ordered his adjutant to give him but frustrated as he was at the disobedience, it was hard to be angry about it. Calidus knew as well as Marcus did that it would be damn hard for the Tribune to get any rest at all once the attack began so this could be his last hours of sleep for days or even the rest of his life if things went badly.

"Fifty more men came in during the night," the adjutant told him.

"That is good news!" Marcus agreed. "Any sign of the savages?"

"Not yet," Calidus shook his head. "I've been talking with some of the red banders who've been out here the longest and they gave me a critical piece of information that I can't understand why no one told us before this. The reds say that the savages don't like to fight at night. It doesn't mean they won't, but it's not their preference."

"No one really likes to fight at night," Marcus told him. "It's too hard to control the action so it breeds more chaos."

"No, that's not what I mean. The savages have a superstition which they take quite seriously. They believe that each of us is inhabited by a ghost and that when the mortal body is killed the ghost walks towards the sun and paradise. If the body is killed at night, the ghost becomes lost because it can't see the sun and so must unhappily wander the earth forever."

Marcus arched an eyebrow at the strange tale. "They can't just wait for morning to start their journey?"

Calidus grinned. "It's not my superstition."

"But if it comes to that, I need to remember that a night attack might be more effective than one in daylight," Marcus summed up. "Good work! Keep the information coming."

He got up to find some breakfast. "It also means my hope that they will go floundering around at night in my manmade lake is not going to happen."

"It could happen," Calidus insisted. "This Teetonka is changing the old rules. He's got the tribes working together. He may be able to convince them that his magic is powerful enough to show the ghosts the road to paradise without the sun."

"But it's still less likely than I had hoped," Marcus grumbled. "How is my lake coming?"

"Faster than we expected. In fact, it's already interfering with finishing the inner wall."

"That quickly?" Marcus asked. The news delighted him. His men could dig in the mud. The *lake* was never going to be deep enough to threaten them, just make it more difficult to attack the inner fort.

"The wall is coming faster too. The new legionnaires we picked up yesterday are really increasing the pace. These are not lazy good-for-nothings like we found everywhere in the Fire Islands and they've seen what the savages can do to an army. They are digging with gusto and their energy has inspired the other legionnaires and the civilians. I think we'll have the wall basically completed by noon and be able to start broadening and deepening the ditch while adding a few feet of height to the wall itself."

"Excellent! And my Gota?"

"They refuse to dig," Calidus told him.

"That's no surprise. Cavalry always think they're too important to do any real labor."

"Severus has them heading out on another patrol—no more than ten miles out, but we need to sweep up any straggling survivors while we still can."

"Just as I would have ordered," Marcus said. In point of fact, those were the instructions he'd given Severus and Calidus yesterday. If they were very lucky and the savages didn't come sweeping in for another day, they could potentially add a lot more survivors to their small fighting force. He had hopes—although he had no idea if they were realistic ones—of picking up another hundred men. That would give him nearly four hundred legionnaires, a couple of score of dismounted Gota horsemen, and more than a hundred civilians to hold the inner fort. While far from ideal, that was enough experienced men to mount a serious defense, even against Teetonka's reported five thousand savages. It wasn't going to be easy, and frankly, if the savages pushed hard enough and long enough they would win, but Marcus was increasingly confident that wouldn't happen. His tricks in the outer fort were setting the savages up for initial failure. That would both weaken their morale and strengthen that of his men. After that, well it was a waiting game punctuated by battles of attrition and his defenses gave him advantages in that sort of fighting that he doubted the savages had much experience with.

They could do this!

All they had to do was hold them off for another seven to eleven days and as the enemy wasn't even in sight yet, that seemed eminently possible.

He found himself whistling a battle song as he went to get his breakfast.

****

Enemy scouts began to appear within sight of Fort Quartus' walls at noon. A dozen men on horseback composed the first group and they hesitated about a mile out for a good hour observing the walls of the fort. Marcus doubted that they could actually see anything happening within the walls but he pulled twenty men off the construction project and got them into their armor just in case he needed a reaction force. What he really needed was his Gota but they were out patrolling somewhere in the surrounding territory and he was forced to get by without them.

Without warning, the savages advanced, picking up speed after half a mile to a fast trot before breaking into an all out charge one hundred yards out. They came straight at Marcus where he stood alone atop the wall in his armor and with his shield. Their bows came up and they began to fire, possibly trying to force him off the wall, or possibly just seeing if they could kill one of the men from Aquila.

"Now, Severus," Marcus ordered in a quiet, almost nonchalant voice as he raised his shield to defend himself.

"Pilum ready," Severus ordered. "Advance!"

Twenty red and black band legionnaires formed in a single rank climbed the steep inner embankment of the earthen wall until they reached the top—startling the savages who were now only twenty yards away.

"Target and throw!" Severus commanded.

Almost as a single body, twenty pilum launched from the line of men taking down three savages and one horse—a damn fine showing.

The raiders immediately left off attacking Marcus to shoot their arrows at the new threat.

"Second pilum, throw!" Severus ordered.

This time, Marcus put his own pilum into the flight. He was quite probably the best pilum thrower in the legion. He had taken the gold in each of his four years at the lycee and had lost none of his skill since then. His four foot weapon flew from his hand and took a savage in the side as his men took down another two men and three horses.

The savages turned and fled as if they feared that his men were carrying even more of the weapons.

Marcus watched them retreat impassively before sending out a group of men to claim his prisoners. Perhaps they could learn something about Teetonka's numbers and plans before they killed the survivors.

****

"Remember that the savages respect courage and one of the ways they test a man's bravery is to torture him to see if they can make him scream," Calidus told Marcus.

"Meaning?"

"I think the savages are genuinely insulted when we offer to make it stop hurting if they tell us what we want to know."

It was an hour before the evening meal and Marcus had gathered his officers for a quick meeting to make certain they were all up to date on the state of the defenses. Some of that was simply a matter of looking around them. The creek had overflowed even better than Marcus had hoped for. The water was already three or four inches deep and would probably double over nightfall. If they could steal another day before the savages attacked, they might have a full foot of water in what the men had taken to calling Lake Defiance. They used the same term—*Defiance*—for the fort because the Gente thought naming castra by number—Prime, Segundus, etc., lacked spirit.

The only problem with the success of the dam was that it made setting up his layered defenses a bit more difficult. It was, as Lord Evorik would say, a pain in the *ass* to dig in ground covered even by a few inches of water. This slowed down the strengthening of the inner wall and complicated the task of laying the scattered lines of shallow trenches Marcus was putting everywhere in the hopes of tripping up the savages and their horses if they came splashing through the water to attack the inner wall. In the hopes of keeping his own men from falling victim to these traps he had marked them with the mounted heads of the savages they'd killed earlier in the day.

Marcus hoped this would be sufficient to warn off his own legionnaires from these pitfalls without alerting the savages to their danger. Of course, it might all be for naught. As of now, all of the pits were perfectly visible through the clear water of the *lake*, but hope springs eternal and at the very least he was keeping the men too busy to think much about their plight.

"So we're not getting any information?" Marcus asked. "I don't want to be holding any prisoners when the attack begins. There is too much chance that they might get free and cause mischief in our rear, so make certain they die before the action begins."

Calidus nodded his understanding and Marcus turned to his least experienced officer. "Lesser Tribune? What is the state of our supplies?"

Cyrus, the officer left behind by the Great Tribune when he set off to relieve Fort Tertium, was the least happy with their circumstances in defending Fort Defiance. When the full scale of the catastrophe to the Great Tribune's relief force had become apparent, he had privately argued to Marcus that Fort Quartus—Defiance now—should be abandoned and they should make a run for the Jeweled Hills. Marcus had squelched his own desire to dismiss the notion out of hand and taken time he truly didn't have to explain to the frightened man that doing so would force them to abandon any survivors of the slaughtered legion and probably compel them to leave behind most of their merchants who would not lightly abandon their wagons and goods. Furthermore, it would complicate reasserting civilized control of the plains as it would cede control of an important water source and the staging area that was Fort Defiance to the savages. These arguments had not terminated Cyrus' objections and Marcus had reluctantly moved him away from the men to work on the supplies to keep his obvious fear from infecting the other legionnaires.

"The supplies in the wagon train help our situation considerably," Cyrus informed them, "The caravan has brought ample numbers of pilum plus sixty replacement shields to bolster our defense. That's not enough to give shields to all of the survivors of the Battle of the Thundercloud, but it helps significantly."

"What about breastplates and swords for the civilians?" Marcus asked.

"Those are equipment for legionnaires," Cyrus reminded the Tribune in what could only be described as a haughty tone of voice.

"In case you haven't noticed," Marcus observed, "all of those civilians will be acting as legion auxiliaries the moment the savages arrive in force. I want them armored and armed to the best of our ability."

Cyrus' lip puffed out as he pouted for a moment, but he did not protest again.

"Severus?" Marcus asked. "Just how many men do we have now?"

"Three hundred eighty-two legionnaires, forty-seven Gota horsemen, seventeen civilians who were already here at Fort Defiance including four women of easy virtue, ninety-six civilian males from the caravan, three women from the caravan and one infant less than a week old."

"That's actually better than I expected," Marcus admitted.

"But not as good as it may appear at first. We lost most of the Dona merchants to the return trip to the south and the Gente do not take orders well."

Señor Capitán Adán bristled with indignation. "Those men will fight with courage and honor!"

"I don't doubt that," Severus said, "but what they will not do is fight as legionnaires. They will fight as individuals who happen to be standing around in a line—not as an army."

Severus' explanation had done nothing to calm the temper of Capitán Adán, so Marcus offered him some mollification to keep the meeting from boiling into an argument about the relative quality of Gente warriors. "It takes a long time to train men to fight as legionnaires, Capitán. Far more time than we have in this crisis—especially when we have had to put all of our time into erecting our fortifications. Have no doubt, everyone here understands that we are stronger with your valiant countrymen beside us than we would be alone."

Without wasting any more time on the older man's feelings, Marcus returned his attention to Severus. "I think under the circumstances the lack of discipline of the Gente warriors will be ameliorated by the need to fight behind the wall. The Gente will not be called upon to maneuver their lines in battle—just to stand fast and kill any savage who dares to climb the wall in front of them."

Severus nodded understanding full well that if any such maneuvering was required it would fall on the legionnaires to carry it out.

"I think when Warrior Atta brings his men back into the fort tonight, we will finish sealing the front gate. We can let men on foot continue to join us if any more make it this far, but I can't risk losing seasoned warriors before the horde attacks my walls."

"I've been giving some thought to that," Red Vigil Honorius announced. "We have had more opportunity to work with the Gota here at Fort ur, Defiance," he grinned for a moment before continuing his report, "than they do further to the south, and I think there might be a role to play for the horsemen inside the fort. I recommend you walk Lake Defiance with Warrior Atta and seek his advice on how best to implement his men. When the savages come over the wall, there will be an opportunity for the cavalry to strike, although how we would get the horses back into the inner fort, I cannot say."

"Hmmm," Marcus considered the idea. "I'll speak to Warrior Atta. If we can do it without losing the Gota, I'm inclined to give it a try."

He turned to his Acting Black Vigil. "Lysander, how are the caltrops coming?"

"Very good, Tribune," the Black Vigil reached into a leather bag and pulled out two pieces of iron about three times the length of a man's little finger and three times as thin. The two pieces had been wrapped around each other so that three of the ends formed a tripod while the fourth stuck straight up in the air. All four ends had been sharpened to points.

"It took my friend a while to get the hang of the forge again, but he's got about thirty of these now with more coming together all the time."

"Thirty are not many," Marcus said. He had begun to picture thousands of these little horse cripplers.

"We will definitely have enough to make the backside of the entrance mound a death trap for the first savages through. Other than that, it depends on how much time they give us. My friend is working all by himself."

"I will speak to my people," Capitán Adán announced. "It is quite likely that someone among them has experience working a smithy. You should have come to me immediately with this idea," he reproached the Tribune.

Marcus had been tired of tiptoeing around the prickly older man before he'd ever promoted him to capitán, but he schooled his face once more and told him, "We would all be grateful if you can find someone to help the smith with his work."

Adán nodded with great dignity.

"Good, so I'll speak to Warrior Atta when he returns. Until then, everyone get back to work."

****

"It's a fucking good plan," Atta agreed in the coarse fashion of the Gota. They were standing in roughly five inches of water—the fort wasn't precisely flat so Lake Defiance wasn't precisely the same depth everywhere—and surveying the ground for a possible cavalry counter-strike. "All of your little traps are being set toward the front of the fort, hoping that the savages will come through on their horses. If we hold my men back at the rear, we should be able to swing around and cause a lot of confusion as the savages pour into the bailey."

"I'm not familiar with that term," Marcus told him.

"Double-walled fortifications are common in the Jeweled Hills," Atta told him. "The territory between the two walls is called a bailey. The territory between the inner wall and the fortified dwelling is called a courtyard."

Marcus nodded and then returned to the matter at hand. "So you ruin the day of a lot of savages leaving their dead bodies behind. What happens then? I can't afford to lose your men from the defense of the inner wall. I can't leave you out here to die. Would your men be willing to abandon their horses and climb the inner wall by hand?"

"No!" Atta gave the response Marcus had expected. "Our horses are like a third hand. We will not leave them behind."

"Then I don't see how we can set you loose in the bailey," Marcus told him. "I can't leave a path into the inner bailey against the numbers we expect to be fighting."

"There is a way," Atta told him. "You could take down the front gates and use them like a bridge across the ditch you've dug around the inner fort. They are made of strong wood. They'll hold my horses and they could be pulled into the inner fort after we've crossed them."

"Remove the gates?" Marcus asked. He knew he was showing his incredulity but it was such a bizarre notion.

"Yes," Atta affirmed. "In your plan of battle, you do not intend to truly defend them. They're only real purpose is to keep the forerunners of the savage army from scouting inside the outer wall too soon. You could build another ditch across the front of the fortress and accomplish the same thing."

"Yes, I could, couldn't I," Marcus considered the idea. At Fort Segundus, lighting had blown the gates to pieces making them worthless. This idea of Atta's preserved them for better use.

He made his decision. "I'll get a crew on the front gates immediately. I want this new ditch dug before dawn—otherwise it might get bloody before we want it to."

Day Sixteen
The Time Things Would Be Hardest

By dawn, a passable ditch and wall had been constructed across the front of the gate of Fort Defiance. Marcus had put the work crew under Red Vigil Honorius and a strong defensive force of ready legionnaires under Severus in case the savage scouts came forward to investigate the activity, but apparently their fear of night fighting held them off.

Marcus kept his crew working now as the sun rose to give the new defensive barrier all the height possible. He thought it likely they would see the enemy arrive in numbers today, although he still hoped they'd wait to make their first attack until tomorrow. On the other hand, Teetonka must have thought them a beaten force after the Battle of the Thundercloud so perhaps seeing no real threat he would be in no hurry to come and finish them off.

Marcus didn't believe this last possibility would long hold up. Once the scouts reported that they were vigorously strengthening the fort's defenses, Teetonka and his savages would come. He had almost succeeded in driving all the foreigners off the Sea of Grass. He would not want to leave an active fort to serve as a forward base for his enemies when he returned south to deal with Fort Prime.

He considered for a moment Tribune Lucanus at the southern-most fort. He'd liked the man and wondered if he yet realized the danger he faced. That might well depend on the fate of those members of the caravan who chose to return to the south. If they encountered another group of savages before they reached Prime, then Lucanus might well remain ignorant of what had happened north of him. But if Burkhard and his people had gotten through, Lucanus would have been able to send warnings to Dona pleading for significant reinforcement.

The war was far from over whatever happened at Fort Defiance. It was just a matter of how many more men would die before Aquila discovered the new threat to its trade routes.

Ahead of him on the plain he could see three different camps of savage warriors. None were particularly close. He wondered if he had been right to focus on the defense and not make a sortie at night against these relatively weak forces. It had been very tempting to go out and strike a first blow, but he had ultimately decided to hold that option in reserve. If the savages held a strong superstition against night fighting, it was quite possible that they didn't consider a night attack a realistic possibility. Making such a move now for relatively little gain would put them on their guard against future attacks, and it might even encourage them to strike sooner so they would not have to face their great fear.

"Severus!"

"Tribune?"

"You're in command here. Keep them working as long as you deem it reasonably safe. I have no problem with the savage scouts coming close enough to see what you're doing so long as they don't actually have a chance to hurt my work detail. I trust your judgment."

"Tribune!" Severus saluted him.

Marcus started to return the gesture when he caught sight of something he hadn't thought about in some time. A hawk flew high above them, flying over the wall and across Fort Defiance. Seneca had told him that it was through the birds of prey that savage shamans performed their farseeing. Were they watching them now? And if so, why was there none of the pins-and-needles feeling that had accompanied the dust storms and the enemy farseeing at Fort Segundus?

He finished the salute and decided to reinforce his instructions. "Remember, we're not planning to defend the outer wall against a serious attack. What these men are doing is more about breaking up the numbers of the attacking force and keeping them from casually observing our new lake and our inner defenses. I don't want to lose men defending this line—we just don't have enough people to do that.

Severus nodded and Marcus started back through the rising water toward the inner fort.

****

"Acting Magus Seneca, I have a question for you," Marcus announced. He'd found the student in the smithy handing a very thin iron rod to one of the three burly men standing over anvils. One of the men held a large pair of shears with which he clipped six inch pieces off the rod. The other two men were heating a dozen or so of the pieces in the forge, before taking out glowing red pieces of iron to bang the ends into rough points and bend the metal against an identical piece to produce a four-pointed caltrop.

The pile of finished objects had grown remarkably from the thirty or so reported last night. Now there were well over three hundred with a new caltrop tossed upon the finished pile even as Marcus watched.

"Tribune?" Seneca jumped in surprise making the older men in the smithy laugh at his expense.

Marcus was so surprised by the number of finished caltrops that he momentarily forgot the reason he had sought Seneca out. He picked up one of the finished weapons. It had not been sharpened to a serious point, but it was still highly likely to cripple an animal who stepped on it. "This is much more than the thirty you reported to me, Black Vigil. How is this possible?"

Lysander chuckled good-naturedly and tried to tousle Seneca's hair, much to the young man's annoyance. "It was your young magus here who did the trick," the older man said much to Marcus' shock.

"Seneca?" he asked and then wished he kept his surprised mouth shut.

"The thing holding us back was making these thin little rods," Lysander explained. "It takes forever but the boy here started poking around in the back of the smithy and found dozens, maybe hundreds of the things."

That made a lot of sense to Marcus. The legion would want the ability to quickly produce a device that crippled horses when it was light cavalry that was the primary enemy. The question was why hadn't Lesser Tribune Cyrus included these rods in his list of the fort's supplies?

"Good work all of you," Marcus complemented them. "Seneca, if I could have a moment? I need some magical advice."

Seneca eagerly followed Marcus out of the smithy.

"You did very well in there, Seneca," Marcus told him. "That discovery of yours may very well be the difference between success and failure in the coming attack. Well done!"

The young man beamed with pride.

"Now I need you to help me understand something," Marcus said. "Back at Fort Segundus you told me that a shaman can see through the eyes of a hawk up to a distance of ten or so miles. Remember?"

"Of course, Tribune," Seneca told him. "But I also said the distance would vary with the strength of the magus. A shaman, or a group of shamans, powerful enough to summon that thundercloud ought to be able to do a simple farseeing though a bird of prey for dozens if not hundreds of miles."

"So why aren't they?" Marcus muttered.

"Excuse me, Tribune?" Seneca asked.

"I said..." Marcus started before trailing off. He didn't want to tell anyone he thought he had *felt* the magic of the farseeing just as he had *felt* the magic in the dust storm. Something had happened to him when that gunk in Kekipi's amulet had sprayed all over him back in the Fire Islands and he wasn't comfortable with anyone knowing about it.

"If I understand your question correctly, Tribune, I think the answer is that Fort Defiance's wards are still intact."

"They're what?" Marcus asked.

"They haven't been destroyed, Tribune. Surely that's obvious, right? Fort Segundus was overrun by the savages. There the shaman sought out the wards and broke them. But they haven't been able to do that here yet. They can't see anything happening within the fort and for maybe a hundred or so yards beyond the outer wall."

"They can't?" Marcus felt like an idiot asking questions that should be obvious to everyone, but the news startled him and added to his sense of hope. Teetonka really was going to be surprised by Defiance's defenses.

"Yes, Sir," Seneca repeated. "We are invisible to them as long as the wards stand."

"That's incredibly good news," Marcus told him.

"I should have brought this to your attention earlier," Seneca apologized. "I didn't realize you weren't aware of this."

"Will the wards help us with stopping other forms of shaman magic?"

Seneca shook his head. "A fully trained and experience magus might be able to manipulate the wards to do something else, but I can't. But honestly, I don't think any of them are likely to be able to stop the lightning this shaman can call. That is really powerful magic. But I've been thinking about it quite a bit and I think there are two possibilities which will increase our chances of withstanding it."

"I'm all ears," Marcus told him.

"First," Seneca told him in a voice he'd probably learned from his teachers, "the enemy shaman will have to be able to see his target to strike it effectively and with the wards in place, he's either going to have to come close or trust to luck as the lightning crashes down out of the heavens."

"That is very good news," Marcus told him. "We need to talk about where these wards are and how we defend them."

"Oh, that's easy," Seneca told him. "One of the ward stones is beneath the praetorium in the center of the inner fort. The other four are at the four corners of the outer fort. I think we're going to lose control of those, but it won't matter if they are destroyed because your inner wall should be within the natural protection of a single ward stone. They will have to kill us to get to that one and," the young man tried to smile bravely, "I don't think it will matter to us then if it is broken or not."

"Very well thought out," Marcus said. "Now what was this second point you wanted to make about our advantages in fighting the lightning shaman?"

"I mentioned it before," Seneca told him. "Weather magic is very complicated. Normally you would have a host of magi working together to manipulate magic on that scale, but from what we've heard it sounds as if Teetonka is somehow doing this on his own. If that's the case, when the battle gets crazy, if we can distract him enough, I might be able to interfere with his control of the lightning storm."

Marcus remembered ignoring this suggestion earlier, but now he gave it his serious attention. "How would you do that, Seneca?"

"I don't know yet, Sir, but magic moves and flows in the air about us and in the earth and water. When the shaman begins to raise his storm, I will light my candles and try and observe what he is doing from a magical perspective. And if I see my chance, I will try and interfere with his working and see if we can't make it blow up on him." He shrugged with a hint of embarrassment. "I'm just a student, Tribune, but my teachers used to complain that I have a gift for making even the simplest of magics blow up in my face. I think that's a gift I'd like to turn on our enemies."

Marcus put his hand on Seneca's shoulder. "You have my permission to move forward with this plan *only* if you give me your word that you will be most cautious. I do not want Teetonka detecting you and bringing his lightning down upon you in retribution. We are in for a long siege and there is no need at all for you to hurry. Do you understand me?"

"I do, Sir," Seneca swore.

"Then why don't you go back into the smithy and see what else you can do to help those men?"

****

The savages began arriving in numbers a couple of hours before dark—and what numbers they were. Traveling in bands of one hundred or so, they appeared everywhere on the plains with the lead forces establishing their camps a few hundred yards in front of the gate and forward walls and the later ones moving on to encircle Fort Defiance.

Camp was not an accurate term by Aquilan standards. The legions fortified their castra every night when they were moving in enemy territory, but these savages basically threw themselves down wherever they stopped. They built campfires out of the dried bison dung that seemed to be everywhere—and that was even stranger than burning the coal rock—but other than that there was nothing to distinguish their campsite from any other spot on the plain.

By nightfall, there were more than a thousand savages strung out around them, but Marcus felt certain there would soon be many more. These men were far too casual in their movements. Their belief in the inevitability of their victory was too great for so few men to hold on their own.

This was also the time things would become hardest for his men. Waiting for an attack would fray their nerves and whittle away their self confidence. As the numbers grew outside the walls their own fears would squiggle and grow. The only things Marcus knew to do to counter this were launch a preemptive strike or keep the men too busy to think and worry. Since the strike would play to the savages' strengths rather than his own, he chose the latter and kept his men digging, broadening the submerged ditch and heightening the wall.

It was not making him popular, but if it helped keep his people safe he could live with that.

They could all live with it.

Day Seventeen
We're Not the Ones Who Are Going to Be Dying

"That's a lot of savages," Lesser Tribune Cyrus noted from his place at the top of the outer wall where Marcus and his officers stood together observing the army gathering against them. Half the legionnaires were now on guard duty—armor on and shields in hand—manning the outer walls as if they meant business even though each man knew that they were not intending to defend them against a serious assault. This was a waiting game and the longer they could convince the savages to wait to start their assault the less time they would have to hold until Lord Evorik returned with reinforcements from the Jeweled Hills.

"We call it a *shitload*," Warrior Atta informed the legion officer. "When the enemy is too great to count and you're shit deep in trouble, use *shitload*."

Every man present, even Acting Magus Seneca, smiled at the Gota warrior's words.

"It is looking to be rather more than the five thousand that I expected," Marcus admitted.

"And they're still coming in," Severus observed in his flat unimpressed voice.

"Can we...can we hold out against that many?" Capitán Adán asked with a definite tremor in his voice.

"Of course we can," Marcus assured him. Then he chuckled and the sound was not in any way forced. "You almost have to feel sorry for the poor bastards. This isn't a legion caught by surprise out in the field. It's the hardest men on the planet dug in behind solid defenses just waiting for the chance to get some of their own back against the primitives who've been torturing their friends and comrades. Mark my words, men," he lifted his voice so that the sound would carry to the closest legionnaires. "We're going to turn Lake Defiance red with the blood of savages. The survivors will remember what we do to them here for a thousand years."

He could see a red bander standing on the wall fifty feet away nod his head in agreement and whisper an affirmation to the man beside him. He was one of fifty-three stragglers who'd made it to the fort yesterday and he'd almost broken down in tears of relief when he'd seen the preparations they were making and learned that Lesser Tribune Cyrus was not in charge of their defenses.

As was so often the case in the legion, the problem was not the men, it was the leaders.

"Capitán," Calidus stepped in. "Perhaps you don't understand what kind of legionnaires you're fighting beside today. I'm sure you've heard by now that Tribune Marcus here single-handedly put down the resurrected Rule of Twenty in the Fire Islands, but did anyone tell you what that means. We were surprised in the field in what our leaders thought was a simple operation to mop up a few poorly organized rebels when we suddenly found ourselves confronting thousands of undead warriors rising up out of the ground to destroy us. Most of them were skeletons, but the bodies of our dead comrades rose up to try and kill us as well. Surprised and isolated from the rest of the legion, Tribune Marcus did not panic. Instead we fought our way through the undead horde and put the Rule of Twenty back in its grave. These savages are undoubtedly a dangerous foe, but they won't catch us by surprise and we're truly ready for them. You and your men should take heart. We're not the ones who are going to be dying by the *shitload*," he winked at Warrior Atta. "The savages are the ones who are about to find they're knee deep in the muck."

"It's time to wrap this up," Marcus observed. He firmly believed that if you spent too much time bolstering the men's nerve you ended up undercutting your efforts. "Red Vigil Honorius, you are in charge of the gate defenses." Not that there was truly a gate anymore but the spot which had once held the great doors had been purposely left weaker than the rest of the wall. If the savages wanted to spend the time, they could knock enough of it down to let them jump their ponies over the ditch in front of it, top the wall, jump down onto the slope of the mound and pour over it into the field of caltrops they were planting on the far side.

Which reminded him. "Calidus, I think it's well past time we finish planting the caltrops. Make certain the area behind the mound is well saturated, then follow the plan with what's left and make those bastards regret bringing any horses into Fort Defiance."

"As for the rest of you, let's get back to our tasks. They could officially come at any time now. Let's be as ready as possible when that happens."

Without waiting for their response he turned and waded through the deepening lake back to the inner fort.

****

The day ground on interminably long as tribe after tribe of savages joined their cousins in making camp around Fort Defiance. The damming of the creek clearly caused some discomfort beyond the walls as the savages were forced—at least for the time being—to get by on the water they carried in skins upon their horses. That water was not going to last very long and thoughts of the thousands of enemy horsemen growing weaker day by day encouraged Marcus to fantasize about holding the outer wall against them despite the differences in numbers. But such an effort needed a thousand men more than he had and so he quickly discarded the overly tempting notion.

As if to prove that he had made the right decision, a group of some one hundred savages suddenly charged the wall on horseback. Legionnaires scrambled to resist them, running from different directions on the wall to concentrate their numbers at the point of apparent attack. Marcus was too far away himself to direct their efforts, but the new black vigil, Lysander, rallied the men quite efficiently and directed a volley of pilum at the savages just as they dropped from their horses, hatchets in hand, and charged the wall, jumping the outer ditch and scrambling up the steep slope toward the legionnaires.

They ran hard against the shield and swords of Lysander's men and a dozen more died in the first seconds that the lines crashed. Then a bizarre thing happened. Many of the savages getting their first look over the wall froze in amazement and paid for their surprise with their lives. A moment later, sixty or so survivors of the assault jumped back down across the ditch and ran after their ponies—not frightened as Marcus' legionnaires incorrectly assumed, but astonished by their look at the waters of Lake Defiance.

They rode to the nearest tribe and spoke animatedly to them about what they had seen, and then they rode on, always pointing toward the wall of the fort and the water behind it. Within an hour, dozens of savages had decided that they needed to see for themselves the strange sight the first group had described to them. But instead of attacking the wall in great numbers, they stole forward singly from all directions, successfully finding gaps in the outer defenses that Marcus did not have the numbers to plug and climbing to the top of the wall to gape at the spectacle of standing water on the Sea of Grass. Then they jumped back down to go and tell their kinsmen what they had seen, starting the whole process over again.

All of this proved to Marcus that his initial concerns about the indefensibility of the outer wall had been correct. He didn't have the numbers to hold it and he quickly gave instructions that Lysander and Honorius were only to direct their men to resist significant groups of sightseers. If the savages wanted to waste the day looking at a man-made spectacle, Marcus was more than happy to accommodate them. The longer he could keep them looking and not fighting, the better for everyone.

****

"Looks like we've survived another day," Severus volunteered in a voice so quiet Marcus could barely hear it.

"Tomorrow things will get violent," Marcus predicted. The savages had come in far greater numbers than the five thousand warriors that the fleeing legionnaires had reported to him. With numbers at least two or three times higher, the chances of successfully resisting had plummeted as the day progressed.

"Probably," Severus agreed. "They can't wait much longer because of the water situation."

"Maybe I miscalculated there," Marcus suggested. In these circumstances, he wouldn't voice that doubt to anyone but Severus, but the Black Vigil had been his mentor since he first entered the legion and he trusted him completely with his confidences.

"No," Severus objected, "I don't think so. The savages are not going to sit out there for a week. Without the spectacle of the lake, they might even have come after you today. The lake gave them something to think about, although I doubt that they really understand what it means for them yet."

Marcus accepted the observation at face value. Severus would never lie to him just to protect his feelings. "If they're probably coming tomorrow, I'm thinking of pulling the men back tonight. If they really charge with all ten or fifteen thousand warriors out there, they'll overwhelm and cut off the men on the wall before they can get back to the inner fort and then we're all dead."

Severus considered a moment before agreeing. "You'll do it under cover of darkness?"

"Yes."

"The problem is," Severus pointed out, "that pulling back off the wall lets them come in and drain the lake without resistance. That would be the smart move on their part. Come in, drain the lake, and let the ground dry out again. What would that buy us—two or maybe three days?"

"I'll take the days," Marcus said. "Is that what you think they'll do?"

"I don't know," Severus admitted. "This is not a civilized army. It's a raiding culture. And raiding cultures move quickly. What *we* would do is dismantle the fort's defenses one by one, seeking to minimize our losses by destroying the enemy fortifications. Depending on the larger strategic situation, we might even be willing to starve the enemy out. But these savages won't necessarily think that way. They are always on the move. They may even be uncomfortable staying in one place for long. And there is always the chance that this group wants to finish here so it can move on Fort Prime. So I don't know—a lightning dash at the walls of the inner fort might seem the best move on their part."

"Lightning," Marcus repeated. "I've seen no sign of thunderclouds yet."

"Nor dust storms," Severus reminded him. "Because of our pilum, I would expect them to at least raise a dust storm before they charge against us. As for the lightning, I could argue it either way, but I think I would want to bring the lightning down on my enemies if only to demoralize them."

"I guess we'll find out tomorrow," Marcus told him. "Make sure you get some sleep tonight because I think tomorrow's going to be a long hard day."

Day Eighteen
Severed Skulls Were Not the Ideal Choice of Weapons

At dawn about eight hundred savages charged Fort Defiance from eight different directions, leaping off their ponies before the ditch and scrambling over the outer wall. They seemed angry, perhaps even insulted, when they encountered no resistance. These bands immediately began moving into the fort toward the inner wall, but not at the headlong speed they had approached the outer wall.

With no resistance encountered, several hundred more savages approached the main gates and began to level the patchwork wall Marcus had erected where the doors once stood. To the legionnaires and their allies great surprise, this workforce was made of women and children. This discovery had tremendous implications for the coming battle and immediately bolstered the defenders' morale. The savages didn't have fifteen thousand men arrayed against them. They were nomads who had brought their families to the siege—a fact that Marcus might well be able to turn against them. Teetonka, if he really was the war leader facing them, had been very foolish to reveal this bit of intelligence. But then, maybe he thought it so obvious that the families would follow his army that it hadn't occurred to him the legion would not already assume they were there. It was always strange fighting a people who were so very different from your own.

"Let's not give it all up without a fight," Marcus suggested. "Severus, give the order to Warrior Atta that his men are now free to operate in the bailey, but remind him that he is not to get close to the mound and all the caltrops we've deployed there."

Severus left to carry out his instructions and Marcus took a few minutes to walk the inner wall, check on his men and bolster their morale if he could.

"Do you see that?" he asked one of the green banders who had been with him since they left Dona. "The savages are mostly women and children. And here I thought for a few minutes they could make us work up a sweat."

The young man grinned nervously but said nothing.

Marcus clapped him on the shoulder. "You'll do fine. It's very hard to assault a prepared position. And it won't even be hard to bury them when the battle's over. You'll already have dropped their corpses into that ditch."

With a gesture he indicated the trench the men had worked so hard to excavate, now filled with water a few feet beneath their feet.

Marcus moved on when the smiles became a bit more genuine.

He found Alberto standing with other Gente looking nervously at the savages spreading out in the space between the two walls. He was one of the men who had received a legion breastplate but his sword was of northern design with a fancy decorated hilt. Still, it would probably kill well enough if Alberto knew what he was doing.

"And how is my little namesake?" Marcus asked him offering to shake the older man's hand.

Alberto licked his lips nervously. "He's got a good appetite. Carmelita says he never wants to stop eating."

"Glad to hear it," Marcus said. He knew almost nothing about children, but figured it could not be a good sign if the babe was never hungry. "You're going to earn a great story to tell him today." He gestured toward the other Gente. "All of you will. You went out to earn a living for your families and will come home mighty heroes."

Shoulders squared at his words. The Gente liked to think of themselves as worthy of great praise.

"Now let me show you something," Marcus said. He made no effort to quiet his voice because he assumed that it would be a rare savage who could speak the Gente language. "These savages are making a major tactical mistake right now. See how they are spreading themselves out. I assume they are doing this because they are used to fighting men with bows—men like themselves who do not use shields or spears. But watch what happens when your Gota neighbors are let loose upon them."

As if on cue, the wooden gates banged down, one plopped at an angle up onto the wall from within the inner fortress and the other from the top of the wall across the ditch. Within seconds, Warrior Atta raced his horse up and down the makeshift ramps with his forty-six men charging after him. In the bailey they plunged directly into the surprised savages spread out in front of them, expertly stabbing with their spears. If only there was some way to let them get the full weight of themselves and their mounts behind the blows, but a man who charged straight into his opponent was highly likely to find himself thrown backward off his horse. A man just could not grip the stomach of his horse strongly enough to keep him in his saddle with a straight on charge.

As more and more of his numbers reached the bailey, Atta wheeled his men and began clearing out the southern side of the castrum. Savages scrambled to get out of the way while others shot arrows from their tiny bows. In the chaos of those early moments, few arrows even came close to their racing targets and many of the primitive warriors slipped and fell as they attempted to maneuver in the eighteen inches of standing water.

Gota rode these men down without mercy, trampling them with the hooves of their steeds, and much to the surprise of even the Gente, the merchants-turned-soldiers cheered at the triumph of their overlords.

After about ten minutes of fighting, Atta turned his men again and went charging back in the other direction, abandoning any apparent attempt to take the gate where women and children fled from the battle and warriors hurried to hold them off with massed arrow fire. Instead Atta led his men back across the southern side of the fort to attack the savages gathered in the west. These were much better prepared for him, and he suffered his first casualties—six injured and two dead, but he broke the savages ranks and sent them fleeing back over the outer wall of Fort Defiance.

When he and his men returned to greater cheers across the makeshift ramp into the inner fortress, they left more than one hundred and fifty dead savages lying in the shallow water behind them.

****

"Why aren't they using the dust storms?" Seneca wanted to know. Except for a major covering force protecting the women and children tearing down the first wall at the former gate, the savages had pretty much departed from the rest of the bailey. "It's good magic," Seneca continued. "It would conceal their movements—keep us from seeing what they're doing and how much progress they're making."

"It would also make it a lot harder on the women and children dismantling that first wall and filling in the ditch," Marcus told him. "I think they'll bring the dust storm before they launch a real attack, but right now they probably figure it's frightening us to see our defenses disappearing."

"Isn't it frightening us?" Seneca asked.

"No," Marcus told him. "We want them to take down that wall, remember? While I don't mind if it takes them a lot of time to do it, I want them to come crashing in here on horseback. That's why you helped make all of those caltrops, right?"

"Right," Seneca agreed with a lot less certainty in his voice.

"Look," Marcus explained. "They are going to lose a lot of horses when they come charging through that gate. I hope that makes them really mad. I want them pouring in here to kill us in a blind rage. We have a few more traps out there to slow them down and really piss them off, but I want them thinking of nothing but killing us by the time they reach this wall."

As Marcus spoke, Seneca's eyes grew wider and wider. "But why? Why make them angrier than they are now?"

"Because angry men don't think," Marcus told him. "Angry men have no discipline. Angry men die on the swords of well-trained legionnaires."

"But there are thousands of them," Seneca protested.

"That's right, and I want to kill the first two or three thousand right then before they get smart and remember the advantages their bows give them, or decide to take their time and soften us up with bolts of lightning. I want them to die and die and die so that the survivors can't stand the thought of having to charge our defenses again."

"But, but won't a lot of us die too if they come at us like that?"

"Men die in war," Marcus told him with just a hint of compassion. "But if we can goad the savages into a rash charge on our defenses, a hell of a lot more of them will die than we will."

"And the dust storm would actually hide what is happening from them," Seneca said. "They'll just keep coming."

"The dust storm probably hurts them more than us in this siege," Marcus explained. "Yes, it hides their movements, but we'll know they're coming anyway unless they raise it and maintain it for days—which helps us because we want to buy time for Lord Evorik to return with a relief force. So it hides their movements, but it also hurts the accuracy of their arrows both because they can't see us and because of the winds that raise the dust. They don't suffer this problem when they come racing in on horseback and shoot at surprised caravans from ten feet away, but that's not what they're facing here. They should be standing back out of pilum range and firing tens of thousands of arrows into the inner fort while their brothers close with those hatchets of theirs. The dust storm really doesn't let them use their arrows to greatest advantage."

"And the lightning?" Seneca asked.

"The lightning worries me most because I haven't faced it before. But if you're right and Teetonka will have to come close enough to see what he's trying to hit, then I think it will be something we can survive. After all, he can't see behind our walls as long as the wards are in place. So he destroys a couple of buildings which we don't need—most of our supplies have already been distributed away from them. Then what—attack our walls? Lightning hits the earth all the time. I would think that that is a very slow way to open our defenses and if he chooses to try that, why can't we build a new inner wall as he does it?" That was actually something Marcus would have liked to have done if he'd only had a few more days.

"I see, so we really are in good shape," the young man mused.

"Seneca, we have five thousand or more warriors who want us dead surrounding this fort. I'm sorry, but there is no way to make that into a good thing. But if we keep our heads and remember our discipline, most of us can survive this attack." He was probably lying. Teetonka had the numbers to overwhelm the legionnaires if he had the nerve to keep attacking. And the lightning, Marcus really didn't know what his enemy could do with that. But it never helped morale to be totally honest about the odds of battle.

****

"They're in," Severus noted, pointing at a lone savage horseman who had just ascended the mound. He was a striking figure, even at this distance, practically naked in his loin cloth except for a fancy feathered headdress which flowed far down his back. In his right hand, thrust high over his head he held a short war spear, again with feathers trailing, and on his chest a pendant gleamed—the sight of which made Marcus' blood run cold.

"I'd think that riding a horse with your bare legs like that would chafe your ass—not to mention rough up your family jewels," Atta observed.

"Everyone listen!" Marcus cut him off. "Who's got the best eyes? I need everyone looking at Teetonka there. Tell me what you see gleaming on his chest!"

"That's Teetonka?" Lesser Tribune Cyrus asked, stopping only when Severus cracked him on the top of his head with his open palm. "Shut up and look! Honorius, you've got good eyes, do you—"

It's an eight pointed star," Seneca reported. "I can see it quite clearly, although I don't understand why. The rest of him is actually a little hazy."

"It's a magic pendant," Marcus said, "and I think it's just like the one Kekipi wielded in the Fire Islands."

"Surely not," Capitán Adán said. "How could it be the same? The Fire Islands are more than two thousand miles away."

"I have the broken remains of the first pendant in my baggage," Marcus told him. "It gave him great power. This may explain why he's suddenly able to call down the lightning. If he comes into range of sword or pilum, don't miss the opportunity."

The savage shaman lowered his spear and two lines of horsemen galloped up the mound passing to either side of him. Instead of weapons, each held two severed heads out to either side of him as they guided their horses with their knees, plunging down the nearside of the mound with reckless abandon—reckless because it had not apparently occurred to any of the savages that they might be charging headlong into a trap.

The first horse screamed and fell hard, its rider launching off its back to fly headlong into the water up ahead of him. The horse directly behind him crashed hard into the fallen animal and tumbled its own rider to the ground. The next savage tried to guide his mount in a leap to the left only to discover that that was where the pit lay that had provided the dirt for the mound. His steed hit water that was closer to ten feet deep than eighteen inches and panicked.

Behind him on the mound, other horses found caltrops and the shrieks of rage of the shaman, Teetonka, were loud enough to be clearly heard in the inner fortress.

"That's my signal," Atta announced. "We can hurt them again now."

He did not wait for Marcus' orders before running to his men and his own trusted steed. Gente merchants-turned-soldiers moved the wooden doors back into position and suddenly the Gota horsemen were back in play charging around the side of the fort at the stunned savage warriors only just beginning to work their way past the field of caltrops and pits. As it turned out, severed skulls were not the ideal choice of weapon to confront the spears of skilled cavalry men.

"It's always gratifying to see one's plans work out so splendidly," Marcus noted. "But I think we're going to see some action soon, so if each of you would rejoin your men we can prepare to give these savages a reception that the survivors will never forget."

Marcus' officers ran for their posts. Had the savages done as they should have and used their thousands of men to climb the outer walls and rush the inner ones while their horsemen charged in through the gates, things might have been getting hairy about now. As it was, their flashy attempt to devastate the defenders' morale had rebounded against them and legionnaires and Gente alike shouted triumphantly as the Gota drove the savages back toward the pits and field of caltrops.

Men and horses screamed as the chaos mounted, but before too long, savages began to spill north off the mound and regain control of the situation. Marcus ordered a horn to be sounded, calling the Gota back and Atta, reluctantly, broke his men free of the fighting and charged back to the ramps into the fort.

One enterprising savage who attempted to beat them up the ramps ended dead in the ditch beneath them with a legionnaire's pilum in his gut.

After the last horsemen returned, Gente pulled the door-turned-ramp back into the safety of the inner fort walls.

The enraged savages did not immediately do as Marcus had hoped and throw themselves piecemeal against his prepared defenses. Instead they splashed about the flooded bailey, screaming their rage at Marcus and his men. Every couple of minutes, one would rush toward the wall to hurl one of his severed heads into the inner fortress. Severus and Cledus put a quick stop to men wasting pilum against such attacks, although Marcus, himself, gave into temptation and showed off his skill by skewering anyone who dared to come within range of him. It was a fine game but it didn't last long enough.

After a couple of hours of gathering their forces between the two walls, Teetonka again lifted his short spear high above his head and exhorted his warriors in their native language. After he finished, three quarters dismounted from their horses and picked up their hatchets.

"Pilum!" Marcus ordered and the men each picked up one of the hundreds of weapons that had accompanied the caravan from Dona far to the south.

"On my order," Marcus shouted even as Teetonka ordered something that must have meant the same thing.

The shaman's spear came down and the men hurled themselves forward, splashing through the water toward the wall. Marcus waited until they were some fifty yards away before ordering the first pilum thrown.

It was difficult to miss with such a horde running toward them.

"Pilum!" Marcus shouted again and the men around him retrieved a second weapon.

"As they reach the ditch, boys!" the Tribune told them. The savages couldn't be certain how deep the ditch was and they were likely to try and hurdle it. Marcus would in their positions and he timed the next throw so that the men would be at their most helpless, leaping through the air.

Sharp steel sliced deep into their chests and then his men were pulling their swords and there was nothing to be done but hack at the head and arms of the countless bastards trying to climb the wall and kill them.

Commanding officers really weren't supposed to get involved in the actual melee, but it was impossible to stay aloof under these conditions. He brought the bottom edge of his shield crashing down upon one man's uplifted face and hacked a hand off the wrist of another attacker. Bright blood sprayed across the evening air coloring the water just as Marcus had predicted.

Men howled on both sides of the wall as death visited the battlefield again and again and again.

Marcus' skin began to prickle and then to hurt as the pins-and-needles sensation overwhelmed him. The wind was blowing hard and he suddenly realized the dust had picked up, cutting down his visibility. Was Teentonka trying to hide another attack?

Marcus stepped back and did his best to assess the battlefield. On all sides of the fort, his line was holding. Men were down but that was nothing compared to the number of dead savages. Teetonka wouldn't be hiding another attack, he was trying to cover a withdrawal.

Evidently, Red Vigil Honorius had just come to the same conclusion. "Don't let them pull back, boys!" he shouted from about five hundred feet away from Marcus. "We've got them where we want them!"

As if to prove his point, he leapt out off the wall into the flooded bailey directly in front of him. A dozen of his men screamed and did the same. The savages recoiled in shock and horror, and began to retreat.

Teetonka on the mound before the gate shrieked what had to be a dozen curses and pointed his short spear directly at Honorius. Bright white lightning leapt from the tip of the weapon and burnt the sky between the shaman and the Red Vigil. Then two hundred men screamed—most of them savages—and dropped dead in the manmade lake.

For a moment, everyone froze in horror as the after flash of the lightning continued to blink in their eyes. Then everyone pulled back hard from the site of the blast—the legionnaires and the Gente merchants instinctively pulling back from the wall while the savages fled the fort entirely.

Teetonka continued to scream at them, going so far as to hit his own people with another bolt of lightning, but nothing could have stopped that human tide. They ran over the outer wall—easy to do from the inside—and did not stop running until they were far out upon the arid plains.

****

"We have triumphed!" Capitán Adán crowed as he joined the other officers at their meeting in the aftermath of the savages' retreat.

"Did you see them scurry like frightened children?" Warrior Atta asked. The two men clapped each other on the back like brothers celebrating the winning of their race horse instead of what they were—antagonistic members of a ruling class and the unhappily governed.

"We stood strong and we triumphed!" Lesser Tribune Cyrus said, joining the celebration. Green Vigil Phanes, who'd learned to keep his head down after his initial conflicts with Marcus, added, "They came at us and then they ran away!"

Only the experienced legionnaires, and Seneca who was carefully taking his lead from Marcus, seemed to understand the siege had not ended.

Marcus let them congratulate each other for another minute before offering his own comments. "You all fought well and I will say as much to the troops when I address them at the end of this meeting. Warrior Atta, you and your men especially outperformed my expectations. You all handled yourselves with the skill and discipline absolutely necessary to winning this siege."

Atta and Adán, at least, had figured out from Marcus' tone that the Tribune thought they were celebrating prematurely. The two legionnaires had not.

"We did exactly what we needed to in this *first* battle," Marcus continued, "exactly what all of our preparations were designed to accomplish. We sucked the enemy in and we killed him by the *shitload*—to quote our Gota friend here."

Warrior Atta smiled, but everyone else was finally on board with Marcus' message. The first battle was won but the siege was not over.

"Now there are two ways this might go," Marcus told them. "One, the savages could attack again tomorrow. I find this unlikely, but possible. We did beat them badly and it will take time to reorganize themselves and rebuild their confidence for another assault."

"You're sure they won't just go away?" Green Vigil Phanes asked.

"Yes!" Marcus made the word as decisive as he could. "Teetonka, the lightning wielding shaman, was so furious at their flight that he struck out at his own men. It's possible that one or two tribes will run away tonight, but would *you* want a man that powerful coming after you and your family for the rest of time?"

Phanes shook his head and Marcus continued. "The second way Teetonka might handle this—the way I would have handled it from the beginning—is to drain the lake while he harasses us with his magic. Now I don't know how much strength it costs him to use his lightning, so he may settle for keeping this dust storm on top of us day in and day out, but he'll harass us, trying to interfere with our sleep and bring down our morale."

"I suspect he will use the other shaman to manage his dust storm," Seneca volunteered. "They might be the ones who raised it anyway since Teetonka didn't seem to want the tribes to retreat." When he saw that he had everyone's attention, he shrugged and added. "Remember that each of those tribes probably has its own shaman. They may also be able to help him summon his thundercloud as he did when he defeated the relief force trying to reach Fort Tertium. That would not only preserve his strength, but probably make it easier for him to bring forth the lightning. It is the only reason I can think of for him to have summoned that cloud when he can obviously generate the lightning without it."

Marcus nodded thoughtfully, "Thank you, Magus Seneca." He had wondered why Teetonka had bothered with the cloud. They were lucky he had lost his temper and used his magical weapon so poorly and even luckier that the shaman from the dry plains had not known what happens when lightning strikes a man standing in water. "So those are the savages' basic options—attack now or take a couple of days to strengthen their position before coming after us again. If they choose the first option, we simply fight and hope the battle goes largely like the first one, but if they do the smart thing we have an opportunity to create a new line of defense that will greatly enhance our own chances of holding out until relief arrives."

"Holding out?" Lesser Tribune Cyrus asked. "You don't see us simply defeating them if they came at the walls again?"

Marcus wished that question had not been asked, but knew that realistically there was no way to avoid it now that it had been voiced. Best to tackle it head on. "It's very difficult to decisively defeat a besieging army from within the siege. They control whether they attack or not, and while we can sortie out against them, we don't have any extra troops to be making that gamble with—especially against our own prepared defenses."

Cyrus looked confused so Severus added, "Our walls and the lake keep us in at the same time they are keeping them out. The dust storm might conceal our movements but..." He shrugged.

"So until circumstances change, it is unlikely that we will be leaving the inner fortress."

Atta started to protest.

"Yes, yes, I know your warriors are ready and eager to sally forth again, but realistically, Warrior Atta, do you truly believe that the savages are so stupid they won't put five hundred archers on the wall to defend their forces when they start draining Lake Defiance?"

Atta considered that for a moment before shaking his head. "No, they'd have to be really stupid not to do that."

"They were over-confident this time," Marcus agreed. "They thought that their numbers and their relatively easy victory at the Battle of the Thundercloud ensured another easy triumph here. Now they know they have to earn another win and they'll be smarter when they come in again."

He raised his voice because even though the officers had gone off a little ways to hold their meeting in silence, there were many ears straining to hear what they said. "So we have to be smarter too. We have to do something else to demoralize them. And the fastest, easiest, smartest thing we can do is to build another inner wall. This way, if they come after us again in all their numbers with Teetonka's magic helping them along, we can bleed them out like we did this time and then retreat to the new inner ring and make them realize they have to do the whole damn thing over again."

He glanced at Severus, silently requesting him to contribute his thoughts.

The Black Vigil chuckled grimly. "It's a hard thing to think you've almost won the battle only to learn you've gained nothing but a few feet of ground. I know. I've been there."

"Me too," Black Vigil Lysander volunteered. "And if I may say, Tribune, it's a clever plan because it won't be as easy for them to come at us on the new inner wall. We have a lot of pilum left and if we station most of them at the inner defenses, most of the area between this wall and the new one will be a pilum killing ground. To properly attack us, they will have to take down huge sections of the—what would you call it—the middle wall. And they'll be doing that after we've just killed another host of them. No one will want to bring that wall down quickly because it means the third assault against our swords and shields will be coming that much faster."

Marcus' impulse to promote the man to Black Vigil had just paid an unexpected reward. The less experienced officers had already traveled from elation to disappointment and fear in this conversation, but Lysander's words had gone a long way to restoring their confidence. "Very well said, Black Vigil," Marcus complemented him. "We can win this siege. There's still a lot of hard fighting ahead of us, but our defenses are strong and our men are stout and disciplined. I won't pretend it's not going to get tough—all sieges get tough—but I guarantee you that the coming battles look a hell of a lot worse from that side of the wall than they do from this side."

The officers nodded confidently, clearly onboard with Marcus' plan.

"Good! Now let's go brief the men. I want the new wall well under way by morning."

Day Nineteen
They Aren't Going Away

Five days, Marcus thought as he surveyed the new inner wall that his men had spent the night constructing. We've held out five days since Lord Evorik left us to seek reinforcements. That leaves only three to eight days more before he thinks he can return with an army of Gota horsemen. We might actually be able to hold out that long. The new inner wall is going up faster than I really expected it to. If we get the whole day to work on it, it will be a serious obstacle for the savages to overcome. If we get a second day, it will be taller and stronger than our current defensive line.

He caught sight of Alberto working hard beside the other exhausted men to erect this new defense and decided to stop and speak with him. The Gente señor had removed his breast plate and his shirt was grimed with dirt and sweat but he did not appear to be injured.

"Señor," Marcus greeted him. "How goes the new defensive works?"

Alberto did not stop shoveling to speak with him. "Too slowly, Tribune, I fear that if they come again today this wall will not be ready for them."

"If they're waiting for the lake to drain," Marcus told him, "I don't think they'll come today. I expected them to start taking down the outer wall last night, but instead they licked their wounds. Keep working! You and your brother warriors will get the job done."

Alberto paused, leaning on his shovel while he tried to catch his breath. "That is good news! I do not like to think what those savages will do if they come over the walls and catch my Carmelita or little Gaspar Marcus." He shuddered.

"We're not going to let that happen," Marcus assured him. "These defenses are sound! Your family will be safe behind them."

Alberto drove the shovel deep into the ground and tossed another pile of earth up on the growing wall. There was something in his eye that disturbed Marcus—a desperate need to believe the Tribune was telling him the truth combined with the fear that he was not.

Marcus touched his shoulder. "Señor, I'm not pretending things aren't bad, but we are going to hold the savages back. Your family will be safe and we're going to get all of that crystal to your father-in-law in time for Lord Totila's daughter's wedding."

Alberto shoveled another load of dirt out of the deepening ditch up onto the wall. "You're a good man, Tribune. I believe you when you say it to me, but..."

"That fear," Marcus told him, "is what pushes us to win. Keep digging the wall. I'll ask Lord Evorik's wives to check on your family when they take a break from tending our injured."

"Carmelita and little Gaspar are already with the Gota ladies," Alberto told him. "They have been most kind, especially for Gota. It's just..."

"I know," Marcus agreed. "So do what you can now, but be sure you rest when you're told to. We can't so exhaust ourselves that we don't have the strength to hold the—"

"Tribune!" a legionnaire shouted as he ran toward him. "Tribune Cyrus sent me to find you and tell you something is happening!"

Marcus suppressed the flash of rage that rose up within him. Didn't Cyrus have *any* common sense? Sending a man running through the fort like this for anything short of a renewed assault was idiocy.

He raised his voice so that everyone around him could hear what he said. "I'd better go check on this. They're probably just attacking the walls or our makeshift dam—which is exactly what we want them putting their time into."

Reassurance offered, he strode quickly off to find Cyrus.

****

"Look at them!" Cyrus pointed at the far wall through which the dammed creek once flowed. Standing atop the wall were several hundred savage warriors, each armed with their short bows and a quiver of arrows, waiting for the defenders to sally forth and try and interfere with the men gathering below.

"Good!" Marcus observed. "They're going to waste time on the lake."

"Waste time?" Cyrus asked.

"You do recall that we wanted them to spend time doing this?" Marcus asked him.

"Yes, but—"

"Would it have been better if they tried to charge us again through the water?" Marcus interrupted him. "Yes, it probably would have been. But no one thought they would be that stupid—not when it's this simple to drain the water away."

As usual, he was answering one man but addressing all within hearing. "But they waited a long time to do it. This is not going to be a simple task for them. It's unlikely it will finish draining by sunset and maybe the outer fort will still be flooded tomorrow morning." The Tribune smiled. "How many of you think the savages will be anxious to come charging up against us again before the lake is totally drained?"

"Not with the way their mad leader was throwing lightning around yesterday," one of the legionnaires on watch duty commented.

"That's right," Marcus agreed. "So we get another day to strengthen our defenses and they get another day to think about how many of them are going to die when they attack us again."

As they watched, a group of male savages made their way to the dam and stood around thigh deep in water looking at all the rocks. Teetonka appeared on the wall in his elaborate headdress and pointed vigorously at the obstruction but the men did not act on his suggestion.

"What's going on?" Marcus asked.

"They don't think that moving those rocks is man's work," one of the legionnaires who had been stationed at Fort Defiance said.

"How so?"

While Teetonka gestured more and more angrily at the damn, the legionnaire stepped forward to explain his comment. "Men's work and women's work are strictly divided on the Sea of Grass. Men hunt, they make weapons, they ride, and they take care of their horses. Women and children do pretty much everything else. Those men think it's beneath their dignity to dig up those rocks."

"Then where are the women?" Marcus wanted to know.

"They probably also think that it's too dangerous in the fort for the women folk to come do the work," another legionnaire volunteered. "I mean, just look at all the bodies floating in the lake water. You'd have to be an idiot not to be worried about what we could do to them if we wanted to."

The man had an excellent point. "Are you saying that Teetonka won't be able to get his people to move those boulders?"

Even as Marcus finished speaking, the sizzle of the shaman's lightning broke the stillness of the morning. The twenty or so savages standing in the water went cruelly rigid and then collapsed in death.

Everyone, savages and civilized men alike, stared at the bodies for several seconds before the legionnaire who had explained the customs of the Sea of Grass to Marcus leapt higher on the wall. "That's the way you crazy savage!" he shouted. "Keep doing that and we won't have to kill anymore of you."

He turned to Marcus with a smirk and never saw the bolt of lightning that picked him off the wall and flung him more than ten feet into the inner fortress.

Teetonka started shouting again, pointing angrily at the pile of boulders. Marcus couldn't understand his language but his intent was inescapable. Slowly, very slowly, warriors put down their bows and made their way down into the water among their dead companions. Then, working together, they began to pry at the submerged stones.

****

"It goes down a lot faster than it came up," Marcus observed.

"That's always the way of things, isn't it?" Severus responded. "It's harder to build than to destroy."

"Philosophy, Severus?" Marcus asked.

The Black Vigil shrugged. "Just common sense." He gestured at the spot where the water poured through the wall again. "It still did what you wanted it to—helped give us our first victory and then bought us an extra day on top of that."

"I'm hoping for a bit more than a day," Marcus said. "A little standing water in the morning would be much appreciated. I want the ground wet when the savages return. We may not get a lot of mud where the grass is growing, but in the trenches and the new walls—anything that makes it harder to climb up to us is for the good."

"It all depends on when they come," Severus told him. "If that Teetonka has any sense—and I'm not sure that he does—he'll wait three days to attack. Today to let the water drain, tomorrow to let the ground dry out and then I'd bring up the dust storm and start pounding us with lightning for another day."

"You think he can use the lightning that long?" Marcus asked.

"We saw it go on at the Battle of the Thundercloud for hours. I'd use it to keep us from sleeping the night before the attack and I'd send my warriors in silently through the dust an hour after dawn."

Marcus thought about it a moment before agreeing. "That's what I'd do too, but you don't think Teetonka will follow that plan, do you?"

"No, I don't," Severus said. "The man is too angry. It's like you told the officers a few days ago. Angry men lack discipline. I think he'll come tomorrow. I think he wants to come tonight, but he'll wait until tomorrow."

"He has to be worried that reinforcements will come."

Severus shook his head. "I don't give much credence to Lord Evorik's eight to twelve days. I don't know how large a force Topacio can raise, but it's going to need to be bigger than the one they sent with the legion to reinforce Fort Tertium. If you're riding to attack five thousand savages you're going to want at least five thousand men. So you've got two choices. You raise a host of Gente infantry to go along with your Gota cavalry, or you reach out to neighboring cities and ask for help from their cavalry. Either way, that takes more than eight to twelve days. We're on our own, Tribune. The way to win this siege is to suck them up against our walls and kill them."

Marcus considered what Severus had said and was disappointed to realize he agreed with him. In his gut he'd always known that the hope of reinforcement was a weak one, but he regretted its loss just the same.

"What do you think about Fort Tertium?" Marcus asked. "Are they dead or still holding out like we are?"

"Could be either," Severus told him. They are deep in the Sea of Grass and currently cut off from resupply. It's actually good strategy for Teetonka to leave them behind and come deal with the relief force and now us in Fort Defiance. Fort Tertium will wait."

"Or they could have rushed them during a dust storm and the whole garrison could be dead," Marcus countered.

"Either one is possible," Severus agreed. "It doesn't make a difference to us either way. We've got Teetonka and his savages here and they aren't going away."

Day Twenty
Outnumbered Ten to One

The wind picked up with the dawn, bringing the now familiar prickling sensation to Marcus' flesh. Someone, Teetonka or his shamans, was using magic. He no longer had any reasonable doubt that that was what the sensation meant. Somehow, surviving the explosion of Kekipi's strange eight-pointed medallion had made him unusually sensitive to the arcane. And that new sensation told him that the primitive magi among the savages—their tribal shamans—were stoking the wind with their magic.

He turned away from inspecting the teams of drivers moving the merchant wagons behind the new inner wall so that he could look out over the middle wall to see what the savages were up to. There was still some water ranging from a foot to a couple of inches covering the ground of the outer fort and it wasn't likely to get a heck of a lot lower unless the savages opened up holes in the southern wall. Even in ground as flat as the plains there were subtle gradations across the bailey of the fort which caused water to pool more deeply in some places than others. There was also, interestingly enough, a noticeable downward slant of the ground which presumably started with the mountains to the north and continued on to the salt pan to the south. The difference within the confines of the fort was probably no more than eight inches but that was sufficient to leave the southern part of Fort Defiance flooded.

As to the savages, they were not really doing anything yet. A few hundred still sat on the walls in groups of fifty or so, ready to shoot at the Gota cavalry if Marcus should try to set them loose in the bailey again. Other than that, there was no sign of them at all until a quarter of a mile or so beyond the walls where their camps began to speckle the landscape. They weren't mounting their horses yet, so for now at least, the wind did not denote urgency.

He went back to examining the wagons. In a perfect world he would move the horses within the walls as well, but a besieged legion fort in the northern range of the Sea of Grass was about as far from perfect as a man could get. No, he wasn't going to have room for all the horses and frankly wouldn't have taken them even if he did. Atta hadn't liked this when Marcus explained it to him, but even the pigheaded Gota warriors could be made to see sense.

When the lightning started, and Marcus had to believe the lightning would come, the horses were likely to panic and there was no way the defenders could cope with more than four hundred frightened horses bucking and thrashing in terror inside the tight confines of the defenders' final stronghold. That would be a recipe for disaster even if the savages wouldn't choose that moment to charge the final walls.

Not that there was room for the animals within the inner most walls anyway. Out here in the middle area, they had space to move around a bit if they needed to. In the inner walls they would be standing together as if in the stalls of some massive stable. Bringing them inside just wasn't feasible and that was before Marcus considered the problem of how they would feed them.

So he watched the drivers park the wagons in small groups, separated from each other as much as was feasible to minimize the chances that all would burn when the lightning started catching them on fire. It was a rare moment of peace for him since the siege first started and he relished it precisely because he knew it wouldn't last.

****

"Tribune?" Seneca Liberus called. "Tribune? Where are you, Sir? Red Vigil Calidus told me you were over here by your Green Banders."

Several of the men laughed as the clearly befuddled Acting Magus stepped right past Marcus as he called out for him.

Green Vigil Phanes took the opportunity to divert attention away from the dressing down he'd just received for the sloppy state of his men's armor. Marcus didn't expect it to be clean under these conditions, but he'd been damn clear that armor would be worn at all times once the dust storm had risen. He wasn't going to let his men be caught unprepared for battle, even if it meant strengthening the new inner wall with a breast plate on.

"What's wrong with you, Seneca?" Phanes snapped. "You just walked past the Tribune!"

Seneca turned at the sound of the Green Vigil's voice and jumped back in shock to see Marcus standing there beside him. "I'm sorry, Tribune. It must be the dust. I just, I didn't see you."

"That's obvious!" Phanes scowled.

Try as he might, Marcus didn't see anything to like in Phanes. He was a lazy little man at heart who enjoyed the power he wielded far too much to ever make a good officer. And he didn't seem capable of learning from his more experienced superiors. "See that your men are properly armored, Green Vigil," he told him. "Acting Magus, walk with me."

Seneca fell in step beside the Tribune as they walked away from Phanes. "Now what do you need?" Marcus asked him.

Seneca nervously licked his lips. "Someone out there—maybe several someones—has started to work some very powerful magics. I've never seen anything like it, although I have read about such things. Frankly, the fact that I can see it without any preparations on my part is really scaring me."

Now that Marcus thought about it, the now-too-familiar pins-and-needles feeling that had returned to him with the wind this morning had become noticeably stronger. "So you think what?"

"That Teetonka is summoning his thundercloud. I think the lightning is going to start falling on us soon."

Marcus nodded thoughtfully. It was the only thing he could think of also. "A couple of times now, you've mentioned the possibility that you might be able to interfere with the storm. Would you expand upon that please?" Marcus actually found the idea implausible. Seneca was just a student after all, but if the lad really could do something to help them he would be foolish to discard the possibility out of hand.

Seneca licked his lips again. "I'm not sure I really can. You see, one of the things we're taught is to see the flows of magic. It takes practice. Experienced magi can do it almost instinctively because we naturally see magic in the world around us anyway. This innate ability—it's not really a sixth sense its sort of part of our natural eyesight—is one of the signs that a person can learn to wield magic. I mean, how can you manipulate something you can't sense? You understand?"

"Yes," Marcus assured him even as he wondered what this meant in regard to his new sensitivity.

"So this is very important in magical combat. One magus decides to throw fire at another and being able to see those weaves of magic coming together lets another magus know what sort of shield to raise to protect himself. Understand?"

Again Marcus nodded.

"I can't do that yet," Seneca admitted. "That kind of instantaneous reading of the magic in the world around us is actually fairly advanced. Part of the difficulty is the speed with which everything happens in combat. But a greater difficulty is the need to be able to read the flows while actually staying alive and doing other things. Students like me learn to read the magical energy by slipping into deep meditative trances. We light candles. We burn incense. We lose our awareness of the conscious world and we start to see things."

He shifted his weight awkwardly from his left to his right foot. "But I can already get glimpses of these flows, you understand? They are so powerful that I'm catching glimpses of them without meditating. And what I see—it's not just super powerful. It's really complex. I sort of imagined that there would be three or four or maybe six lines of magic shooting up into the thundercloud and that I could watch in my trance until I got the timing right and then push at one of those strands with all my might and knock the lightning bolt away. Maybe I could even hit the savages with it. Then Teetonka and I could have a little duel—not me trying to kill him, but me trying to deflect his blows. But…it's way too complicated. It's like he has already spread out a huge net around him and I just wouldn't know where to begin."

Marcus nodded thoughtfully. He hadn't really expected Seneca to pull a rabbit out of the hat to save them, but he appreciated the young man's integrity in telling him the truth. "What would happen if you pulled one of the strings of the net?"

Seneca shook his head. "I honestly have no idea. It's so complicated that losing one or two strands for a short time might not have any impact at all. Alternatively, it might cause things to blow up on him, although that seems unlikely. What I'm almost certain would happen is that in a net this big, he would not only detect my interference but locate where I was physically attacking him from. And with a man as powerful as Teetonka that probably means I'd be dead pretty quickly after I tried."

There was fear in the young man's eyes but not cowardice. Marcus felt fairly confident that he would go ahead and attack Teetonka's spell if the Tribune asked him to. But what purpose would that serve at this time?

"If you think you can do it safely, you can meditate and observe the net, but you are not to interfere with it without my permission. Do you understand? You're the only person available to me who can help me understand the magical side of this war. I don't want you risking yourself without my permission."

The Acting Magus saluted Marcus.

"Good! Now if you're convinced the lightning is coming, I have to move forward with building the next phase of my defenses."

Without another word, Marcus stalked off toward the makeshift hospital that Lord Evorik's wives had erected in the center of the fortress.

****

"Tribune Marcus!" Señora Carmelita cried out as he entered the Praetorium. The building was nominally the legion headquarters in Fort Defiance, but the Tribune had not used it as such. He spent his days checking on his men, the enemy and the state of his improving defenses. He had neither the staff nor the desire to sit in this building and send other people out to do his checking for him. So when he'd asked the Gota Ladies Hilduara and Riciberga to take charge of the care of his wounded, he had given over the Praetorium to their needs.

Now he was thinking better of his moment of generosity.

"It's good to see you, Señora," he greeted Alberto's wife. "It's very generous of you to volunteer to help with the wounded. How is your new son doing?"

"He's sleeping right now," Carmelita told him. "Would you like to see him?"

Marcus actually had no time for looking at babies, but he knew it would crush the young mother if he turned her down so he agreed to follow her into the main hall of the building where the wounded lay on the floor and her child in a crib made out of the drawer of an elaborate dresser which the Great Tribune might have brought with him all the way from Aquila. Like most new babies, Gaspar Marcus Lope was a tiny little thing, fortunately sleeping peacefully at the moment. The most notable thing about him was a shockingly full head of rich black hair—not at all the bald thing that described the couple of handfuls of other babies that Marcus had seen over the years.

"Quite a handsome young man," Marcus praised her. "I think he gets his chin from his father, but that cute little sleeping smile must come from you."

Carmelita beamed with pride and pleasure at his words, but fortunately, the two Gota women had come over to see why he was visiting.

"Ah, Lady Hilduara," Marcus addressed the senior of the two wives. "How are my men doing?"

"We've only lost one more man since your last visit, Tribune," the noblewoman informed him.

Marcus knew that that meant his lethal casualties had risen to fifty-two men—far more than he could afford to lose but far less than the twelve to fourteen hundred savages that he estimated they had killed so far. Those numbers were extraordinary and had been helped along by the excellent cavalry work of Warrior Atta and his men, and even more so by the temper of Teetonka in striking down a couple of hundred of his own men.

"And the injured?"

"I've already sent back to you those who can fight. I don't think you can count on getting any more."

That was worse news. While there were only thirty-one men still out due to injuries, combining them with the dead meant he'd lost eighty-three of his five hundred ninety-five defenders. Most of the losses—although by no means all—had been from the civilians, but every man down made it more difficult to continue to hold his walls.

Marcus decided to get right to the point. "My magus tells me that the savages have begun to gather another thundercloud. I have been thinking about how to handle this and worry that by putting you in this building I have actually made you more vulnerable to attack rather than providing you with more protection as I intended. These two buildings can be seen from beyond the wall and while they are safe against arrow fire, they are not safe against lightning."

Both of the Gota women nodded solemnly as if they had already considered this problem.

"So what I propose to do is to dig a large pit and, time permitting, roof it with the walls from this building. The pit will not be visible to Teetonka and his men. The roof will give you some protection from arrow fire. Do you have any objection to this plan?"

"Six of the men really should not be moved," Riciberga told him, "but I think we have no choice. We will have them ready when you give the word."

"Good," Marcus said. "I'm also going to move the rest of our supplies out of the Quaestorium and into similar pits. Anything we think might be useful to you will be moved into the hospital pit with you."

Task accomplished Marcus left the women and set about getting men to start the new construction.

****

When they'd seen the first thundercloud in the distance after emerging from the salt pan it had looked to be a relatively tiny thing. Now, watching the clouds flow toward them from the hills, the roiling mass of darkness seemed anything but small. It covered the sky, not just for a mile or two but for dozens with more clouds being drawn to the coming storm like iron filings to a load stone.

Upon the surface of the clouds, lightning crackled, forewarning everyone of what was to come and Marcus could see the vision insidiously worming its way into his men's morale. He had to do something so he took a gamble and summoned all but a few watchers off the wall to address them.

When they aligned before him the difference between the three groups of his troops could not be more apparent. The legionnaires formed his center rank and stood in perfect lines, backs rigid and silent as the tomb. The Gota stood making a great show of their bravery, nonchalantly conversing in low tones while pointedly ignoring the thundercloud approaching them from the north. But the civilians, they stood in little groups staring at the clouds with fear on their faces. It was the civilians Marcus needed to worry about now, but he could not humiliate the proud Gente by making it too obvious that he was singling them out for their fear. Still…

"That's right," he said approaching them. "Take a good look at that cloud." He raised his voice. "All of you do the same. There's no use in pretending it's not coming. We've made some preparations for it that I'll explain in a minute, but the odds are some of us are going to die by lightning bolt and all of us are going to get damn sick of the thunder blasting out our eardrums."

He gestured at the cloud. "So go ahead and look. Teetonka has killed fifteen of our men with lightning." Someone groaned which was actually precisely the response Marcus was hoping for. "Of course he's killed five *hundred* of his men that way so his men are probably more nervous about those clouds than we are."

Warrior Atta laughed and the sound cut through the tension in the men—even Marcus' highly disciplined legionnaires—and suddenly everyone was laughing with him.

Perfect!

"We probably can't count on him continuing to murder his men by the hundreds, but, who knows? Sol Invictus is with us! He looks down upon us from his fiery seat in the sky and he has to be pretty happy about the way we've faced up to our problems and thrown a thousand of those bastards into their graves."

For some men, laughter gave way to cheers.

"Now the lightning is going to come, but Teetonka can't see what he's shooting at. So we're going to spread you men out on the wall and pull some of you back a little bit away from it to shelter and rest in the small pits we've been digging everywhere and leave only about one in fifty of you—camouflaged with dirt and mud so that Teetonka can't see you—to keep watch on our savage friends. For the rest of you, let the lightning fall. He's not going to have an easy time hitting you. I'm far more worried about the savages' arrows because, let's face it, a few thousand of those launched at the same time almost have to hit something."

That took the men back a moment, but before fear could set in again, Marcus gave them the solution to that problem. "That's why the Aquilan legions use such large shields. They defend us from arrow fire in battle and at rest. Those little holes we've been digging are big enough for four men to squeeze into, but the opening can be covered with two shields. So when we're ready for you to charge out and defend the walls, you might have to pull six or ten arrows out of your shields, but you're not going to be pulling them out of your bodies, understand?"

Men nodded—the experienced legionnaires with quiet confidence, the civilians and the Gota with slow understanding.

"I won't lie to you," Marcus told them. "It's not going to be fun to sit back and let them fire arrows and lightning at us. Once in a long while, they almost have to get lucky and hit something or someone. But this storm will not break us! When the savages charge that wall again, we will leap to our places and kill them with pilum and sword until they run screaming back out onto the plain just like the last time!"

This time the cheers were both heartfelt and prolonged.

****

Almost with the severity and suddenness of extinguishing a lamp, the black thunderclouds rolled between the earth and mighty Sol Invictus and left Fort Defiance covered in darkness. For a moment, all work froze as men accustomed themselves to the new conditions, then—just as they started to move again—a bolt of brilliant white lightning carved its jagged path out of the heavens to rip into the roof of the Praetorium.

Chips of wood shot into the air followed a moment later by a flickering tongue of flame which the men stared at with the same sickly fascination that a sparrow stares into the eyes of a hungry snake. Then the thunder boomed seeming to shake the very ground with its fury.

Men flinched away from the building—the apparent epicenter of the blast—with even Marcus' prized Black Banders holding up an arm or their shields as if to protect themselves from the noise.

"This is going to be worse than I thought," Marcus muttered before bellowing to his men in his loudest voice. "All right, then! Now you've seen the show you get back to work! Watchmen face outward! Are you going to let the savages sneak up on us! The rest of you—back to your holes or your jobs! We've probably got a few hundred more blasts like that coming and I for one hope they're all as useless!"

Calidus and Severus picked up the Tribune's shouts, followed very quickly by Atta and Lysander and finally by Capitán Adán. Phanes and Cyrus remained silent as if trying to prove that they were the weakest links in Marcus' command. Severus could be counted on to drag Phanes back in line, but as for Lesser Tribune Cyrus, no one but Marcus had the rank to deal with him.

He quickly crossed what he was now thinking of as the inner bailey to find the man cringing as he sheltered in the four man holes that had been dug as protection against the arrows and bolts from heaven. "Lesser Tribune!" Marcus shouted.

Cyrus looked up with a disturbing combination of loathing and fear.

"A word please, Lesser Tribune Cyrus!" Marcus made the words sound like a request but both men knew they were an order.

Very reluctantly, Cyrus began to climb out of his hole.

The prickling of Marcus' skin peaked and he braced himself against the next bolt. Like the first stroke of lightning it impaled itself on the roof of the now abandoned Praetorium, which suited Marcus just fine. Let Teetonka waste a thousand bolts on the building. Let him spend all his strength smashing it into the ground. It made no difference to Marcus. His wounded had all been moved out.

As the thunder rang in his eardrums, Marcus turned back to Cyrus only to find him cowering back in the bottom of his hole.

Something would have to be done. He hated to break the man on the eve of the next battle, but he had to consider the real possibility that leaving him in command could undermine all of his men.

"Lesser Tribune!" he snapped with absolutely no compassion in the tone of his voice.

This time there was more loathing than fear in the junior officer's gaze—except that here, in these conditions, Cyrus wasn't a junior officer. He was second in command.

"I asked for a word, Lesser Tribune. Don't make me repeat myself a third time."

Even more reluctantly, the frightened officer pulled himself up to the surface next to Marcus.

"Walk with me," Marcus told him aware that every eye around them was watching the conversation. Fortunately, the peals of thunder had been so deafening that none of the men could likely hear them.

"You're putting me in a very difficult situation," Marcus told Cyrus when they had moved a hundred feet away.

"Tribune?" Cyrus asked.

"You're showing the men you're frightened. It's all right to actually be scared, but you're never permitted to show it."

Cyrus looked at Marcus as if he was utterly insane, but the Tribune did not waver from his purpose. He was actually trying to save the Lesser Tribune's life, because if he could not get him to change his ways, Marcus would have no choice but to execute him, shaming both the man and his family for all time.

"I can't afford to lose you, Lesser Tribune, but you're no use to me hiding in your hole."

Cyrus reached out to grab hold of Marcus, but the next bolt of lightning struck the Praetorim and the Lesser Tribune jerked back in fear as if he thought he was about to be burned. "We can't fight that!" he shouted, pointing at the burning building.

"We don't have to!" Marcus reminded him. "We only have to endure it until the savages come a calling."

"But we'll die!" Cyrus screamed, attempting to be heard over the bellow of thunder.

Marcus waited for the sound to fade away. "Maybe we will and maybe we won't," he halfway conceded. "But do you know what is sure to kill us? Ignoring the walls while Teetonka plays magus on our heads. If we're not ready when the savages charge, we are all dead. And you can't be ready to fight hiding in the bottom of your hole like a toddler who's just wet his pants."

"We can't—" Cyrus started to protest.

This time it was Marcus who grabbed him. "You're the second ranking man in this army—a Lesser Tribune. The men look to you for an example and you're *failing*! Now get back to your men, stay out of your hole, and do your job!"

Cyrus' eyes had grown almost mad with fear and for a moment Marcus didn't think he had the courage to do as he was ordered, but the man took a deep wavering breath and saluted. "As you command, Tribune."

He'd started back toward his men and Marcus turned toward his next task when the next bolt of lightning struck, illuminating the shadowed world just long enough for Marcus to see Cyrus draw his sword.

With a howl of fury definitely tinged with madness, the Lesser Tribune threw himself at his superior officer. Marcus leapt back, drawing his own blade to fend off the attack. The two swords clang together as a new crack of thunder split the night.

The failure of Cyrus' initial attack only increased his look of desperation. He hammered at Marcus with his blade and it was everything the Tribune could do to keep his own sword fending the attacking weapon away. This was not how Aquilans were trained to fight. They stood in ranks—shield on the left arm to protect the body—not twisting and hacking with only naked steel to defend them.

Men peeked out of their holes in the earth to see what was going on and the damned perimeter guards assigned to keep watch on their enemies did the same. Marcus needed to put an end to this before the savages figured out that no one was paying attention to them anymore. He also needed to end it before Cyrus managed to cut or kill him.

He gave ground looking for some way to turn the tables on his opponent. There were pits scattered about the landscape but as none of the men watching them had come to help Marcus he suddenly feared getting too close to them. What if the men inside grabbed at his ankles in the insane belief that Marcus' death would make them safer? No, he had to—

Marcus tripped, falling hard on his backside and then rolling quickly to the left just before Cyrus smote the ground with three feet of sharpened steel.

The Lesser Tribune recovered faster than Marcus, swinging viciously at his superior officer who barely deflected the blade. Eschewing the sword, Marcus kicked out and hit Cyrus' shin, but his opponent was wearing his grieves and the blow didn't really hurt him. He chopped at Marcus' foot, then in a backhand stroke took a cut at his face which Marcus only avoided by flinging himself flat on his back.

Then he took a chance to end everything, rolling back into a sitting position just as his opponent stepped closer to finish him. The point of Marcus' sword drove hard into the other man's stomach just below the breast plate.

Cyrus' eyes widened with shock and pain, but Marcus wasted no time looking at them. He kicked again, this time against the ankle and succeeded in knocking the Lesser Tribune down, He then let go of his own blade so he could grab Cyrus' sword arm by the wrist and just hold on until the bleeding man grew too weak to attack again.

"You damn fool!" Marcus hissed at him. "Outnumbered ten to one and you waste your life attacking *me*?"

He clambered to his feet, fury coursing through his veins. "What are you all staring at?" he bellowed even as the lightning flashed again. "You men on the wall—get back to watching, damn you!"

His hands shook with rage at the idiocy of the whole thing. What good would killing Marcus have done Cyrus? Did he think the savages would accept their surrender and let them march away? Did he think he could run, slipping past the savages camped around them in siege? Or did he really think hiding in a hole was going to somehow see him through to safety?

He grabbed his sword still sticking out of Cyrus' belly and pulled it free. "Of all the stupid ways to waste your life," he mumbled as he wiped it on a relatively clean part of Cyrus' shirt.

"What are you looking at?" he growled again at the nearby men before pointing at one of the survivors of the Battle of the Thunder Cloud. "You, Eolus, you're Acting Red Vigil. Take charge of these men. Keep someone on the wall watching at all times and the rest of them in the pits ready to come out and slaughter these savages when they finally work up the nerve to come at us again."

Eolus saluted. "You men—get out of that hole and drag the Lesser Tribune's body into an unused pit. As for the rest of you, get back under cover. Not you, Diomedes, you have the watch, don't you? So get back to watching then!"

Still shaking, Marcus strode away.

Day Twenty-One
We Are Legionnaires!

"Here they come!" one of the watchmen shouted. "They're coming at the wall!"

The previous night had been the hardest Marcus ever recalled surviving. The lightning had hammered them all through the darkness—first thoroughly destroying the Praetorium and Quaestorium before ranging farther—catching some of the wagons on fire and finally, inevitably, striking among the horses and starting the stampede Marcus had worried over. Panicked by the blast and the screams of the electrocuted horse, the hundreds of other animals had bolted in all directions, a great many trying to jump the wall only to come down in the ditch on the other side breaking their legs and dying most piteously.

If only more had met their end like that because the others raced about the middle bailey stumbling into pits where their thrashing weight killed dozens of legionnaires and Gente auxiliaries—far more than the lightning would directly take and almost as many as they lost in the first rush of the walls.

Marcus knew he should have simply killed the animals. Had he any idea how much damage they could really do he would have done it despite the protests of the Gota and the Gente, but he had foolishly stayed his hand and given Teentonka an important victory. Had the savages not been paralyzed by their ridiculous fear of the darkness, they would have lost the whole fort right then. But despite the screams and obvious confusion behind the middle walls, the savages had not left their camps to attack them.

Now morning had come and it looked like Teentonka was ready to make up for lost time.

Marcus permitted himself a cold grin. He was about to find out that he'd missed his opportunity.

****

"Pilum…throw!"
"Throw!"
"Throw!"

Black Vigil Severus' initial command echoed around the perimeter of the fort on the tongues of the other officers. A flight of pilum shot out at just over one hundred yards and savages screamed as they fell before the sharp points.

"Pilum!" Severus was already shouting. Half the men under his command immediately picked up another weapon while the men beside covered them with their long Aquilan shields. A few arrows glanced off the protective barrier or stuck into the dirt wall but most shot over the legionnaires and their allies as if the savages had been so shocked to see so many living men appear to defend their walls that they had loosed their arrows without properly aiming.

"Pilum!" The other officers repeated the Black Vigil's commands all the way around the walls of the fort.

"Throw! Severus demanded just a bare two seconds later.

A second flight of some two hundred pilum killed another fifty or so savages.

"Pilum!" Severus ordered even as the steel points were sinking home.

The survivors, and there were still *thousands* of surviving savages charging the walls from all four directions, continued to race forward. With a well-trained legion, Marcus knew they could get in two more throws, but with this group he hoped Severus had the sense to stop at one.

"Throw!" the Black Vigil commanded.

The savages were mere steps from the ditch now and almost every one of the pilum hit them. There was almost literally no place that wasn't lined with bare flesh.

"Swords!" Severus shouted, "and *kill* the bastards!"

All around the wall, Marcus could see swords leaping from their sheaths and men stepping up to do battle. It helped their confidence that they had done this before. They knew the savages would break because they'd seen it happen. But there was a difference between this morning and then that Marcus hadn't described to his men. Last time, the savages had thought they'd have an easy victory. Today they knew they'd have to pay the price for their glory.

Men died—mostly savages it was true—but they weren't killing them on the ten to one scale that would have made this attrition equal.

Lightning struck the wall and a legionnaire died.

Marcus stepped forward immediately to fill the hole, driving his sword hard into the gut of the savage that tried to reach the open space ahead of him. He shoved the dead man back with his shield and struck again at another. The ditch began to fill with the bodies of the dead while men screamed and died on both sides of the wall.

Maybe he should have pulled them back to the new wall immediately, but that left them no ground to give and their enemy emboldened. They had to throw them back one more time—force them to eat ruinous losses so that when the time came to retreat again the savages were cowed at the thought of having to die on the new wall as they had on this one.

Thunder drowned out the sounds of men dying for a few blessed seconds. Then the screams returned and Marcus added to them by hacking down another man.

The lightning struck beside him again, taking not a legionnaire but one of the savages—as if accuracy with this powerful magic was simply too much to be expected.

As it had during the first attack, the sight of one of their own falling to their leader's power caused a shock of horror to jolt through the savages within sight of the tragedy. It was an extremely minor reaction, but Marcus saw what it was and understood what it meant before there had been time for the thunder to start rolling.

Shock and fear had momentarily stolen the momentum from the attackers and Marcus felt in his gut that if he acted right now he could turn the tide of the entire battle.

Screaming "Aquila!" at the top of his lungs he leapt onto the wall and then down onto the men who two seconds earlier had been clambering over the ditch to attack him. His sword cut down two savages and his shield slammed back a third. An excited shout rose up on the wall behind him and, Eolus, Sol Invictus bless him, the legionnaire who'd become Red Vigil after Marcus' fight with Cyrus, leapt off the wall after him.

Savages already shocked by the lighting strike on their comrade staggered a step backward into their fellow tribesmen.

Other legionnaires leapt off the wall as Marcus, screaming incoherently in his fury, killed two more men. As he pressed into the mass of savages, a growing flood of his precious legionnaires charging behind him, a single savage's nerve failed and he turned and fled.

That one break in the attacking fervor was all it took to convince half a dozen more that victory was not to be theirs today.

As they turned, half of them died beneath the swords of legionnaires, but the attempt to run convinced others that it was time to get the hell out of there.

The flight of these first savages infected the whole line as more and more turned and fled as more legionnaires and the first of the Gente auxiliaries leapt off the wall and into the ditch, killing as they came.

Familiar screams rained curses down upon them, followed by a jagged bolt of three-pronged lightning which killed many but didn't come anywhere close to hitting Marcus' people. Teetonka actually seemed more incensed by the broken courage of his fellow savages than he did by the actions of the defenders who were killing them. A second bolt crashed to earth, followed by a third and a fourth far more rapidly than any succession of blasts that had rocked the fort over the long night.

Thunder claps burst without break, seemingly overlapping each other and the wind picked up markedly, gusting like the great storms that sometimes struck the Fire Islands from the wide and endless sea. Rain began to fall for the first time since Marcus had entered the Sea of Grass, but the winds were so strong that rather than fall vertically, it seemed to blow horizontally and struck like small pebbles.

The legionnaires, with their large shields, began to struggle to keep their feet, until one after the other they let the great wooden kites go and watched them fly across the fort and over the walls into the great grassy plains.

Lightning continued to fall into the ranks of the fleeing savages, but the breaking weather was so severe that Marcus' men were ceasing their pursuit at the very moment they could do the most damage. "Form on me!" Marcus shouted, but he could see there was no hope that his men could respond to his voice. He, himself, couldn't hear it. And with the near total blackening of the sky under the raging clouds, they could barely see him either—at least not between the strokes of lightning.

Then a new bellow rose up over the thunder as the winds erupted into ever greater violence. Dozens of bolts of lightning flashed out in every direction, not apparently directed, but spinning off from a huge funnel cloud that was forming out of the storm above their heads. Marcus had never seen anything even remotely like it before and when the bottom of the funnel suddenly extended toward the earth it literally obliterated some fifty feet of the outer wall out of existence.

Then the cloud began to dance, its earthbound end squiggling chaotically about them, now descending on these legionnaires now ripping apart that group of savages. In the total fury of this unimaginable horror, all remaining military discipline fled Marcus' soldiers, including himself, as each man tried to find some safety from the terrible storm.

****

Marcus peeked out of the ditch which he had flung himself into in his effort to get back to the middle walls of Fort Defiance. The funnel cloud had departed after what seemed like hours but in reality might only have been a couple of minutes of dealing death and devastation to the fort and the surrounding savage camps. He wondered if that chaos was what Teetonka had really wanted—if in his rage, the savage shaman had decided to destroy everyone? Or had things just gotten out of control for him in the end? There was no way to know, for if Marcus ever got close enough to speak to the bastard he was not going to waste time talking. He was going to hack him to death with his sword!

He looked around him and saw sporadic destruction everywhere. The outer wall had been destroyed in at least three places, the middle wall in two more, and the inner wall which he could see through a hole in the middle wall had a great gaping gash in it to let the savages through. Except…there were no savages to be seen—at least not living ones. Their dead bodies had been flung about the fort by the winds, outnumbering Marcus' soldiers by at least five to one. The full fury of that funnel cloud must have caught the lot of them at the outer wall, pressed into a seething mob as they tried to overcome this final obstacle to their freedom and well, it truly didn't look like a continued siege was going to be a problem for Fort Defiance.

He risked attracting attention to himself, not that he thought it was much of a risk anymore. "Who's alive? Report in now!"

A face almost immediately appeared over the edge of the ditch a few dozen yards away from him. "Tribune? Is that you, Sir?"

Marcus didn't waste time with the obvious answer. "Are you injured, legionnaire?"

The man climbed out of the ditch totally covered in mud from the brief but furious rainstorm. "No, Sir, I just…the wind…and the rain…and that strange cloud…"

Other men were reacting to the sounds of their voices, picking themselves off the ground and out of the ditches.

"I know! But it's over now—"

He broke off when he realized that the prickling sensation was as strong as ever. "At least I hope it's over. Now run to the outer wall and report back to me on the savages. Let's not make any assumptions."

The man saluted and ran to do his bidding while other men began to pick themselves up and see to the wounded.

A low rumbling, much like thunder began to fill Marcus' ears. He immediately looked to the sky, but the near total blackness of the clouds was dissipating and no bolts of lightning were readily apparent within it.

A voice called to him from the gap in the inner wall. "Is that you, Tribune?"

Marcus turned to find Calidus coming toward him. "I'm glad you survived, Calidus. How are things on the far side of the fort?"

"We didn't break them there like you did here," Calidus told him. "But then that strange funnel cloud came and caught part of my line and a whole mess of savages and scattered everyone."

"So you held?"

"Yes, but the wall is smashed. We're going to have a terrible time—"

"Tribune!" the man who'd run to check on the savages shouted. "They're massing, Tribune! They're massing!"

Almost unable to believe the report, Marcus ran toward the man to see what he was reporting with his own eyes.

A mile or so out on the plain, Teetonka had somehow managed to gather about him a crowd of warriors. There were not thousands this time, but even the hundreds he had pulled about him seemed an almost inconceivable feat in the aftermath of that funnel cloud. Could their fear of their leader really be that great?

Even as Marcus watched, the crowd of tribesmen began to walk back toward the fort, preparing a final assault against the walls that could no longer repel them.

"Everyone back to the inner fort!" Marcus shouted. "Right now!" All legionnaires, all Gente, all Gota, get your asses back to the inner fort. These savages have got no brains and we have to kick their heads in one more time."

Men stared at him in astonishment but Marcus was already running back toward the damaged inner wall. There was a huge hole in its southern face—that was where he'd have to make his stand. He'd line up his legionnaires as if they were still a hand and set the auxiliaries to guard the walls around them in case Teetonka tried to get fancy.

To the north of him, the rumbling noise continued to grow louder.

"Severus! Severus! Are you alive?"

"Tribune?" a familiar voice called back.

"Good, gather up your men and get to me. Lysander? Capitán Adán? Warrior Atta? Green Vigil Phanes? All of my officers assemble with your men right now!"

Compelled by the urgency in Marcus' voice, men began to run toward him—not just his officers but every functioning man left in Fort Defiance. Right out in front of them came Señor Alberto who grasped Marcus' hand and immediately started babbling at him. "Thank you! Thank you, Tribune! Your genius has saved the lives of Carmelita and my son and even the Gota women and the men in your hospital. Digging that pit—getting them out of the building—it was genius! They are all alive! Thank you! Thank you!"

"Señor, shut up!" Marcus snapped. "I'm glad your family is safe, but they won't be for long if we don't get organized. The savages are returning, understand? Now where is Capitán Adán?"

"He's injured, Tribune," another of the Gente men informed him. "I saw it happen. That horrifying cloud brushed against him and flung him through the air like a wood chip. I think he has broken his arm and he is bleeding. He cannot—"

"Señor Alberto," Marcus cut the man off. "We may have only minutes before the savages are on us again. *You* are now in charge of the Gente, Teniente! Take them now and gather up every injured man you find and *get them into the inner fort before the savages arrive!* Run now! Don't talk! *Go!*"

Still looking shocked, Alberto began to get the Gente moving. "You heard the Tribune! All Gente, spread out and find the wounded. Let's go!"

"Warrior Atta!" Marcus finally caught sight of the man in the growing crowd of perhaps one hundred fifty or so men. "Are there any horses left in the fort? Can you give me any kind of mobile defense?"

"My men are already search—"

"Atta, Atta," a Gota warrior came charging up on the back of what was probably a draft horse, not a war steed. "It's a great wall of water coming from the north! We must hurry! We must—"

"A flash flood?" Atta asked with obvious horror.

He ran to the wall and clambered to the top to get a better view. Marcus followed him, as did just about everyone else still standing around. To the north—still many miles away—was a thin dirty blue line of something—the evident source of the growing rumbling sound.

Something close to panic lit Atta's eyes as he grabbed hold of Marcus' muddy shirt. "Do you see it, Tribune? That line is a raging wave of water! Why did no one think of this? Yes, the fort is built on the lowest of hills but the land around us, we are in an old river bed. The storm was so fierce and you can see that it is still raining in the hills. The water will race right past us on its way to the salt pan. It will…"

His voice trailed off but Marcus did not need him to finish the sentence. It would smash right against the broken walls of Fort Defiance and wash away everything in its path. The outer and middle baileys for sure, but maybe not the inner fort. It just might hold—"

"Tribune! The savages have begun to run, and even more are coming now!"

Of course they were coming faster. They'd seen the wave too and their only chance of surviving was to take the inner fort before it got here.

"New plan!" Marcus shouted. "Or rather, the same plan but move even faster! Gente get our injured into the inner fort! Legionnaires, find shields if any are left and form ranks at the broken inner wall! Gota, you are our mobile defense. The legion will hold the break in the wall but you must spearhead the defense of the rest of the fort. I don't think we're going to have to hold for long!"

Men began to run to do his bidding. Screams split the morning as badly injured men were unceremoniously picked up and hauled to the only place that might offer them safety. Marcus maintained his perch on the wall, alternating his attention between the line of death approaching from the north and the mob of killers charging him from the east. Most of the added numbers coming toward him were the women and children who also badly needed a safety Marcus could not afford to give them. What a horrible, horrible day this would be even if the legion survived to see night fall again...

The savages penetrated the outer wall and Marcus' men fled before them. He had only enough men to form one thin defiant line across the gaping hole in his final defense and no more than four shields among all of them. He set Severus and Lysander to hold his wings and himself in the middle. Calidus and limping Phanes he placed halfway between, hoping they could bolster his exhausted line.

"We are legionnaires!" Marcus reminded his men. "For centuries we have held the line of civilization, pushing back the barbarian hordes, standing for everything that is just and good in the world." He raised his voice even louder. "Now is the time to prove we are worthy of our ancestors! Now is the time to prove we are *legionnaires!*"

The first savages crashed against them and there was no more time for shouting. Marcus caught the wrist of a warrior swinging a hatchet at him and thrust his trusted sword blade deep into the man's gut. Beside him, a legionnaire died, and the whole line staggered backward. A Gente stepped up beside him, working his longer sword blade with quiet skill as he plugged the hole in the human wall. To Marcus' left, a Gota jumped in to fill another gap. The line ceased to buckle, but then the women and children added to the press and the sheer weight of numbers pushed them back again.

They couldn't hold, but they had to—

A roiling wall of water battered itself against the fort's weakened defenses and chaos broke out as the foaming wave front burst into the outer and middle baileys and swept dead, injured and still-running men and women away before it.

A smaller wave, a mere tendril of the infinitely more powerful surge, cut through the gap in the southern face of the inner wall and flattened attacker and defender alike without totally sweeping either group away. Then the great force of the passing wave was gone and men struggled to their feet to resume the battle. There were no sides anymore—no lines—just a chaotic mess of foes striking out at each other not in the hope of ultimate victory but just to hold on to life for a few more precious moments.

Marcus hacked and whirled and stabbed and dodged and hacked again. Blood sprayed through the air all around him and the screams of rage and death blocked all other sound from his eardrums. He backed into someone, then rebounded forward thrusting his blade deep into another savage's stomach. Dying, the raider clutched at Marcus' sword and pulled the weapon—still imbedded in his own flesh—from the Tribune's hand.

Ten thousand needles seemed to stab into Marcus as a familiar young Aquilan voice screamed in agony. Whirling about Marcus met the eyes of Teetonka—no longer wearing his feathered headdress—but fully recognizable due to the eight-pointed star hanging around his neck.

Staggering with exhaustion, the great shaman dropped the nearly unconscious body of Seneca Liberus and muttered something incredulous in his native tongue. Without taking time to think about his action, Marcus reached out with his quick hands and snatched the man's star amulet off his chest, yanking as hard as he could to steal the amulet.

The enchanted chain did not break but Marcus' efforts pulled the shaman off balance making him stagger even closer to the Tribune.

Marcus took advantage of the opportunity to drive his knee solidly into Teetonka's balls and when the shaman doubled over, he followed up with a brutal blow to the man's chin.

Despite the pain, the shaman's eyes sparkled as if the power of lightning were rising inside of him. He lifted hands that crackled with power and—screamed.

The shaman's body went rigid for a moment, then he whirled about, turning his back to Marcus and exposing a dagger sticking out of his flesh just above his kidney. Teetonka grabbed hold of Seneca with hands alive with the same heavenly energy he'd used to destroy the praetorium and the young man's whole body lit up so that Marcus could see the skeleton outlined beneath his flesh.

The legionnaire did not hesitate! Pulling the dagger free from the shaman's back, Marcus spun Teetonka around to face him. Electricity coursed into him, grinding his teeth together and standing his hair on end, but he fought through the pain and drove the dagger straight into the amulet decorating Teetonka's chest.

This time it was the shaman who screamed—a sound so loud and piercing that it interrupted the fighting all around them. Lighting rippled up and down his body and then the amulet burst and otherworldly gunk poured out of it just as it had from Kekipi's broken amulet in the Fire Islands. Marcus reacted a little bit faster this time and rather than be bathed in the stuff he was only clipped by the stream—at least until Teetonka fell backward and the magical slime sprayed up into the air to come down on Seneca and him both like the rivulets of an oily fountain.

Marcus tried to shield Seneca with his body but couldn't stop the student from being soaked in the slime as well.

Day Twenty Eight
I Regret to Inform You

"You're a bit late," Marcus told Evorik with a huge smile on his face.

The Gota noble eschewed the expected bumping of fists to wrap Marcus into a bear hug. "Goddamn politics!" he muttered in Marcus' ear. "Everyone agreed that sending a relief force was important, but the damn jockeying for precedence caused half the nobles in Topacio to delay raising their forces while they waited for the Thegn to name *them* to head the expedition. If my brother hadn't decided to lead it himself, we would still be shitting on ourselves back in the city."

Marcus pulled back from him. "Your brother, *Thegn Alaric*, led the relief force?"

Evorik grinned. "Marcus, my friend, let me introduce to you my half-brother, the mighty and all powerful Thegn of Topacio, Alaric the Third."

Marcus came to full attention and saluted the man who was an older, grayer, version of Evorik. "Thegn!"

With a respectable lack of pomposity, the man grinned at Marcus. "I've heard a lot about you in the last two weeks, Tribune." He glanced wryly at his half-brother then winked at Marcus as he mimicked Evorik's voice. "Tribune Marcus is an amazing leader. He'll hold the fort no matter how many savages they throw against him. He got us through the salt pan, for Fulgus' sake. Though the heavens, themselves, fall upon him, he'll be standing in Fort Quartus if we just get moving!"

He paused and looked about them at the still-shattered fort. "It looks like the heavens did fall."

"They did indeed," Marcus agreed, "but fortunately, I was not standing alone when this happened but was shoulder-to-shoulder with the stout men of the Jeweled Hills and my own legionnaires."

The Gota behind Alaric grunted with approval. While there were Gente infantry with the relief force, Marcus saw none standing among the officers. He remembered Atta's surprise that he had promoted Adán to Capitán and wondered how badly he had violated local custom. Well there was nothing to be done about it now.

"If I may, Thegn Alaric, I would like to introduce my officers to you."

The Thegn graciously consented and Marcus guided him toward the ranks of his battered army. His legionnaires stood in perfect formation, backs as straight as pilum. Beside them stood the Gota in similar rank but not bothering to display the motionless discipline of the Aquilan men. Finally came the civilian Gente in their far looser lines. At a nod from Marcus, all the surviving officers stepped forward.

"As you know, Thegn Alaric, an army is only as good as its officers and I have been blessed by Sol Invictus, the Unconquered Sun, Himself, with the very best of men to support me here at Fort Defiance. First, please meet my legionnaires, Black Vigils Severus and Lysander and Red Vigils Calidus and Eolus." Phanes had died in the final battle as the water gushed in upon them. Marcus would have to write a letter to his family. He'd mention none of the lad's weaknesses and only the courage with which he had performed his final duties.

The Thegn nodded respectfully to each man, then stepped forward and shook hands in the Aquilan fashion—palm to wrist—with each of them. "Well done! I see the heads of savages everywhere on what's left of your walls. Well done indeed!"

When the Thegn was ready, Marcus introduced the next man. "Next comes the heart of my Gota cavalry, Warrior Atta—a brave and capable leader of brave and capable men."

Atta received a grin from the Thegn and the two men bumped fists in the Gota fashion. "I'm sure you will have some fucking good stories to tell, Warrior Atta!" Alaric told him. "You'll dine with me tonight so I can hear all of them!"

Atta's already broad grin nearly doubled in size.

The leader of Topacio hesitated as if he thought perhaps the last two officers had stepped forward by mistake. He glanced back at Marcus.

"And my final two surviving officers," Marcus told him, "Capitán Adán Nacio and Teniente Alberto Lope, both of the city of Amatista. Like my other officers, they led from the front and held the line. We could not have defeated the savages without them."

Cheers broke the stillness of the afternoon as the Gente infantry in the relief army went wild with excitement.

Alaric turned to Marcus and lifted an eyebrow at the reaction, then turned back to the two Gente officers and held out his fist to them. Shocked, first Adán, left arm in a sling, and then Alberto bumped the fist of the Gota ruler.

"Well done!" Alaric's voice bellowed out across the front of the fort. "Evorik, everything you said about this Tribune appears true to my eyes. He is another Juan Pablo Cazador, bringing the best out of Gota, Gente and foreigner alike. Well done!"

Marcus nodded at the complement. "Your words are very generous, Thegn Alaric. And it is good to hear that my half-brother is so well respected in your land."

Evorik frowned. "*Was* so well-respected, my friend." He stepped forward and placed a comforting hand on Marcus' shoulder. "I regret to inform you that your brother, Señor Juan Pablo Cazador, is no more."

"What?" Marcus asked. He couldn't quite make sense of the Gota's words.

"He's dead, Marcus," Evorik told him. "Your half-brother has been murdered."

Excerpt from *Legionnaire Book 3: The Jeweled Hills*

Chapter One
What Was Really Happening?

"Who enters the Hall of Beremund, Thegn of Amatista?" Ulphilas, the Herald of Amatista, stepped forward and answered in a voice that filled the entire Hall. "One who claims to be Tribune Marcus Venandus, Patrician of the Republic of Aquila far away on the Continent of Austellus."

"Claims?" Marcus whispered to the man standing next to him, Lord Evorik of Topacio. Like Ulphilas, Evorik was a Gota nobleman, part of the ruling class of the intensely independent Jeweled Cities of the north. He wore a fine silk shirt with one of those funny silk squares peeking out of the strange pockets the Gente and Gota wore over their right breasts. A rearing horse had been embroidered onto the corner of the square in gold thread. Thick bands of gold and silver adorned his arms and a topaz stud marked his right ear. Finally, a couple of impressively gaudy rings shone on the strong fingers of both hands. But any veneer of civilization all these accoutrements might have created was destroyed by the wild and unkempt red beard that fell from his chin to the middle of his chest.

"It's part of the custom here," Evorik whispered back.

"Who can verify this foreigner's claims?" the original man asked the Hall without moving to permit Marcus, Evorik and their companions to enter. Behind the clearly important official stood seventy or eighty men milling about in a disorganized mass. Almost all were Gota who differed from Evorik only in that they wore amethyst studs in their ears. Behind them on a high-backed wooden throne sat the gaudiest barbarian of them all, presumably Thegn Beremund.

The Herald made a sweeping gesture with his hand to indicate the men who accompanied Marcus. "I have brought witnesses, Master of Horse, to testify to his identity before the Thegn."

Marcus knew that the Master of Horse was one of the top officials in the Gota government. In the old days, when they were semi-nomadic wanderers, such a man spent most of his time in the saddle. Today he ran much of the government of the Thegn and probably seldom left the city.

"Who are these witnesses?" the Master of Horse demanded. "Let them step forth in the order of their worth."

That was the sort of instruction that probably caused fights to break out in the Hall, but no one challenged Evorik's right to speak first. The Gota stepped a pace in front of Marcus. "You all know me. I'm Evorik of Topacio, brother to Thegn Alaric and brother-in-law to your own noble Lord Totila." He grimaced as he said the last name lest anyone get the wrong impression that he liked his brother-in-law. "I have ridden with this man," he gestured toward Marcus, "across the Sea of Grass, fought the savages with him, and entrusted my two wives to his protection when the need came to rally a relief force to teach the savages another lesson. He is Tribune Marcus Venandus."

Marcus found himself wondering why this could possibly be necessary. Surely every visitor to this Hall was not required to prove his identity. And it seemed even more foolish in Marcus' case as the Thegn had evidently sent out Ulphilas to fetch Marcus to tell him about the Siege of Fort Quartus—or Fort Defiance as its defenders had begun to call it. Surely he didn't trust the Herald so little that he thought he would bring him the wrong man. So what was really happening?

Herald Ulphilas had met Marcus as he traveled with the wagons of the caravan less than half a day out of Fort Defiance and pretty much commanded him to travel back to Amatista with him with all possible speed. The Thegn had heard of the battle and wanted the details. Marcus hadn't wanted to leave the wagons which secretly included a significant amount of treasure he had captured in the Fire Islands so many months ago, but Evorik had urged him to do as the Herald requested. So Marcus had turned responsibility for his wagon over to his trusted men and agreed to journey ahead with them to Amatista.

Marcus was in the north by the strangest of coincidences. Exiled for the *crime* of making his superiors look foolish he had fortuitously received a letter from his older half-brother, Juan Pablo Cazador, asking him to journey to the Jeweled Hills to help him with a somewhat mysterious problem. So Marcus had sailed north with his trusted officers, Black Vigil Severus Lupes and Red Vigil and Adjutant, Calidus Vulpes, but their journey had been blocked by pirate activity in the Narrow Sea. So they had chosen an alternate route, by wagon caravan across the Sea of Grass, and run smack dab into a tribal war to *purge the grass* of all foreigners. Marcus had been forced to take command of first the caravan and then the shattered remnants of the Fort Defiance garrison to hold the savages at bay. He'd done this so well that by the time the Gota army finally arrived to relieve them the savages were broken and their leader dead.

The Master of Horse turned toward the throne and the Thegn nodded to him.

He turned back to the Herald. "I accept this witness. Do you have any others?"

"I do indeed," Ulphilas assured him. "Warrior Atta served bravely at both the Battle of the Thunder Cloud and the Siege of Fort Defiance. Warrior?"

Atta stepped forward, the younger man's beard dangling only a couple of inches below his chin. "After the savages treacherously surprised us at the Battle of the Thunder Cloud, I followed the orders of Lord Ildefons and led my men back to Fort Defiance to warn the remaining legionnaires of the disaster. I found that this man," he pointed to Marcus, "Tribune Marcus Venandus, had taken charge of the fort after leading a caravan of wagons across the salt pan to try and warn Fort Defiance that Fort Segundus had been destroyed by savages and that Fort Tertium was almost certainly under attack."

"But you do not know that this is actually Tribune Marcus Venandus," the Master of Horse pressed Atta on the details as he had not pushed against Evorik's telling.

"If you are asking if I knew the Tribune by sight before meeting him at Fort Defiance, the answer is clearly *no*. But there was no question in the caravan as to this man's identity. He joined the wagons at the beginning of the trail in Dona and was well known not only to the legionnaires but to the merchants and drivers of the wagons. I am also told he was treated with great respect by the Tribune in charge of Fort Prime. Even discounting his strong sense of honor and the superior qualities of his character, there can be no denying that he is who he says he is."

The Master of Horse nodded and returned to questioning Herald Ulphilas. "Are there other witnesses who can attest to this man's identity?"

Only a lifetime spent in strict military discipline prevented Marcus from showing his exasperation. What in Sol Invictus' green earth was going on here?

"There are, Master of Horse, but the circumstances are unusual and I will need your permission before daring to bring them forward to testify."

"Explain!"

"My next two witnesses are Gente señors—merchants of good standing within our city."

"Then what is the problem with their testimony?" the Master asked.

"They were promoted by the Tribune to the ranks of *capitán* and *teniente* despite the fact that they have no Gota blood in their veins."

"And how did they perform in these duties?"

The whole Hall pivoted to stare in shock at the Thegn whom, Marcus gathered, was not expected to speak at this point in whatever the hell it was that they were doing here.

"I am told," the Herald began.

"Let Warrior Atta answer!" the Thegn interrupted. "He is an eyewitness to their worth or lack there of."

Both Capitán Adán and Teniente Alberto bristled at the questioning of their honor, but Atta looked suddenly nervous as he was called to testify on their character. "It was a dark time, Great Thegn. The Tribune, he kept telling us that if we held together and trusted him we would hold the fort for as long as it took Lord Evorik to bring reinforcements. But I did not believe him. There were more than five thousand savages arrayed against us and their leader, the Shaman Teetonka, had just broken the mighty cavalry troop of Lord Ildefons and our legionnaire allies through treachery and a fearful rain of lightning. I believed that within days I would be rejoining Lord Ildefons in the Hall of Fulgus and not the least because more than a fifth of our men were Gente like these—of questionable worth and character."

Both Adán and Alberto started forward in protest but the strong hands of Gota warriors clapped down upon their shoulders and silenced them.

"But I was wrong," Atta continued. "The Gente fought as men possessed and between the battles they worked tirelessly to strengthen our defenses. And these two men were ever in the thick of things, both in battle and at work."

The Thegn turned his attention from Atta to the two Gente señors, studying their faces from across the room. Then he sank back into his chair. "Well said, Warrior Atta, I will take your counsel under advisement but for the time being, both of these men may speak as if they hold the ranks of *capitán* and *teniente*."

A murmur broke out among the Gota present and it was not a totally pleasant sound, but Adán and Alberto both looked well pleased by the Thegn's words.

Thegn Beremund waved his hand. "Get on with this shit!"

The Master of Horse immediately turned to the Herald. "You may proceed."

"I call Señor Capitán," his mouth twisted in a grimace of distaste as he pronounced the rank, "Adán Nacio to testify to the Tribune's identity."

Adán stepped forward. He was an older man who wore an embroidered vest in addition to his silk shirt and fine black boots and trousers. His left arm was in a sling—broken when he was clipped by the whirling storm of Teetonka and thrown far across the bailey at Fort Defiance. "I became aware of the Tribune shortly after the caravan started on its way. He was treated with great respect at Fort Prime by the other legionnaires and not one of them questioned his identity. I have heard," he looked apologetically at Marcus, "an ugly rumor that he was traveling north because his father, Vitalis Venandus, a man well-known to the city of Amatista, had gotten into political trouble back in Aquila and that his enemies in the Senate, unable to touch the father took vengeance by exiling the son."

That was, unfortunately, an all-too-accurate way of describing what had happened to Marcus. His superiors had gotten themselves and an entire legion killed by rebellious natives they'd thought to use to wipe out one irritating subordinate. Not only had Marcus and his men survived the treachery, they had wiped out the rebellion and single-handedly saved the province. Had Marcus had a normal father, his actions would have gained him praise throughout the Republic, but unfortunately, Vitalis Venandus' never-ending schemes for greater power had allowed the patrons of his now dead superiors to twist the heroism of Marcus and his men into a semblance of treason. The problem would be straightened out eventually, but in the meantime, Marcus had been forced to absent himself to foreign lands.

"Señor Teniente Alberto Lope," the Herald called. "Have you anything to add?"

Alberto stepped forward. "All that I can add is that Tribune Marcus is an excellent man. In addition to his extraordinary abilities in battle, he is honorable, thoughtful and compassionate."

"And you know that he is actually Tribune Marcus Venandus how?"

"He told us he was—my wife and I," Alberto said. "Everyone in the caravan knows he is Tribune Marcus Venandus. So did the Tribune at Fort Prime. I don't understand why this is in doubt."

Neither do I, Marcus thought. But he kept his mouth shut and let this idiocy play itself out.

"Finally I have student of wizardry, Seneca Liberus, as witness," the Herald said. "He is a citizen of Aquila come to Amatista to study with Mago Efrain Estudioso."

"At last, and you knew the Tribune before he joined the caravan?"

"No," Seneca admitted. "But Black Vigil Severus did, as did Red Vigil Calidus."

"And these men are where?" the Master of the Horse asked.

"They were left behind to bring the Tribune and Señor Teniente Alberto's wagons to Amatista. Señor Teniente Alberto's wife has recently given birth to a child and cannot drive their wagon on her own."

Marcus had had enough. "May I ask what this is about? I was invited to this Hall by Herald Ulphilas. I did not ask to come here. My brother is apparently dead so there is truly no reason for me to have come to Amatista at all. My presence is a courtesy to you, Thegn Beremund. Why are you insulting me with all these questions to my friends?"

Thegn Bermund rested his chin on his hand, quite obviously studying Marcus.

The Master of Horse turned to Evorik. "He doesn't know why he's here?"

The Gota lord shrugged. "As I indicated to Thegn Beremund in my letter, it seemed simpler this way. Aquilans are a strange breed of men and one can never be certain how they will act when taken out of their accustomed roles."

Marcus turned on his friend. "Lord Evorik! I demand—"

"Not in my court!" Thegn Beremund snapped.

Marcus whirled back around to face him. "Is this a court then? Am I accused of some crime? Perhaps saving the lives of Amatistan citizens upsets the Gota rather than—"

"Marcus," Evorik's voice was as low as the hand on the Tribune's shoulder was light. This was clearly not an attempt to coerce him, but to reason with him. "You can trust me, my friend, as I once trusted you with the safety of my wives. Nothing bad is happening here. Just cooperate with the inquiry and you have my word, all will be well."

Against his better judgment, Marcus took a step back, but he made no effort at all to keep the frown off his face.

Slowly, Thegn Beremund sank back into his slouching posture upon his great chair.

The Master of Horse resumed questioning Seneca. "And can you testify that this is in fact Tribune Marcus Venandus."

"Yes," Seneca said. "In addition to the reasons put forth by the others, I spoke with Magus Jocasta at Fort Prime. She was familiar with Tribune Marcus and Black Vigil Severus by reputation and expressed no doubt as to his identity."

"I've heard enough," the Thegn said. "Tribune, come here."

Still angry, Marcus strode forward to face the throne. He neither bowed nor even nodded his head in respect. He was a citizen of the Republic, not some barbarian kingdom.

"I am not trying to insult you, but as Thegn of Amatista I need to know without doubt that you are who you say you are. Can you think of some way to prove this to me?"

"No!" Marcus answered without taking even a moment to consider the question.

"He has letters," Lord Evorik said. "He mentioned them to me on the trail. His brother and he have been writing letters for a great many years."

"At last," Beremund said. "We are getting somewhere. And can I see these letters?"

"I left them with my wagon," Marcus told them.

"They're right here, Thegn Beremund," Seneca called out.

As Marcus turned on him, gaping, Seneca pulled a sheaf of parchments out of his bag. "Lord Evorik asked me to bring them for you when we left the caravan," the younger man explained.

The Master of Horse took the parchments from Seneca and carried them to the Thegn who gestured at several men. Within moments half a dozen of them were reading the documents, calling out dates, and mentioning the names of the senders.

Marcus felt his face flushing with rage again.

"His promotions," the Thegn grumbled, "and the official decree of exile. He has letters from Señor Juan Pablo Cazador that had to have been sent years before the man's death." He pushed the parchments into the hands of the Master of Horse. "Does anyone here doubt he is who he says he is?" He looked at each of the men before settling on one with a graying beard and a beer belly. "How about you, Totila? You were the one who found this too convenient. Any real doubts now about this shit?"

"No," the Gota lord said. "What's more I'd say he's the best solution to our problem."

"He's the *only* solution," the Master of Horse said.

"Very well then," the Thegn said. "I am satisfied that this is Tribune Marcus Venandus standing before me. In keeping with the customs of the Gota, the Gente, the laws of Amatista and the expressed written wishes of Señor Juan Pablo Cazador, I hereby confer upon Tribune Marcus Venandus all the property of his half-brother within the city and state of Amatista and," he broke off and looked at Evorik. "It's my understanding that Thegn Alaric agrees to recognize his ownership of all Señor Juan Pablo's property in Topacio as well?"

"That is so, Thegn Beremund," Evorik agreed. "It is, after all, the will of Señor Juan Pablo."

"Very well," the Thegn continued. "Said transfer also includes all the responsibilities of the Tribune's half-brother as they are recognized under the customs of the Gota, the Gente and the laws of Amatista and Topacio. Tribune, I confer upon you the title of *señor* and—"

Marcus had been listening to the Thegn with a growing sense of horror. He had not come to Amatista to collect the estate of a brother he had never even met—especially a *merchant* brother. And now this barbarian thought to insult *him* with the merchant's title? He made his opposition known in the explicit terms these coarse barbarians seemed to love. "What the *fuck* do you think you're doing?"

Shocked silence broke across the Hall.

"I am a *patrician* of Aquila and you think to insult me in this way?"

"Tribune," Evorik said as he tried to grab hold of Marcus' arm.

Marcus shook him off. "I do *not* engage in commerce. I fight wars! And I win them! How dare you suggest that I am no more than a common merchant?"

"They're not trying to insult you, Tribune," Evorik said. "It's a simply enormous estate and—"

"You say that as if I can be bribed!" Marcus raged at him. "Better to go live with the savages in the Sea of Grass than to compromise my honor as a—"

"Clear the room!" Thegn Beremund shouted.

Marcus whirled around to see the Thegn was off his throne and shoving his nobles angrily out of his way. "You, Evorik, stay! And you Totila! And you!" he pointed at several men in the room including Adán and Alberto and began pummeling the others out of his hall. Seneca ducked behind Atta and managed to evade the guards now forcing the others out.

When the room was cleared, Marcus started to protest again, but the Thegn whirled on him.

"You shut the fuck up!" he snapped as he stuck his finger into Marcus' face. "You have no idea what's happening here—no idea how fragile the peace is or how important your brother was to the survival of Amatista. We are surrounded on all sides by enemies except for brave and loyal Topacio to our south. Our community is completely riven with factionalism. The dons hate the señors, and both groups hate the Gota, and everyone despises the Qing. But that isn't bad enough, is it? Because every fucking one of these groups has a dozen factions within them fighting with each other to see who can come out on top. It is a fucking impossible situation which when it breaks loose will have us killing each other in the streets despite the fact that our enemies are waiting their chance to swoop in and steal everything we have."

The Thegn lowered his hand and stalked several paces away before whirling around to face Marcus again. "But it hasn't broke loose for ten years because your fuckingly-stupid genius of a brother came along and found a magic that would pull us all together—Gota, Gente and Qing all striving together toward the same end. He tricked us into *building* something for Amatista instead of pulling our fair city down again and now we can't survive without it."

He glowered unhappily at Marcus. "Now he's dead and we don't know what to do. To make it worse, the whole silk trade is already dying—has been dying for more than three years. It began with *bandits* in the hills that always seemed to know when and where the silk wagons were going to roll. Obviously someone within Amatista had been helping them but they're too well funded to be operating completely on their own. Diamonte, Aquamarina, Morganita and Granate—they're all in this against us."

The Thegn had finally reached a subject that fully interested Marcus. "Are you saying that all four of these city-states have united against you?"

"Yes and no," the Thegn hedged. "They are all aligned against us but they're not truly united. You see, everyone wants our silk for themselves."

"So they cooperate to strangle you, but they block each other from moving in for the kill," Marcus theorized.

All of the Gota nodded.

"I don't understand what this has to do with me. Your cavalry is famous throughout the upper continent. Clean out the bandits—"

"That will probably bring our enemy city-states into the open," the Master of Horse noted. "They have expressed concerns that we not use our bandit problem as an excuse to mobilize an army on their borders."

"The city walls look strong," Marcus pointed out from his passing observation as he entered the city gates.

"But the silk is spun in the countryside where the mulberry leaves are grown. We can't pull those back into the walls. We cannot afford to be invaded—not with the economy in tatters and our industry on the verge of collapse."

"And it's collapsing why?" Marcus asked again. He really had trouble understanding how the relatively new silk trade could have become so important so quickly."

"Amatista, like Topacio, does not have very good farm land. We have always depended heavily on grain imports from the coast and from the central cities of the Jeweled Hills to feed our people. This is one of the reasons we have always been among the poorest of our neighbors, but the silk changed that. Despite the complaints you hear, everyone in Amatista has benefited from the silk trade. We developed a favorable balance of trade for the first time in my lifetime. We were paying off our creditors and developing true independence.

"Then the bandits came and we began to fall behind again. Then we had two weak harvests in a row and we started hemorrhaging our newfound gold and silver trying to buy enough food to feed our people—especially here in the city. Our warehouses are overflowing with bolts of silk but we aren't able to get them to the markets in Ópalo. But it's not just the silk traders who suffer but all the tradesmen who cater to them are hurting as well. And now the bandits have expanded well beyond the silk caravans crippling the rest of our trade. Unrest is growing. Everyone expects me to fix this problem without realizing that raising an army to fight the bandits will likely get us invaded and our city plundered."

Marcus suddenly understood why his brother had reached out to him. Juan Pablo had needed caravan guards who could defeat the bandits without looking like a traditional Gota army and he had been counting on Marcus with his legionnaire's experience to train those guards for him.

He did not share this insight with the Gota. "Your problems are quite serious," Marcus admitted before lying, "but I really don't see what they have to do with me. I am only a visitor to your city. Nothing you've talked about has anything to do with me."

"Bullshit!" the Thegn said. "It has everything to do with you. Señor Juan Pablo was the glue that held the silk trade together. He has been dead less than a month and already what is left of it is falling apart. Everyone is fighting with each other. No one wants to let someone else be in charge. The Gota cannot let their inferiors give them orders. The greedy Gente are already trying to grab up more of the profits. The Qing are enraged at the way both groups treat them and it won't be long until they start looking to start over in a new city as they did here in Amatista. *We* can't manage this without Juan Pablo, but *you* might be able to. You're an Aquilan. You're totally outside our normal disputes. And the Gente and the Gota both already think highly of you for your actions at Fort Defiance."

"Your arrival also simplifies the inheritance situation," the Master of Horse explained. "There are differences in Gente and Gota custom here that greatly complicate the situation. The problem is that Señor Juan Pablo had no children—not even a girl." He started ticking off points on his fingers. "So each of his wives' families want their dowries back and are making claims on other parts of his fortune. His creditors are also moving in because they see that the silk trade is about to fall apart and want to recover what they can from his property. Add to that that his many cousins on his mother's side are laying claim to everything he accumulated and, well, without a single heir to keep the fortune together the whole silk trade may splinter and die anyway."

The more they told Marcus, the less pleased he was with the entire situation. He wanted nothing to do with it. "I am not a merchant," he reminded them, but no one was listening.

"You on the other hand," the Thegn said, "enter our city at the perfect time. You are the half-brother of Señor Juan Pablo and under Gota law that makes *you* his heir under these circumstances."

"But not under Gente law?"

The Thegn shrugged. "When there is a conflict, Gota law decides the dispute, but there won't be a conflict because *you* are specifically mentioned in the Señor's will. He obviously believed you were coming and made his plans accordingly to protect his fortune and his city. You see, you are the perfect solution to the problem—a well-respected outsider to step into your brother's boots."

"Except that I refuse," Marcus told them. "I am not a merchant. I know nothing of commerce. I refuse to dishonor my family by becoming the one and engaging in the other."

"From what I'm hearing," a tentative Aquilan voice ventured, "Señor Juan Pablo Cazador wasn't really a merchant either."

Everyone turned to stare at the young student of magic, Seneca Liberus. "I mean, most commerce is a relatively simple affair. A landowner's servants grow crops and sell them to a merchant who sells them to hungry people." Seneca's voice seemed to find more strength as no one cursed at him or told him to be quiet. "Or in a more complicated case, a weapon smith buys ore, transforms it into a sword, and sells it to a soldier."

"A weapon smith is really a craftsman, not a merchant," Marcus complained. "He adds value with his own skill to the metal. It's an honorable profession."

Señor Capitán Adán opened his mouth to protest, but Lord Evorik with a quiet shake of his head convinced him to be quiet.

"Well let's look at an even more complicated case then," Seneca suggested. "A normal cloth merchant—not one of these silk merchants—buys wool from a shepherd, gives it to a spinster to turn into thread, then gives the thread to a weaver to make cloth, then gives the cloth to a dyer to color, all before selling it for his profit. But the merchant isn't really important to the process. What I mean to say is that any other merchant can fill his role. Correct me if I'm wrong, but that isn't the case with this silk trade. It's a new and complicated way of raising revenue for Amatista that involves complex management of both the ruling Gota and the subject peoples, the Gente and the Qing. Señor Juan Pablo held a monopoly on the profession because the tax revenues are so important to the Thegn and it took royal authority backing him to make his plan successful."

The Thegn nodded thoughtfully and Seneca continued.

"Well that's not much different from the monopolies the Senate gives out back home in Aquila. They don't give them to merchants—they give them to *prefects* charged with important tasks for the state. Mining monopolies, shipbuilding monopolies, salt monopolies—all of those go to influential and capable patricians because no one of lesser status can be trusted with them. The government here has obviously never had to deal with a situation quite like this before and so the Thegn had never had to create a special rank to manage these government monopolies. Since Señor Juan Pablo was already a merchant when he came to them, it's understandable why they continued to work under the auspices of his already existing title, but I bet it caused problems among the Gota, didn't it, Thegn Beremund?"

The Thegn laughed. "Not just among the Gota but among the Gente dons as well. None of them liked taking *suggestions* from a señor."

"So the problem here is one of titles, isn't it? Thegn Beremund offered you your brother's title because he thought of it as just one more possession that Señor Juan Pablo was passing on to you. But the title isn't really appropriate, is it? But if he were to adopt a new title, such as *prefect*, creating an office that reported directly to him—that would show everyone just how important and unique he thinks this monopoly is."

The Master of Horse, Lord Totila and Herald Ulphilas all frowned at this suggestion, but the Thegn smiled at the thought. "That is an easy solution, isn't it? I will make a new title. Now—"

"But I know nothing about silk," Marcus protested.

"If I may, Thegn Beremund," Adán asked.

The Thegn graciously permitted the Gente merchant to continue.

"It is not uncommon for important officials in the Thegn's court to lack an intricate understanding of the day-to-day details of the offices they manage. They hire clerks and other specialists to help them. In this case, Señor Juan Pablo will have had a staff. And if you need assistance in evaluating them and managing them, your valiant deeds on the Sea of Grass have earned you many friends who can help you, not the least of whom are Teniente Alberto and myself." He bowed respectfully as he made the offer. "We would be honored to return the gift of our lives with any small services you might require."

"I don't say this about the Gente very often," the Thegn observed, "but that was fucking well said, Capitán. If Tribune Marcus accepts the responsibilities his brother handed to him, you and the Teniente may keep your military titles, although you will no longer be in active service."

Both Gente señors beamed even as the Gota frowned again.

"Thank you, Thegn Beremund," Adán bowed again. "Your wisdom is like a pearl of great price gleaming in the tarnished streets of our once fair city."

"Don't make me regret my gift by spitting bullshit at me," the Thegn grumbled before turning back to Marcus.

"So what do you say, Prefect? Can you step into your brother's shoes and help us save the city he loved so much."

All of Marcus' instincts told him to refuse, but it occurred to him that if he followed that impulse and tried to stay in the north, Beremund and Alaric of Topacio could make life very difficult for him. And where else could he go in the north? To the enemy cities that would hate and distrust him because of his relationship to his half-brother?

He tried one more time to make them see sense. "I'm a military man. I know nothing at all about managing something like this."

"If you don't, you fucking should!" Evorik told him. "You are quite adept at training men and inspiring them to fight, but your superior officers have to do much more than that. They spend more time managing local politics and arranging their supply lines then they do working with the men. This will be good experience for you."

"I just…it all tastes so unseemly."

"If your brother had owned only large agricultural estates would you have any qualms about this?" Evorik asked him.

"No," Marcus answered honestly.

"What if he had some wine presses and a couple of mills which his tenants used? Would those be a problem?"

"Of course not."

"There's no fucking difference between that and this," Evorik told him.

Marcus chuckled humorlessly. "My friend, I did not know there was a lawyer hiding beneath that beard."

"Your employees will be like your clients back home," Seneca tried again.

Marcus turned on him. "And why do you want me to accept this…office?"

Seneca retreated a step, taken aback by the sudden burst of temper. "It's the Qing, Tribune. Not these refugees in the city, but the real Qing Empire. I've heard your stories about the Fire Islands. I saw the eight-pointed star around Teetonka's neck on the Sea of Grass—just like the one you recovered from Kekipi in the Fire Islands. And now from what the merchants say they are interfering in the Jeweled Coast too—sabotaging their efforts to use the refugees to start up the silk trade on this shore. When I put it all together, I see the Qing working to weaken and isolate the Jeweled Cities of the north. What if they intend to expand across the Bottomless Sea to get a foothold here? How can that be good for the Republic to let our friends in the north fall?"

The young man's words struck hard because they rang so true. Marcus had seen that the Qing were stirring up trouble against the Republic but he had not made the perfectly reasonable leap to recognizing that their target might well be the Jeweled Cities. Seneca was absolutely correct. It would be a disaster for the Republic if the Qing were to establish a physical foothold on this continent. Their navy was already one of the greatest in the world. If they added all the ports of the Jeweled Coast…"

"So you'll do it then," Thegn Beremund asked.

Slowly Marcus nodded. "I guess I will."

"Good!" Evorik threw his arm around the shoulders of the Tribune—now Prefect. "If the Thegn has no objection, then Herald Ulphilas and I can take you to your new home to meet your wives."

About Gilbert M. Stack

Gilbert M. Stack has been creating stories almost since he began speaking and publishing fiction and non-fiction since 2006. A professional historian, Gilbert delights in bringing the past to life in his fiction, depicting characters who are both true to their time and empathetic with modern sensibilities. His work has appeared in more than a dozen issues of *Alfred Hitchcock's Mystery Magazine* and is available online. He lives in New Jersey with his wife, Michelle, and their son, Michael. You can find out more about Gilbert at www.gilbertstack.com.

Other Works by Gilbert M. Stack

Legionnaire
1 The Fire Islands
2 The Sea of Grass
3 The Jeweled Hills (coming April 5, 2018)
4 The Battle for Amatista (coming in June 2018)

The Pembroke Steel Series
1 Lazarus Key
2 Hearts of Ice and Other Stories
3 The Shore and Other Stories

Novels:
Forever After
High Above the Waters
Panic Button
Ransom

Among Us
Hiding Among Us (with Marc Hawkins) Coming Soon
Missing Among Us (with Marc Hawkins) Coming Soon

Short Stories
What Child Is This?

Contact Gilbert M. Stack

You can find Gilbert M. Stack at:

www.gilbertstack.com
https://www.facebook.com/GilbertStackAuthor/
https://www.goodreads.com/GilbertMStack

And subscribe to his free newsletter either on the home page of his website or at:

gilbertmstack@gmail.com

Just send a quick email with the phrase "Subscribe to Newsletter" in the heading.

Printed in Great Britain
by Amazon